A Time to Heal

Other books by the author

A Time to Love,
book one in the Quilts of Lancaster County series

and coming in Fall 2011
from Barbara Cameron and Abingdon Press
A Time for Peace,
book three in The Quilts of Lancaster County series

A TIME TO HEAL

Quilts of Lancaster County Series

Barbara Cameron

Abingdon Press fiction
a novel approach to faith

Nashville, Tennessee

A Time to Heal

ISBN-13: 978-1-4267-0764-3

Published by Abingdon Press, P.O. Box 801, Nashville, TN 37202

www.abingdonpress.com

Cover design by Anderson Design Group, Nashville, TN

Library of Congress Cataloging-in-Publication Data

Cameron, Barbara, 1949-
 A time to heal / Barbara Cameron.
    p. cm. — (Quilts of Lancaster County series ; 2)
 ISBN 978-1-4267-0764-3 (pbk. : alk. paper)
 1. Amish--Ficton. 2. Lancaster County (Pa.)—Fiction. I. Title.
 PS3603.A4473T54 2011
 813'.6—dc22
                          2010051907

Printed in the United States of America

1 2 3 4 5 6 7 8 9 10 / 16 15 14 13 12 11

For my family

Acknowledgments

Thank you to my family and friends who are so supportive of my writing. I know it can't be easy to listen to me talking on and on about characters who feel like real people to me!

Barbara Scott, my wonderful editor, deserves a BIG thank you for her enthusiasm for the series and for her intuitive comments to improve it. Thank you so much, Barbara.

I can always count on Judy Rehm, friend and Bible scholar, for her support and for helping me to express a biblical truth better.

I so appreciate Linda Byler who takes time away from her own writing to read my manuscripts and help me make my stories authentic. Linda, I wish you the best of luck as your books enter the market. I know you will enjoy great success!

Each day when I sit down to write I think about the people who encouraged me when the dream God planted in me started to bloom . . . the high school English teacher who moved up to a higher grade each year as I did so that we had four wonderful years together. At the time I wondered what that was about, God. Now I know that it was for the day Mrs. White would read something I wrote and encourage me to write a short story for extra credit. Then there was Charlie LaPoint, the very cranky but gifted newspaper editor who alternately terrified me (I was just out of high school!) and pushed me to be a better writer, insisting to the managing editor that I should be promoted to intern reporter and when I messed up, stuck up for me. And finally, Vivian Stephens, the editor who bought my first novel and set me on this path.

As always, God, the master author of the book of my life, gets the biggest thanks. And the glory. Thank You!

1

*F*ree.

They couldn't keep him caged up any more. He took a deep breath of the summer air, warm and fragrant with the scents of earth and the crops growing in the fields on each side of the road.

A man could get to feeling dead inside living in the place he'd been, trapped in a prison of despair and pain, shut away from the rest of the world. He'd gotten out and he would never go back.

He had enough scars to last a lifetime.

His surroundings were so different from the small rural town in Kansas where he'd grown up. But there was a similar feel to this landscape with the crops ripening in the fields and, most of all, the huge barns that cast shadows over neat farmhouses, as if asserting their importance. Work came first.

The old-time farm equipment looked weird. Modern-day efficiency ruled the fields back home. And the buggies—well, they were the biggest surprise. He knew the Amish drove buggies. He'd seen photos. But the reality made him feel as if he'd stepped back in time, not just stepped out of the prison he'd been in for so long.

Dusk began falling as his military boots marched toward their goal. He set his backpack down and pulled a wrinkled map from his pocket, studying it for the hundredth time. Excitement quickened his step even though he felt exhausted and hungry. She wouldn't be expecting him. Might not even appreciate the surprise. But he'd felt compelled to come here. It might mean trouble, but he'd never backed down from a problem before.

He heard the sound of horse hooves clip-clopping behind him, interrupting his thoughts.

"Need a ride there, *sohn*?"

He turned and looked up into the friendly face of an Amish man whose grizzled beard blew in the cooling late summer breeze.

"No, thanks," he said. "I don't have much farther to go."

He watched as the Amish man nodded and called to his horse, and the buggy moved on down the road.

Forced to rest a short while later, he ate the jerky strips and apple he'd bought at a convenience store earlier. A meager meal but he'd had worse—sometimes none at all. The ability to enjoy God's country outside made it a banquet.

He pitched the apple core into the nearby cornfield. It'd make a meal for some mouse or other tiny animal. He tucked the jerky package into his backpack and stood. Pain shot through his knee. He winced and then worked out the kinks before he tried walking.

Not far now. The farmhouse perched on a small hill ahead. He recognized it without even looking at the number on the mailbox. She'd described it so well.

He didn't know if he'd get a welcome. After all, they hadn't met under the best of conditions. Perhaps he should have written and asked if he could come visit. But he hadn't wanted to know she didn't want him to. If she refused to see him, he'd find a place and see for himself what she'd talked about.

But as he looked around him, as he breathed the air of freedom and walked alone and unfettered, he knew that he'd found what he'd been searching for all these years.

Paradise.

◈

Hannah stepped out of the buggy, reached back inside to lift the covered tray, and smiled. She couldn't believe they'd be celebrating Joshua's birthday again. Time seemed to fly by. Parents often said that. She hadn't believed them before now. But Joshua was eight already.

Balancing the tray on her hip, she opened the door to the schoolhouse and stepped inside. Joshua turned and waved before he resumed working with another scholar. Several other children smiled and waved shyly but they, like Joshua, returned to their work without needing a reminder from Leah, the teacher.

"I thought I'd come a little early to see if you could use some help," Hannah said as Leah walked over to greet her.

"I knew you would. I can't tell you how grateful I am for all the time you volunteer here."

Hannah glanced around the room. Nothing had changed since she'd attended this very *schul*. She'd sat at that desk over there by the west window, done her sums and written sentences on the blackboard, and heated her sandwich on the radiator as they all did in the winter. She'd celebrated birthdays here, performed in little plays with the other scholars, and fallen in love with Samuel Lapp. She had been in seventh grade; he, in eighth.

Unfortunately, Samuel hadn't known she existed even though he sat just two rows away.

Leah held out her hands. "Let me set this down for you. What kind did you make?"

"Half yellow, half chocolate. I put in two chocolate cupcakes just for you."

Leah's eyes lit up. "You know me so well."

Hannah laughed. "I should. You always bargained with me for anything chocolate if I brought it in my lunch." She glanced around. "What can I do?"

"Daniel and Jacob could use some help with their addition and subtraction lesson."

Hannah walked over to the table where Daniel and Jacob were hunched over their tablets. "Can I help you with your addition and subtraction?"

"Could we have a cupcake first?" Daniel responded, his grin full of charm.

She shook her head and tried to look stern. "Not until it's time. And besides, Joshua's *mamm* and *daedi* aren't here yet."

Jacob looked up at her and frowned. "Jenny isn't his real *mamm*. She died."

Daniel smacked his arm. "Hannah knows that. Don't be a *schtummer*! Jenny's his new *mamm*."

"I'm not a dummy!" Jacob said. He hit Daniel on the arm, and the two glared at each other.

"That's enough," Hannah said. "Time to get to work or the two of you will sit here while the rest of us eat cupcakes."

Groaning, they hunched over their lesson again. Hannah hid her smile while she watched Daniel, tongue caught between his teeth, worry over a problem. When he held up the paper and showed her his answer, she nodded with approval.

The door opened and Jenny walked in. Hannah watched as her *schwei* made her way across the room. Sometimes she still couldn't believe that this glowing, healthy woman was the same one who'd come home a pale, shattered version of herself just two years ago. Now, only those who knew what Jenny had been through could detect the slight limp in her walk and the small scar that lingered on her face, evidence of the injuries she'd suffered.

But everyone could see how she radiated happiness and could feel the aura of peace that surrounded her. Some of it came, Hannah knew, from Jenny working so hard to overcome her injuries. Some of it came from her deepening faith and her love of the Plain community into which she'd been accepted. And some of it came from the man she'd married—Hannah's widowed *bruder*, Matthew.

Praise God for that. Matthew had changed for the better after he and Jenny had married.

Hannah remembered how Jenny had once asked her what she looked for in a man. Had she made up a wish list? Jenny had wanted to know. Hannah, having never heard of such a thing, shook her head and laughed a little at the thought.

But Hannah had no interest in any of the men here in Paradise, and she'd started to wonder whether she would ever marry and start a family of her own. She feared that she'd become *en alt maedel*—an old maid.

Hannah joked with this sister of her heart that the man who would become her husband would just have to show up if she were ever to become a wife and mother.

Now, as Hannah glanced around at all the sweet faces of the children who surrounded her, she felt a small pang. If she wanted *kinner* of her own—and she realized more and more these days that she did—maybe she would have to settle for one of the men who'd tried to court her.

No one was home.

Chris couldn't believe it. He'd come all this way and no one was home. Why hadn't he thought this could happen?

But he'd figured that life on a farm kept you mostly on the farm. That had been his experience growing up on one. He hadn't gotten away from it except to go to school—time he'd begrudged. What did he need algebra for anyway? Would it help him to run a farm? Simple math, geometry—okay, he might need those. But algebra? And English? He spoke it just fine, thank you very much. Agricultural and 4-H classes after school—now that was different. He could use those for his future, he'd told the guidance counselor.

After a brief stint in the military, a tradition in his family, he'd come home to help run the family farm. Marry a home-town girl, have kids with her, enjoy the American Dream.

But things hadn't quite worked out that way.

Now, as he stood knocking on the front door of an empty house, Chris felt like it was just one more example of how his life hadn't worked out the way he'd planned.

Letting his hand fall to his side, Chris glanced around. Now what? He had money, but it was too far to walk to a motel, and besides, they had to come home soon, didn't they? He would wait. He'd prayed about coming here for so long, he refused to walk away.

He strolled around the house, spotted the barn, and felt a smile creep over his face. The barn had always been one of his favorite places, aside from working in the fields with the sun warm on his back.

Pushing open the doors, he nodded in satisfaction at the sight that greeted him. The interior was spotless, with horse tack hung neatly on a nearby wall and the stalls cleaned and lined with straw.

The loft beckoned. It had been his favorite place on their Kansas farm. He climbed the ladder. Once up top, he took off his backpack and slung it down on the hay.

Sitting on the edge of the loft, he remembered all the times he'd felt bigger than himself, high above the ground. Sometimes he'd just wanted some time alone; sometimes he'd dreamed about all the places he longed to see.

Now he'd seen them, but there was only one place he wanted to go after visiting the woman he'd come so far to talk to. He wanted to go home, see if he could live there again, make peace with his family.

His whole body ached. He closed his eyes and rotated his head. He'd pushed too hard today. Opening his eyes, he glanced at the hay heaped invitingly behind him. Many a fine nap had been taken in his hayloft.

Glancing down, he saw that he'd left the barn door open. He would hear if someone came in with the horses. Lying back, he groaned with pleasure as he relaxed. No bed had ever felt softer.

Pulling his backpack closer with one hand, he reached inside and pulled out his Bible. He opened it to his favorite passage—actually, Vince's favorite passage in Ephesians, for he'd marked it by folding the page down—and read, "I pray that He would give you, according to the riches of his glory, to be strengthened with might by His spirit in the inner man."

He had riches. Sort of. He hadn't had anything to spend his money on with his enforced time off. Of course, the passage didn't mean just money. He understood that.

Strength? He supposed he had some of that although most everyone could use more. He'd survived things he'd never thought he could. Only now did he understand that it was because of the grace of God.

His eyelids drooped, and he forced them open. He couldn't fall asleep. Blinking, he continued reading. This wasn't his Bible, but when his buddy Vince got shot right in front of him, he'd taken it, tucked it into his pocket, and protected it ever since.

Lying in the loft reminded him of times as a kid when he'd sneak away to get some space—some time to read and think. The minute he got home, the rest of the day he spent on chores. Not that he didn't like living and working on the farm. But sometimes a guy needed to get away for a little while.

Dust motes danced in the sunlight streaming through the opening to the left of the loft. The aches and pains he'd noticed from his long, unaccustomed walk eased, and lethargy stole over him.

Peace. This was the peace he hadn't felt in two years. The Bible slipped from his fingers and he slept.

꒰ꕤ꒱

Hannah frowned when she saw the open barn door. She distinctly remembered shutting it before she left earlier. Matthew was a real stickler for keeping it shut, and the *kinner* knew that.

Daisy's nostrils flared, and she jerked at the harness when Hannah stepped inside the structure. The horse seldom behaved in a skittish way. Hannah murmured to calm her and glanced around. Did some animal hide inside?

When Daisy reached her stall, she shied away, but Hannah held on to the harness and pulled her toward it. Finally, the horse settled and went willingly.

After Hannah fed and watered the horse, she turned to leave the barn and heard a faint sound. Stopping, she listened, wondering if an animal had indeed gotten into the barn. One of the farm cats might need to chase down a mouse. There, she heard it again, from up above her head. Looking up, she watched as a piece of hay drifted down like a feather from a crack in the wood.

"Is someone there?"

Perhaps one of her nieces or nephew had climbed up into the loft. They weren't supposed to, but then again, *kinner* were *kinner.* Well, if they were being mischievous, she'd just surprise them.

She tiptoed over to the ladder and began climbing it. She'd just reached the top rung when suddenly a man's face appeared above her.

With a shriek, she stepped back and into air. Her hands slipped on the wood and she felt herself falling. His hand shot out and grasped hers, held, while her legs banged against the wood.

"I've got you. Hold on!" he commanded, holding out his other hand. "Here, grab hold! I won't let you fall."

Grasping his hand, she stared into eyes that were a deep, dark brown, intense and mesmerizing. He pulled her up into the loft almost effortlessly. She lay there, her heart thumping and her breath shallow.

"I'm sorry I scared you," he said. His face loomed over her. "I must have fallen asleep up here. Are you all right?"

An *Englischer.* Dressed in a T-shirt and jeans, he wore his sandy brown hair quite short. She'd never seen him in these parts. Her heart rate, already fast from the near fall to the barn floor, beat faster.

"Who are you?" she stammered. "What are you doing here?"

Before he could answer, he heard someone enter the barn. "Hannah!"

She dragged her gaze away from the man's eyes. Matthew!

Chris felt his heart jump into his throat when he heard the male voice. He muttered a curse. All he needed was some angry husband or boyfriend.

The woman sat up. "I'm up here!"

She brushed the hay from her clothes and began climbing down the ladder, moving slowly and carefully.

"What were you doing in the loft?" he called up.

She glanced up at Chris and bit her lip, then resumed descending the rungs.

With a deep sigh, Chris pulled on his backpack and moved to the edge of the loft.

He heard an exclamation he couldn't understand and the man thundered, "Who are *you*?" He picked up a rake and strode toward the loft ladder.

Chris looked down. "Chris. Chris Matlock. I'm coming down."

He'd had a gun shoved in his face more than once, had been trained to take on any enemy, and had held his own. He could face one stern-looking Amish man with murder on his mind.

Well, maybe not murder, Chris acknowledged as he glanced now and then over his shoulder as he descended the rungs of the ladder. The Amish were known for their peaceful manner and forgiving natures, weren't they?

He hoped what he'd heard was correct.

"Matthew! What are you doing?" the woman named Hannah cried out. Chris hesitated on the steps.

Turning, Chris jumped down the last two rungs and held his arms in the air. But instead of reassuring Matthew, he still advanced on him with the rake in hand.

"Let me explain," Chris said, striving for calm. "It's not what it looks like."

2

The other man's eyes were hard and his mouth was drawn in a grim line.

He wore the same Amish clothing Chris had seen others wearing today: black broadcloth trousers, a dark blue cotton shirt, work boots, and a black large-brimmed hat.

"I've never seen you before today, you're up in the loft with my sister, and it's not what it looks like?"

Matthew turned to Hannah. "Did he hurt you?"

"Let me explain," Chris repeated, making eye contact and keeping his voice calm and steady. "It's not what it looks like."

But the Amish guy didn't look like he bought it. Chris took measure of the man. Matthew was tall and sturdy, about the same height and weight as Chris, and looked to be in good shape from farming as opposed to weight training like Chris.

He could probably take him, especially with the special training he'd received in the military. But he didn't have any desire to fight this man. He would react the same way if he caught some stranger up in a loft with his sister.

The woman called Hannah grabbed her brother's arm. "Matthew, he saved me from falling! I thought the *kinner* were up there playing, and when I saw him my foot slipped on the ladder and I almost fell. He caught me. Matthew, listen to me!"

When Matthew turned to look at her, Chris grabbed the rake and tossed it aside. Matthew jerked back and Chris held his hands up in the air again.

"I'm not interested in fighting you, but I'm also not interested in you overreacting and hurting me," Chris said. "Now, if you'll let me explain—"

"Matthew? What's taking so long?" Another woman hurried into the barn, one who looked familiar despite her Plain clothing.

Chris grinned and stepped forward. "Jenny!"

To his utter shock, he felt his arm grasped and pinned behind his back.

"Don't touch my wife!"

"Matthew!" Jenny cried. "What are you doing?"

"I found him with Hannah up in the loft—"

"Stop it!" Hannah shouted. "Just stop this right now! This man didn't try to hurt me and he was *not* doing something improper!"

Chris blinked and then glanced at Matthew and at Jenny; he saw that they were staring open-mouthed at Hannah. Evidently, neither of them had been expecting such a reaction.

"I know you," Jenny said, looking at him. She frowned and bit her lip. "Give me a minute; I'll remember."

"The veteran's hospital," Chris said.

"Yes! You're Chris!" She turned to Matthew. "I met him when I went to the veteran's hospital for tests. Before my last surgery."

Turning back, she beamed at him. "Chris, this is my husband, Matthew. Matthew, this is Chris. I'm sorry. I don't remember your last name."

"Matlock."

"And this is Hannah, my sister-in-law."

Chris nodded at Hannah.

"Last time I saw you, you were in a wheelchair," Jenny said.

"You too."

"Yes, those *weren't* the days, huh?" She sighed and then smiled. "I'm putting supper on the table. Why don't you join us and tell us what you're doing here in Paradise."

Chris glanced at Matthew and saw that the man still regarded him with suspicion. Many of the Amish men he'd seen that day all seemed to wear a rather stern look, but this one could top them all.

Jenny slipped her arm into Matthew's and looked up at him. "Chris talked me through an anxiety attack while I waited for the doctors. I don't know what I would have done if he hadn't been there."

Matthew's expression softened as he looked at his wife, then at Hannah, and he nodded slowly. When he looked at Chris it seemed to him that the other man looked less grim. "*Ya*, join us, Mr. Matlock."

"Chris," he said, relaxing.

"Chris," Matthew said after a moment.

Turning, Matthew started to walk out of the barn, but his foot kicked something. He bent down, picked up a black book, and turned to the first page. Then he frowned.

When he looked at Chris, the suspicion clearly returned. "I thought you said your name is Chris Matlock," he said in an accusing tone.

Chris took his Bible from Matthew's hands.

"It is. This belonged to a friend of mine."

He tucked it into his backpack and, without looking at them again, walked out of the barn.

Hannah watched as the stranger left.

"I think you've offended him," she told her brother quietly.

"What do you expect from me?" Matthew demanded. "What was I supposed to think?"

"I think you should apologize."

Throwing his hands in the air, Matthew turned and strode from the barn.

Looking at Jenny, Hannah raised her brows. "I haven't seen him like that in years. Not since a boy picked on me in school one day."

Jenny looked thoughtful. "Not a bad thing to see even if Chris didn't deserve it."

She glanced at Hannah, reached over, and plucked something from Hannah's hair that peeked from under her *kapp*. With a twinkle in her eye, she handed a piece of hay to her. "I can't wait to hear what happened up in that loft."

Hannah put her hands on her hips and frowned. "Not you too!"

Her sister-in-law slipped her arm through Hannah's and led her from the barn.

"Oh, I can't resist teasing you. To think the prim and proper Hannah got discovered up in a loft with a handsome man."

"You make me sound—stuffy."

Laughing, Jenny shook her head. "You're not." She glanced at Hannah. "It's just that you're usually a bit reserved, that's all. Though you surely weren't when you shouted at Matthew. I saw a new side to both of you today."

"He was—maddening. There's no need for Matthew to get upset. I wasn't in any danger."

Jenny squeezed her arm. "I know. I chatted with Chris for probably no more than a half hour that day at the hospital, but

I got a really good feeling about him from the way he talked me down from that anxiety attack. He knows what it's like."

Hannah frowned. "You said the hospital had veterans?"

"Yes. He was in the military. The Army. He might still be a soldier for all I know and on R&R. A vacation," she explained. "I have no idea."

"Army?" Hannah didn't realize she'd stopped walking until Jenny stumbled and caught herself. "He's a soldier?"

She supposed that explained the man's strength, for he'd caught her with one hand, held her, then reached down with his other hand and pulled her up and over onto the loft floor with little effort.

Time had stood still as she'd stared up into his eyes, terrified to feel herself hanging high above the barn floor, her feet dangling in the air.

Then, as she lay breathless on the hay, she'd continued to stare into intense brown eyes boring into hers, and she'd felt a connection—a soul-to-soul connection—with this man like she'd never felt with another.

Matthew had asked if Chris had hurt her, but from the time he'd grasped her hand she had known she was safe with him. She didn't know why. She just did.

Hannah's cheeks warmed as she remembered how his hand had touched her cheek. He had looked so concerned.

Jenny nudged her. "What are you thinking?"

"Nothing," she said. Bemused, she walked toward the house with Jenny.

∽૭

Matthew caught up with Chris just outside the barn. "Wait!"

Chris stopped and turned.

"I didn't mean to sound suspicious."

"Sure you did," Chris said without rancor. "But I don't blame you. I'd be the same about the people who mattered to me."

"*Verdraue*—trust—is hard with outsiders," Matthew said slowly. "But if Jenny thinks you're entitled to that trust, that's good enough for me."

Matthew walked up the steps to the farmhouse and held open the door. "*Willkumm*."

Chris stepped inside, and the warm, delicious aromas of food cooking greeted him. An older woman stood at the stove, stirring a pot with a big wooden spoon. She glanced up and smiled. "Well, *gut-n-owed*. Who have we here?"

"Someone who knows Jenny stopped by for a visit," Matthew told her as he took off his hat and hung it on a peg near the door.

He gestured for Chris to come closer. "Phoebe, this is Chris Matlock. Chris, this is Phoebe, Jenny's grandmother."

Phoebe held out her hand and Chris took it. Despite her slight frame, she had a firm grip. Her faded blue eyes were kind but shrewd. She had drawn her gray hair back from a center part and tucked it under the same white cap thing as the other women wore. She also wore a dark gray dress.

She gestured at the long benches on either side of the kitchen table. "Have a seat, Chris."

Phoebe was even smaller than Hannah. Her movements were quick and energetic. As she flitted around the kitchen she reminded Chris of an energetic little bird.

He took off the backpack, tucked it under the table, and sat at the enormous wooden farm table that reminded him of the one back home—big and roomy, with scars from frequent use.

"How about a cup of coffee, Chris?"

"That would be wonderful, ma'am. If it's no trouble."

He breathed deeply of the delicious aromas emanating from the stove. His stomach growled. He hoped no one heard, but when Phoebe smiled and he saw the twinkle in her eyes, he figured she had.

She set his coffee before him and pushed the cream and sugar closer. There was no artificial sweetener on the table, he noted. Not that he ever used it.

"You're joining us for supper, aren't you?"

"I've been invited," Chris said, glancing at Matthew. "If it's not too much trouble."

"A friend of Jenny's is always welcome. Did you work with her in television?"

"Uh, no, I—" He jumped and broke off as he heard a clatter at the top of stairs.

Phoebe smiled. "That's not a herd of buffalo, just the *kinner.*"

Three children came into view, with hair the color of summer wheat and big, blue eyes like their father. They looked like what his mother always called "stairsteppers"—children with just a year or two between them—with the oldest, a girl, appearing to be about ten, a boy of about eight, and the youngest, a charmer, a little girl he guessed to be about six.

"This is your mother's friend, Chris, come to visit," Matthew told them. "This is Mary, Joshua, and Annie."

They greeted him and then eyed him with curiosity as they moved quietly around the room, getting out plates and flatware to set the table, pouring glasses of iced tea, and helping Phoebe place serving dishes of food on the table.

The kitchen appliances surprised him. He knew the Amish rejected the use of electricity, so he'd expected a wood-burning stove instead of a modern one run by propane. Their refrigerator, too, ran on the same power.

Chris's mouth watered as he watched the platter of meatloaf join the dish of mashed potatoes, a ceramic boat filled with brown gravy, and a big bowl of mixed vegetables. When Phoebe drew a pan of rolls from the oven and the sight and scent of them reached him, he decided he was indeed in Paradise.

Jenny walked in with Hannah. "You did everything!" Jenny exclaimed. "You were supposed to take it easy."

Phoebe shrugged. "You'd just about finished cooking. I'm just putting it on the table."

The two younger women went to the sink to wash their hands and then seated themselves. Matthew asked for quiet for the blessing, and when Chris glanced in Hannah's direction, she smiled at him before she bent her head. Chris did the same, feeling a familiarity with the ritual from his childhood, grateful for the meal since he hadn't eaten much that day, too eager to make his way here before dark.

But his stomach decided to let him know how empty it felt at just that moment, so he quickly piled food on his plate, hoping no one noticed the noise.

But when the children giggled, he grinned. "Sorry. Bet my stomach will be real happy in a few minutes when all this wonderful food hits home."

Joshua passed him the bowl of mashed potatoes. "*Mamm* makes good potatoes. She makes everything good. Well, she's still working on her biscuits."

"You'll never let me live those down, will you?" Jenny said with a shake of her head. "Just because the wildlife wouldn't even eat them when we threw them outside on the lawn."

"Your cinnamon rolls are the best," he said loyally, then he dug into his meal and didn't say another word.

Chris couldn't help being surprised to see Jenny dressed in Amish clothes, with a plain high-necked dress with long sleeves. Her dress was a rich blue, though—not dark like

Phoebe's—and the color made her skin glow. The happiness he saw in her eyes convinced him that he'd been right to come here to talk to her.

She reached to wipe Annie's chin with her napkin, and Chris saw that she didn't wear a wedding ring. A quick glance at Matthew's left hand showed that he didn't either.

Some men didn't wear a wedding ring, but he'd never known a married woman who didn't wear one. Wondering at that, he looked away and saw that Hannah watched him. She frowned.

Jenny was full of questions. "So when did you get out of the hospital? What are you doing now?"

She stopped and bit her lip, then grinned at him. "Sorry. It's the reporter in me. I was born asking questions."

"You talked when you were borned?" asked Annie, looking at her. "I thought babies couldn't do that."

"It's an expression," Joshua said. He rolled his eyes, caught his father looking at him, and bent his head over his plate again.

"You're one of *Mamm's Englisch* friends?" Mary asked him as she passed the basket of rolls. "Were you with her overseas?"

Chris shook his head. "I was overseas but I did a different kind of work."

He hesitated and glanced at Jenny and Matthew, wondering if he should say any more. But although they didn't signal him with their expressions that he should censure what he said, he decided to change the subject.

"I met your mother at the hospital here in the States." He spread butter on his second roll. "These have got to be the best rolls I've ever eaten. The whole meal is wonderful."

"Have a second helping," Phoebe invited, handing him the meatloaf platter.

"I already have," he confessed.

"Three shows you really appreciated it," she told him with a twinkle in her eye.

"And you were *hungerich*," Annie told him. "Your *bauch* went groowwwl like a lion!"

"Annie!" Matthew looked stern.

"No, she's right!" Chris said, laughing. "I guess I was really hungry for supper, wasn't I?"

"So did you come here for vacation, Chris?" Jenny asked as she got up to serve dessert.

"Yes," he said. "I remembered you'd told me you lived here and decided to look you up. I wondered if you could show me around a little."

"Oh, I wish you'd let me know you were coming. I have to be in New York for a few days this week," Jenny told him, looking distressed as she stood beside the table with a pie.

"It's okay. I should have called or written first."

Jenny placed the pie on the table and began cutting it. "Maybe Hannah could take you around?"

He glanced at Hannah and glimpsed a frown before she quickly schooled her features into a bland mask.

"Of course," Hannah said politely.

"There's no need if you're busy—"

"I'd be more than happy to do it," she insisted, handing him a plate with a piece of pie on it. "Here, you must try Jenny's pecan pie. It's her best pie."

She handed him a plate with a slice on it and met his eyes. In them he saw wariness instead of the aware, intense look he'd seen when she'd lain breathless on the hayloft and stared up at him.

Something had changed in the minutes since they'd left the barn. And it hadn't been for the better.

Perhaps her brother's suspicion had rubbed off on her.

But Hannah couldn't help wondering if she really wanted to be with this man again for any length of time. Jenny had said he'd been a soldier—might still be—and Hannah had lived her whole life as a member of a Plain community. They were as opposite as opposites could get.

She didn't blame him for being a soldier. That wasn't her business. God alone—not man or woman—was the sole judge of man. But what would she have to say? Would he judge her and her community the way she'd so often seen others do? Had he come here to see them as a tourist attraction?

Yet there was something that didn't seem quite right. He didn't seem like the "type" of person who came to visit the area as so many had done in recent years. Some were interested in a more surface type of visit—look at some farmhouses, eat a number of Amish meals, buy souvenirs. It was as though they had a set of expectations, a list of what to see in a limited time.

Others came to see how Plain people lived a simpler life, one less materialistic that they envied or emulated in these times when people were cutting back or trying to save money. Or learn about connecting with family again, to what and who was important to them. Connecting to God, to spirituality too.

The latter didn't seem like Chris's purpose. Connecting to God that is. Just in the brief time she'd been around him, she could sense some tension . . . he seemed troubled. He'd looked disappointed when Jenny had said she couldn't guide him around the area and started to say something, then stopped. When someone wanted to visit, to spend time with a person, wouldn't you think they'd send word ahead?

What, she wondered, was his real purpose? Jenny was an attractive woman, a friendly one. Had he come because he'd been interested in her and didn't know she was married now and shared a family with Matthew? She'd seen his curious glance at her left hand, then Matthew's.

Hannah glanced at Matthew. He'd welcomed Chris into his home and invited him to eat at his table, yet she hadn't seen her brother fully relax as he normally did at the end of the day. It might not be obvious to someone else, someone who didn't know him, but Matthew still regarded this other man with some caution.

Jenny sensed it. Hannah could tell because she saw Jenny glance at her husband and pat his hand resting on top of the table more than once. It didn't seem like her touch was affectionate so much as reassuring.

Now that he'd finished eating, Joshua turned on the bench and regarded Chris. "What country were you in?"

Jenny nodded when Chris glanced her way. "Afghanistan."

"He was there as a soldier, Joshua, not as a journalist," Jenny told him quietly.

"You got hurt. That's why you were in the hospital where Jenny went, *ya*?" Mary asked him.

"I was at a different hospital, but she came to it once for tests, and I met her there."

Annie, always the sensitive *kind*, patted Chris's hand. "Are you better now?"

Chris nodded. "Yes, thank you."

"Did you kill anyone?" Joshua asked, studying him with an intensity that Chris found a little unnerving.

3

Chris felt the eyes of everyone sitting at the table bore into him.

He waited, searching for the right words, desperately hoping one of the parents would step in to say that children—especially such innocent, protected children—shouldn't hear the truth.

Back when he'd made the decision to follow his father and his grandfather before him into the military, he'd been so convinced that what he was doing was the right thing for him—that he was doing it for all the right reasons. Now he wasn't so sure.

He glanced at Jenny and saw that she stared at him but gave no indication of what answer she felt he should give her son. Neither did Hannah. But Matthew . . . Chris saw that his host wore a troubled expression. Maybe after the man had distrusted him so much earlier, out in the barn, he wanted Chris to look bad because he'd been a soldier and that was against the beliefs of the Plain people.

No, he told himself just as quickly. He didn't know Matthew, so it wasn't fair to believe that the man judged him.

Matthew gave Chris a slight nod, then turned to Joshua. "That's enough, *sohn*. It's not polite to ask guests a lot of personal questions."

Joshua hung his head. "I'm sorry."

"It's okay. Kids are curious. I was always like that as a kid." Jenny smiled at Chris.

"*Mamm?* May I clear the table?"

When Jenny nodded, Mary began picking up plates and flatware and stacking them in the big farmhouse sink.

Later, Chris would wonder why he happened to be looking at Mary just as she walked too close to the stove with the plates. Her elbow hit the handle of the percolator, knocking it off the stove top and sending the hot pot flying toward her.

Jumping to his feet, Chris pushed Mary aside and took the brunt of the pot slamming into him, splashing his chest with scalding hot coffee. His breath whooshed out of him as the searing liquid soaked his shirt. A curse leaped to his lips as the pain blistered his hands and his chest, but he bit it back, not wanting the children to hear.

Matthew jumped up. "Are you hurt?"

Chris pulled his shirt from his skin. He would never have believed coffee could be so unbelievably hot.

"Oh my," Phoebe cried. "I thought I pushed that back far enough on the stove."

"Here, get your shirt off," Hannah said urgently.

She tugged it away from his skin and over his head before Chris could object. Then she grasped his hand and pulled him to the sink, turned on the cold water, and splashed handful after handful on his bare chest.

"Ice," Phoebe said as she looked over his reddened skin. "We'll get some ice. Mary, grab a clean kitchen towel there, put some ice in it."

When Mary continued to just stand there, tears welling up and splashing down her cheeks, Phoebe turned to Joshua. "Get the ice, go, quick!"

"I'll do that," Jenny said. "Matthew, get the first-aid kit. Annie, you go on upstairs and brush your teeth and get ready for bed."

"But I want to help," Annie protested.

"Annie, listen to your *mamm*," Matthew told her.

He retrieved the kit from a cabinet near the stove and then moved to the side of the sink.

"That looks really bad," Matthew said, studying the skin that had already bubbled up and blistered.

He turned to Jenny. "Do you think I should call a driver to take him to the emergency room?"

"No need to fuss. It's just coffee," Chris insisted, embarrassed by the attention but in a lot of pain. It hurt like someone had just pulled the skin off him, but compared to what he'd been through when he'd been injured overseas, it should feel like a cakewalk.

"Jacob Yoder got a third-degree burn last year when he knocked a coffeepot over and the hot coffee spilled all over his hand," Hannah told Chris. "You don't have to pretend it doesn't hurt because you're a man."

He raised his brows in surprise. As he'd noticed earlier, this was no shy, docile, Amish miss.

"I'm not pretending," he said, staring at her directly. "I'll be fine."

She kept splashing his skin with cold water, and once, when her fingers accidentally brushed his skin, she pulled them back as if she'd been burned and looked away.

Chris clutched the edge of the sink as Hannah continued to splash water on his blistered skin. He willed himself not to curse in front of the kids.

Then, in the midst of all the pain, he felt a small hand pick up one of his. When he glanced down, he saw that Annie pressed it to her lips.

"I kiss it make it *besser*," she said and grinned, showing a gap in her two front teeth.

He looked at Hannah and she nodded and smiled slightly. "She's a sweet child."

"Here, try this," Phoebe said, dampening the towel with ice in it and handing it to him.

Chris sat down at the table and held the icy compress to his chest. He felt a little uncomfortable sitting in the kitchen with his shirt off. He heard a gasp and looked over his shoulder. Hannah stared at his back, her eyes wide. When her glance flew to his, he saw the shock in them.

"What—" she began, then she shook her head. "How did you—" She stopped but he saw the curiosity in her eyes.

"Like I said, the coffee's nothing," Chris said. "Really, there's no need to fuss."

His words came out more harshly than he intended, and he watched her flinch and turn away. He started to apologize and then he heard a sniffle and saw that Mary stood by the door, her cheeks wet with tears.

"I'm sorry, I'm sorry," she whispered.

"It was an accident," Chris said. "Just an accident. And I'm fine."

But she'd already spun on her heel, and then he heard her running up the stairs.

"I'll talk to her," Jenny said. She hurried after Mary.

"I'm sorry that I've gotten everyone upset." Chris started to his feet, but Matthew's hand descended on his shoulder, staying him.

"Sit. You saved my daughter from a really nasty burn," Matthew said. "Let's make sure you won't suffer the effects from it too much yourself."

Chris glanced down and lifted the ice away from his chest. The skin had reddened where the coffee had spilled on him and a few blisters had formed, but it didn't look as bad as he expected. The cold water Hannah had splashed on the burn had helped even if the pain still took his breath away. But no one needed to know that.

He looked around. "What happened to my shirt?"

Hannah lifted the wet lump that was his T-shirt from the sink and squeezed the water from it. "I'll wash it and hang it on the line to dry. Do you have another with you?"

"Yeah, in my backpack." He pushed it out from under the table with his foot and started to reach for it.

"I'll get it out for you," she said as she bent down.

"No! I can manage."

~⬨~

Hannah blinked at his brusque tone and slowly straightened. "I'm sorry. I just meant to help."

She chided herself for her impulsiveness. Why hadn't she thought he might not like her rooting around in his backpack? But as she watched him unzip it and pull out a shirt, she thought he'd overreacted.

Then again, she didn't know any *Englisch* men. Maybe they were different from the men in her community.

"So what do you think, Phoebe? Should I take Chris to the emergency room?" Matthew asked.

Phoebe studied him. Her eyes were kind but shrewd. "We should let him decide that. What do you think, Chris?"

"I'm fine. It feels much better now."

"Well, I think you might be exaggerating there but we'll abide by your decision," Phoebe said, and she looked at Matthew for confirmation.

He sighed. "Okay."

"Of course, if you feel worse at any time, no matter how late it is, you need to tell us so we can get you some relief," Phoebe said.

"Yes, ma'am."

"Joshua, could you go get a tube of burn ointment in my medicine cabinet?"

"*Schur*," he said. "Be right back."

He started to tell her they didn't need to go to any trouble but stopped when she looked at him. "Thank you." Nodding, she picked up the percolator and went to the sink to pour out the small amount of liquid inside. Then she set about making fresh coffee, making sure the pot sat on the back burner so no one could accidentally knock it off the stove.

Hannah pulled out several plastic storage bowls and filled them with the leftovers from dinner, trying not to watch how Chris's chest and shoulders rippled as he pulled on a button-front shirt and let it hang open while he returned the ice pack to his chest.

Jenny re-entered the room and sat down at the table.

"Is Mary okay?" Phoebe asked.

"Yes. I told her it was an accident and that no one blamed her for it. She'll be down in a minute to do the dishes."

"Let me do them," Chris said.

"No, you're a guest in our home," Matthew told him. "*Ach*, there you are, Mary."

Hannah watched her niece walk into the room and give Chris a shy smile. "Thank you for keeping me from getting hurt," she told Chris.

"You're welcome."

Mary glanced at her, seeking approval, and Hannah smiled. She loved being invited over for supper here. She missed living here and taking care of her nieces and nephew since Matthew had remarried. Once a week, she and Phoebe walked over from the house they shared next door and visited for supper. Hannah loved those evenings.

"Chris, where are you staying?" Jenny asked.

He shrugged. "I don't know. When I started here, I thought I'd play it by ear, look for a place after I stopped here to visit with you. I didn't count on falling asleep in the hayloft, or taking up so much of your time at supper."

"Don't say that. We loved having you," Jenny told him.

Hannah glanced at the kitchen window. It had grown dark outside while they lingered over supper.

"He can stay in the *dawdi haus* tonight."

Everyone looked at Matthew.

Hannah stared at her brother, not believing her ears. What a turnaround he'd made after his earlier suspicion of Chris. When he glanced over and saw her expression, Matthew shrugged, tilting the cup in his hand and silently sending her a message. He was obviously grateful that Chris had saved Mary from a bad burn.

She looked at Chris and her cheeks reddened when she realized he watched her.

"*Dawdi haus?*"

"It's an addition to the house that grandparents use when they've sold the farm to a son."

"That's very generous of you, but I wouldn't want to put you out," Chris spoke up.

"You're not putting us out," Jenny said, sending her husband a smile. "And besides, you might not thank us after you see it. Matthew hasn't finished his renovations yet."

Joshua returned with the burn ointment and then dashed up the stairs when Jenny reminded him of bedtime.

The floor thumped above their heads. Jenny and Matthew glanced upward, then at each other.

"Your turn," she murmured. Her husband headed upstairs.

She turned to Chris. "C'mon, I'll show you where you can stay tonight."

But before they could leave, Matthew called down the stairs for her.

"I'm coming!" she called.

She turned to Hannah. "Would you mind showing Chris the *dawdi haus*?"

"*Schur.*"

She stood and watched Chris lift his backpack. As he did, he couldn't hide the wince of pain that crossed his face.

"You'll need bedding," Phoebe said. "I'll get some." She went into another room and returned with an armful of folded sheets.

Taking the bundle from her, Hannah turned to Chris. "Ready?"

"Got your back."

"What?"

He smiled slightly. "Sorry, it's just an expression from my Army days."

"Oh."

As Hannah opened the connecting door to the *dawdi haus*, she said, "No one's used it in a long time."

They stepped inside.

"Matthew's done some work in the kitchen but he doesn't have much time until the winter when he isn't working in the fields. It's kind of small—just a living room, the kitchen, a bathroom, and this is the bedroom."

She walked into it and placed the bedding on the dresser, pleased that the place didn't smell musty from being shut up.

Chris looked around and nodded. "This is like what we call a mother-in-law apartment."

"When the son takes over the farm and moves into the farmhouse, his parents move here so they're close if they need any caring for. We won't be needing it for that. My parents are dead."

"I'm sorry. It's tough to lose family." He thought of his grandmother.

"*Danki*. But they've been gone for almost seven years now."

Going to the closet, she pulled out a quilt and placed it on top of the bedding on the dresser. "You might need this. Sometimes the nights get cool."

Chris threw his backpack on the floor near the bed and walked over to the dresser. He stroked the patches on the quilt.

"This reminds me of my grandmother."

"She quilted?"

"Yeah. Don't know where she found the time. She helped my grandfather with the farm and had six kids."

Hannah studied the way his big hand stroked the patches on the quilt. "It's something many of us enjoy doing—in my world and yours. And it's not just about making something warm for our families. It's a way to bring beauty into our every-day lives, to have something of our own, something creative."

"When we talked at the V.A. hospital, Jenny told me a quilt brought her here. She said her grandmother sent one to her with a note that said to come here to heal."

"*Ya*. I remember."

Chris walked over to stare out the window.

"Is that why you've come?"

Chris jerked around and stared at her. "I'm all healed. I came to look around, see a place I've heard about. It's been a long time since I had a vacation."

"Many people come here. Couples. Families. School groups. Even tourists from overseas. But not single men, Chris. Not single men."

"Oh yeah? Why else would I come?"

It was so quiet she could hear the ticking of the clock in the other room. "I don't know," she said finally. "But I hope it's not because you want Jenny. She belongs to my brother now."

❧

He met her stare for stare.

"I know she belongs to your brother. I didn't come to 'steal' her."

She folded her arms across her chest, eyeing him warily. He hadn't ever met a woman so determined, or so protective of her family.

"Maybe I shouldn't stay," he said slowly. "I don't want to cause any problems."

He had already brought one family enough grief. One man's wife had alternately begged and screamed at him, and the child whose hand she held . . . He hadn't been able to forget the look of confusion in his eyes. At four, the child had been too young to understand what had happened to his father in court.

For the second time that day, he turned to leave the property. And felt her hand on his arm.

"Wait! Don't go."

Turning, he looked at her. "I'm sorry," she said. "Maybe I'm being too—"

"Suspicious?"

She laughed and shook her head. "Cautious, not suspicious. I don't want the people I love hurt in any way."

"I'm not here to hurt anyone."

"No," she said with a sigh. "So far you've actually kept two of us from serious injury today. First me, and then Mary." She sobered. "I know I would have broken some bones if I'd fallen from the loft. At the very least."

"You thanked me for that."

"No," she said, looking at him directly. "I don't think I had a chance to do that. Big brother came along ready to beat you up."

She didn't think she'd ever look at the hayloft the same way again. When she'd heard a noise, she'd thought it was just one of the *kinner* being mischievous. Instead, she'd surprised a man—a strong, mysterious man. The strength of his grip had saved her from falling and hurting herself. What she'd felt when he touched her, when he looked deep into her eyes— that had shaken her more than she cared to think.

When he looked at her hand on his arm, she let it go.

"I can sleep anywhere. Haylofts. In the woods."

"No one who's a guest in our home will sleep in the hayloft or in the woods."

"I slept in far worse places overseas."

Hannah flinched. "I don't want to think about that."

He shrugged.

"You saved Mary from a serious burn too. I think that's what really convinced Matthew that you were a good person, that you instinctively jumped up to protect her. I can't let you leave and walk through the dark to find a motel."

Hannah walked to the closet and double-checked its contents. "There are more blankets in here if you need them."

"The quilt should be enough."

She watched him stroke the quilt again.

"It'll feel real homey tonight, I'm sure," he mused. "I stayed with Grandma one winter when my mother was in the hospital. Grandma made me a quilt and she'd tuck me in at night. It felt like a warm hug."

He turned. "The quilt got lost in a move and Grandma's not around to make me another. Maybe I should buy one in town before I leave."

"I teach people how to make them at a shop in town," Hannah said. "It's just part-time."

"Is this one you made?"

She nodded. "There are a lot of places you can buy one. I'll tell you where to go."

"Great."

"Well, I guess I'll go then. Sleep well."

"You too."

She felt a blush stealing into her cheeks. Nodding, she turned and instead of exiting through the connecting door hurried out the entrance of the *dawdi haus*, wanting a moment to herself but not sure why.

Stars twinkled overhead as she walked back to the front of the house. The air was indeed turning cool, but she welcomed the change from the heat of the summer and all the work that was involved in harvesting and canning.

When she walked into the kitchen, the dishes had been done and Phoebe and Jenny were chatting as they sat at the table.

"Perfect timing," Hannah joked.

"Our guest all settled?" Jenny asked her.

"*Ya.*"

"He was very kind to me in the hospital. I don't know what I would have done if he hadn't come to my rescue during that anxiety attack."

Hannah nodded. "You told us that."

"Just thought I'd remind you. It seemed like you were a little distant with him at supper."

"She glared at him," Phoebe said, and she and Jenny laughed.

"I guess I did," Hannah admitted with a grin. "He told me I was suspicious of him."

"Well, well. He was direct."

Hannah laughed. "Oh yes, very direct. But so was I."

Obviously curious, they sat and waited for her to go on.

"You might as well know that I accused him of coming here to steal you away from Matthew."

Jenny and Phoebe looked at each other and then Jenny laughed. "That's pretty outspoken even for you."

"Yes, well." She glanced at the floor and then up at them. "You can't blame me. Good-looking guy comes here unannounced wanting to see my sister-in-law . . . what would you think?"

Jenny's eyebrows rose. "Hmm. Good-looking, huh? You noticed?"

"Is that why you were gone so long?" Phoebe asked, her eyes alight with mischief.

Hannah threw up her hands. "Oh, never mind. I'm going home."

4

Chris lay staring at the ceiling, his arms folded under his head on the pillow. He didn't know where Hannah had gotten the idea that he'd come here with romantic fantasies about Jenny, but he sure hoped Matthew didn't think the same thing. He had enough problems without having his host think that was why he'd come to see her.

Jenny appeared so different from the way she'd looked last time he'd seen her. Then, she'd been pale, in pain, sitting in a wheelchair, and hyperventilating as she waited for the results of her medical tests. He'd been able to relate since he'd gone through the same thing.

Now she glowed with health, moved about easily, and looked so happy with her husband and her ready-made family. He felt a moment's envy that she'd found someone who loved her. Found a home. Found family. Found a community

He had a home back on the farm. Had family—his dad and brothers. He'd gone there after his release from the hospital, but it didn't feel right. He wasn't ready to settle there again. He didn't know when he would be.

Sleep eluded him. The burns on his chest still stung like crazy, but he felt so tired after the unaccustomed exertion of the day that he should have slept. Instead, his mind kept replaying the incident in the hayloft with Hannah.

He couldn't help but remember Hannah staring at him in shock, then disappearing from sight as she slipped from the ladder. His stomach clenched as he recalled jumping up and reaching for her, wondering if he'd be able to grab her hand or whether he would witness her fall to the ground below.

Then, when he pulled her up and she lay gasping for breath, he'd had an opportunity to look at her, really look at her. He thought she was one of the prettiest women he'd ever seen—with her clear ivory skin, wide blue eyes, and full rose-colored lips that bore no trace of cosmetics. Lips that had spoken such hard words of distrust just a short time ago.

No shy, meek Amish miss. Jenny had asked Hannah to show him around the area tomorrow. No doubt Hannah would be polite, as she had been this evening. But she'd watched him at supper, watched his interactions with her family, and now he knew why.

Well, she could believe what she wanted, but he wasn't interested in romancing her sister-in-law. He hadn't come here for that reason at all. And he didn't intend to tell her his reason for coming, either.

He wondered what the next day would bring. After so many months cooped up in a hospital, his injuries holding him hostage in a wheelchair, he wanted to live, not just exist. He hadn't fought all that pain and the surgeries and the depression and despair just to waltz through the rest of his life. He'd survived when others he knew hadn't.

That didn't mean he thought he was special and had some big purpose to accomplish—some big contribution to society to make. But it meant that he had to make the time he had been given worth something. Others hadn't gotten it.

He thought about that a lot. Especially after Vince had been killed and left him his Bible. Vince had talked to him about God and Jesus and about their love for him. Chris didn't understand why he'd lived and his friend had died. Vince had been the one with the connection to God. He was such a good person. Wasn't he more worthy of life?

His counselor called it survivor guilt. A lot of people—especially soldiers—felt this way.

Chris had no idea that he wouldn't be able to talk to Jenny alone. Now he had to think of how he could stick around without arousing suspicions.

And the woman he would be playing tourist with the next morning—he'd have to be careful around her if he didn't want to make anyone suspicious of his motives.

The burns on his chest had made wearing a shirt to bed a bad idea. Now, as Hannah had predicted, the night had turned cool and he felt cold under a top sheet only.

He reached for the quilt, unfolded it, and spread it over the bed. Pulling it up over his shoulders, he wrapped himself in the scent and soft fabric of bedding that had been dried outdoors. Finally at peace, he slept.

The next morning, Mary opened the door when Chris knocked. "*Guder mariye*, Chris." She smiled and explained, "It means 'good morning.'"

"Good morning to you too." He stepped inside and inhaled the wonderful breakfast aromas of bacon, eggs, cinnamon, and coffee.

He nearly stumbled over the suitcase that sat near the front door.

"*Mamm's* leaving for New York City right after breakfast." She shut the door. "Did you sleep *gut*?"

"Very *gut*, thank you."

She stopped and so he did too. "Chris? Do the burns still hurt?"

Chris stared at her. The child looked like a little angel with her long moss-green dress and almost white-blond hair worn in pigtails. Her big blue eyes gazed up at him.

"They don't hurt at all," he lied.

She smiled and slipped her hand into his. "*Gut.* Are you *hungerich*? We made cinnamon rolls."

"Sounds wonderful." He looked at her. "How do you say that in Pennsylvania Dutch?"

"*Wunderbaar.*"

Chris said the word, and she giggled at his pronunciation.

"What's all this mirth first thing in the morning?" Matthew asked sternly as they entered the kitchen.

Then Matthew waggled his eyebrows and sent Annie into a fit of giggles.

"Silly *Daedi*," she said, sitting at the table. She scribbled in a notebook. "Mirth means funny. Right?"

"Right."

She looked up at Chris. "I'm keeping a book of words," she told him seriously. "I'm going to grow up to be a *schreiwer* like my *mamm*. A writer," she explained with a giggle.

Tucking her pencil into the notebook, she plunged her spoon into a bowl of oatmeal.

"That's a stupendous idea," he said.

Annie's eyes grew big. She pulled the notebook open and got out her pencil. "Stupendous! I don't know that word! I have to look that up. It sounds like it means really, really good. Right?"

"You bet."

"Help me spell it?"

"S-t-u-p-e-n-d-o-u-s." He hoped. For confirmation, he looked at Jenny who grinned and nodded.

"Have a seat," Matthew told Chris.

Jenny glanced over from the stove where she used a spatula to lift fried eggs from a cast iron skillet.

"Good morning." She picked up the percolator and walked over to pour him a cup of coffee.

Chris breathed in the scent. It smelled like heaven. "Thanks."

"Hannah should be over soon. I'm not sure if she told you that she lives next door with Phoebe."

"*Mamm?*"

Jenny glanced at Mary and some unspoken message seemed to pass between them. Jenny nodded.

"Chris, how are the burns this morning?"

"Not a twinge," he lied. "The burn ointment you gave me worked really well."

Mary smiled and sipped from a glass of milk.

"I hope you like bacon and eggs?" Jenny asked.

"Love them."

They said a prayer for the meal and then passed around platters of eggs and bacon. The cinnamon rolls were bigger than a man's hand, warm from the oven, and they oozed spicy, sugary sweetness and ribbons of white icing. Chris took one and wondered if he'd be rude to take more. Manners kicked in, and he passed the basket.

"We made lots and lots," Mary told him shyly, giving him a conspiratorial smile as if she'd read his mind. "You can have as many as you want."

The children chattered about Jenny's trip but didn't seem worried about her being away.

"*Mamm's* going to talk to her editor about her new book," Annie told him. "It's not a storybook. It's to tell people what's happening to kids who aren't fortunous like us." She frowned and looked at Jenny. "Fort—fort—?

"Fortunate," Jenny said, her smile gentle as she touched the little girl's cheek. "They aren't as fortunate as us."

She took her seat at the table and served herself as she listened to the children.

Chris waited for the children to ask her to bring them back presents, things, the way kids he knew did when their parents had to go away for work. Instead, the children talked about school and chores and what they'd be doing while she went out of town.

All the while, he saw that Jenny and Matthew quietly held hands beneath the table and spent a lot of time smiling at each other. Even if he didn't know they hadn't been married all that long ago, he'd have figured them for newlyweds. But he hadn't expected an Amish man would display his feelings about his wife.

The front door opened and then closed.

⌒⊚⌒

Hannah walked in and noticed Chris sitting at the table eating breakfast.

She sighed inwardly. So, she was still going to have to play tour guide. Well, she'd do it for Jenny but she wouldn't like it a bit. The quicker he was gone, the sooner she could get back to her daily routine.

Hmm. How quick could she make it? She poured herself a cup of coffee and couldn't help smiling as an imp of mischief tugged at her imagination.

She made the mistake of looking at Chris just then and their gazes locked. His eyes narrowed as he studied her.

Hastily, she glanced away, and this time found Jenny watching her. Her sister-in-law's eyebrows went up, but Hannah shook her head.

"So do you have any idea where you want to go or what you want to see today?" Jenny asked Chris.

He cast a quick look at Hannah and then shook his head. "I think I'll let Hannah plan our itinerary."

"Itin—rrary?" Annie looked like a reporter as she held her pencil above her notebook.

Chris grinned at Annie. "Itinerary. It's a plan for a trip you want to take. You make a list of all the places you want to see so you don't forget anything. Your mother will have to help you spell that one, I'm afraid."

Jenny smiled and spelled the word for Annie.

"My *mamm's* going on a trip, right after breakfast," Annie announced. "And she's got lots of lists."

"I'm a little obsessive about being organized, I guess."

"A little?" Hannah teased.

"Obsessive?" asked Annie.

Jenny bit back a smile and then spelled the word.

Hannah gave in and placed a cinnamon roll on a plate. Jenny still didn't make a lot of different types of food but those she did she made well. Cinnamon rolls were in the top five best recipes made by Jenny, Hannah decided as she bit in.

Jenny made a face at Hannah. "So I needed some help adjusting to running a household with three children and helping Matthew with the farm where I could and still meet my writing deadlines. You were a tough act to follow."

Hannah shrugged and felt a little embarrassed at Jenny's praise. After all, she needed to do the same when Amelia, Matthew's first wife, had died.

"I enjoyed helping Matthew with the *haus* and the *kinner*. And I'll be happy to help in any way while you're gone."

She turned to them. "Starting now. Isn't it time to leave for *schul*?"

The children got up, took their plates to the sink, and then swarmed Jenny with kisses and hugs.

Hannah's heart warmed as she watched Jenny fight back tears while hugging them close.

"I'll be back in no time," she said. "I promise."

"We know," said Annie, and she gave Jenny a big smacking kiss on the cheek. "Bye!"

A quick scurry of feet, and the three children raced out the door. It slammed behind them and left utter silence.

"What a wonderful sound," Matthew said, grinning. He sighed and took a last sip of his coffee. "Let's get you off and I can have a nice, quiet house all to myself for a while," he told Jenny.

"Well!" she pretended to huff. "Maybe I'll just stay there a few extra days."

"Maybe I'll come after you if you do," he responded and her smile faded.

"That would be so awesome," she breathed. "Do you mean it? Just the two of us?"

"I can't manage it right now, during the harvest. But we can go away for a few days this winter."

"How would we manage that—" She broke off and looked at Hannah. "Do I sense a plot here?"

Hannah smiled. "See, I can keep a secret."

Jenny rushed to Hannah's side and threw her arms around her. "Well, I guess I won't mind this once." She sighed. "I feel like we're sisters, not just sisters-in-law."

The two women smiled at each other, and Jenny started clearing the table.

"Let us do that," Chris said, standing and picking up several plates to take to the sink.

"But you're a guest," Jenny protested.

"I'm used to doing chores," he told her. "I grew up on a farm." He returned to the table to gather up the silverware. "Besides, you need to get going, right?"

"Thanks, Chris." Jenny stood and looked at her husband. "Can you help me with my suitcase?"

He jumped up. "*Ya*, of course."

They hurried up the stairs, and the bedroom door shut with a click.

Hannah watched Chris glance down the hall. She was sure he'd seen the same suitcase by the front door she had when she'd come over this morning.

When he turned back, Hannah caught his look and smiled.

"They still act like newlyweds," she said with a reluctant smile.

"It's good to see her looking so different from the way she was at the hospital." Running water in the sink, he squirted in dishwashing liquid.

"It was a hard time for her," Hannah said, picking up a dishcloth and joining him at the sink. "Matthew told me that Jenny was injured when a car bomber targeted her because of her news reporting. He said they didn't want the truth to get out about how civil war had harmed the children there."

He rinsed a plate and handed it to her.

"Why were you in the hospital? What happened to you?"

"Enemy with a bomb," he said shortly.

"So the two of you have a lot in common."

She'd made it a comment, not a question. So she didn't feel any surprise when he nodded and stayed silent. But when he handed her another plate to dry, he looked into her eyes and he sighed.

"Yes." He handed her a cup, then pulled the plug and let the water drain from the sink. "That's it. Are you ready to go?"

Hannah knew when someone didn't want to talk. Obviously this man who'd been so free to talk to the *kinner* and Jenny and Matthew a few minutes ago didn't want to talk to her.

Well, he didn't want to talk to her about whatever had caused those awful burn scars on his back. It had always seemed to her that most people liked to talk about their physical problems. Emotional ones too. But this man was a mystery.

She loved mysteries. Okay, so maybe she was a little bit nosy. But there was nothing wrong with that, was there?

She hung the dishcloth to dry. "I'll get the buggy."

❧

Chris watched her start for the door and then realized that he'd be kind of crass to let her go do all the work while he sat and waited for her to pick him up.

"I'll help you."

"I don't need—"

"I'll help you."

"Did you have horses on your farm?" Hannah asked him as they walked over to Phoebe's barn.

"Two."

She didn't wait for him to open the door like some women did but reached for it. Their hands touched and she jerked back and looked at him in surprise as if he'd given her a shock. Taking advantage of her surprise, he opened the door and followed her inside.

"This is Daisy," she told Chris. "And Daisy, this is Chris."

The striking chestnut mare had big, expressive brown eyes. "Aren't you a beauty?"

"And such a flirt," Hannah said as Daisy rubbed her nose against Chris's hand.

He looked at Hannah. "I heard somewhere that sometimes people here buy retired racehorses to pull their buggies. Did Daisy used to race?"

Hannah nodded. "She's like the wind."

The horse looked bigger than he expected, but Hannah quickly harnessed her and led her outside.

Chris glanced up as he heard the wheels of an approaching buggy. Jenny waved to them as they passed.

When he returned his attention to Hannah, Chris whistled when he saw that she had finished attaching the buggy to the horse.

"That was fast."

"I've been doing it a long time." She climbed into the buggy and waited for him to take a seat.

The buggy felt like a flimsy contraption compared to an automobile, but Chris supposed that if it were made of the things that cars were made of, it would take many more horses to pull it. The inside looked spare, with simple, cloth-covered seats.

Hannah called to the horse and they were off, almost racing past farms and open pasture. Chris absorbed the clip-clop vibration of the horse's hooves against the road, the gentle sway of the buggy, and the presence of the woman who sat beside him in her demure dress. A woman who glanced at him from beneath dark lashes, a smile playing around her lips.

"So where is your list, *Englischman*?" she asked.

It took Chris a minute to focus on what she'd said. "List?"

"You said you were here to look around, to learn about the Plain people. Tourists come here with expectations, with a list of things they'd like to do and see. So where is yours, Chris?"

He shrugged. "I don't have a list."

"I see."

"I'm not here to steal Jenny away," he said, reminding her of her accusation the night before.

"*Nee?*"

"Huh?"

"No?"

"No. I just thought I'd play it by ear. Before I got your services as a tour guide, I mean." He met her gaze. "So I'll leave it up to you."

"*Allrecht.* I'll take you to the places I think you'd expect to see then."

"Great," he said.

They traveled a little farther without speaking. Then something made him glance over at her. He blinked. Was it his imagination that she looked like she was trying to hide a smile?

She must have felt him looking at her for when she turned her head and found him regarding her curiously, she carefully schooled her expression.

❧

She took him to a bakery filled with tourists eagerly buying traditional baked goods, and they chatted with a friend who worked there.

Chris looked at the vast array and couldn't decide what to get. He'd never seen so many different varieties of cookies, cakes, and pies. A lot of people were buying something called shoofly pie. Chris took a sample, but it tasted overly sweet to him.

The door opened and half a dozen people swarmed in. Where had all these people come from? There were tourists everywhere.

And Hannah was right. There were groups of people—families and senior citizens—but no single men like himself.

"What do the children like?" he asked Hannah while he waited to be served.

She laughed. "Everything. I don't think I've ever found a sweet they didn't like."

"But what's their favorite? They must have one."

"Whoopie pies."

"How about you?"

"I don't want anything, thanks."

"What about Matthew?"

"My brother's a big kid. He'll eat a whoopie pie with the *kinner* if you bring him one."

He bought a dozen pies so there'd be enough for the children and anyone else who wanted them. Then they joined the throng of tourists who moved toward a store that advertised local crafts.

Hannah led him from shop to shop that specialized in Amish crafts, leather goods, and foodstuffs. He couldn't ever remember shopping so much in his life.

"I thought I might buy a quilt like the one on my bed, but I haven't seen any I like as well as that one."

"Don't rush. There are shops we haven't visited yet."

He groaned. "I thought we'd gone in every store in town."

"Such a *faulenzer*," she said, shaking her head.

"I have a feeling that's not a good name to be called."

She laughed and shook her head. "Lazy person."

When they finally returned to the buggy Hannah had hitched near the first shops, Chris sank onto the seat with relief. One of the bags in his hand slipped and landed with a plop on the floor, spilling out the handmade Amish doll he'd bought. He bent to pick it up and stuff it back in the bag when he saw the tag on its back.

"Made in China," he read.

Hannah tried to stifle her giggle. Chris lifted his eyes to stare into Hannah's and found them filled with laughter.

"You knew."

She covered her mouth with her hand and then dropped it and laughed out loud. "That particular shop is what some people call a tourist trap. I figured it would be the kind of place you expected."

He stared at her and nodded slowly. "Yeah, I guess I did."

"Sometimes people only see the . . ." she seemed to search for the word. "Stereotypes."

"Like people sometimes do when they find out I served in the military," he said quietly.

Her smile faded. "*Ya*, I guess so." She was silent for a long moment. "I'm sorry. I guess I don't know what to think about you, Chris."

Leaning back in the seat, he glanced around, then met her gaze. "Why don't you show me what you love about your area?"

Hannah smiled at him. "*Schur.*"

She drove him by several farms and talked about the crops that were raised here during the different seasons. She stopped the buggy and gestured at the fields in front of them.

"We have alfalfa and corn and soybeans and lots of differ-ent kinds of vegetables. Even dandelions."

"Dandelions?"

She nodded. "Lots of people love them in salads."

"They're weeds. I'm not eating weeds. Or flowers."

She laughed. "They're delicious in salads. And you should try dandelion gravy."

"Weed and flower gravy. I don't think so."

"If it was the right season for it, I'd make you some and change your mind."

Sighing, she called to Daisy and got the buggy moving again. "It's hard work farming, but the people who do it don't want to do anything else."

"Like Matthew."

"Yes, he's truly a man who loves the land." She fell silent for a moment and then she glanced at him. "And what about you?"

"I missed it—working the farm—while I was away."

"Are you going back?"

He dragged his attention from the passing landscape. "To the farm or the service?"

"Either."

"I'm not reenlisting in the Army."

A tense silence fell between them. He felt like a cloud swept over then, shutting out the sunlight.

5

$\mathcal{H}$annah wondered if she should suggest they return home, but after a few minutes, it seemed his mood lifted.

"The farms look so prosperous here."

"Most of them do well. But land has become expensive here, so some Amish families have moved to other states."

She pulled the buggy over and they watched men working in the field. Hannah slanted him a look, wondering if she should ask him again if he intended on returning to his childhood home.

"And what about you?"

"What about me?"

She rolled her eyes. "Getting you to talk about yourself is like pulling teeth."

"I always thought that was a weird expression."

Hannah muttered under her breath.

Chris laughed and tried to stretch his legs. "Not much leg room in these things, is there? Anyway, no, I don't like talking about myself."

"Sorry, I'm just trying to be social."

"Are other Amish like you?"

"You mean other Amish people or other Amish women?"

"Women."

She held up her chin. "I just have a natural curiosity. Besides, we do love a good conversation. We love to visit with our friends and family."

"Since there's no television or computers."

"Because we don't want there to be," she told him with a touch of curtness, then realized she sounded prim and fussy.

He glanced at her. "Sorry."

"No, I'm sorry. I know I sounded defensive."

She paused and then looked at him. "I've seen television a few times, in a store in town or at an *Englisch* friend's home. I found some of the programs to be . . . interesting. I can see why our church leaders are worried about it coming into our homes. It was hard to walk away."

They traveled for a few more miles, both of them silent.

"Listen, I'm hungry," Chris said. "How about you?"

"Yes. I can fix us something back at the house."

Chris shook his head. "No." He glanced around. "Everyone's done enough—especially you. I'm sure you had a lot to do this morning, but you gave it up to take me sightseeing."

"*Geyan schona*," she said simply.

When he raised his eyebrows in question, she raised her shoulders and let them fall. "So willingly done. There are many places to get something to eat. It's one of the reasons people come here—to eat the food that the Amish make. That and to buy some craft item like a quilt—"

"Or a doll from China," Chris finished for her. He shot her a grin to show he could laugh about it himself.

"But really, there's no need to go to a restaurant. I could—"

"No, I don't want to put you to any trouble."

"It's no trouble to prepare a meal for a guest. We're known for our hospitality."

"I insist," he said firmly. "It's my treat."

Hannah had noticed that, like her brother, Chris liked good food and a lot of it. Soon, she pulled the buggy up to a restaurant that advertised Amish cooking and efficiently hitched Daisy to a post. While the restaurant didn't appear as large as some they'd passed, she knew of no better food locally.

"More Amish eat here than tourists," she told him.

"I'm game. I figure any place where the locals eat has good food or it would be out of business in no time."

They walked up to the door and Chris opened it before she could.

⁓꩜⁓

A feast of delicious scents greeted Chris as they entered the restaurant.

He'd always been a good eater—after all, most guys were and he worked hard—but eating MREs on the battlefield wasn't his idea of a gourmet meal. And the hospital food tasted like cardboard. Not that the hospital cafeteria could be blamed. The pain of his surgeries had taken the edge off of his appetite.

Now, he found his mouth watering as he smelled the rich aromas and glimpsed the food being served at nearby tables. His appetite increased.

When the hostess led them back to an empty table, Chris quickly pulled out a chair and seated Hannah. It wasn't just a gesture of courtesy. Combat had taught him never to sit with his back to other people or to the entrance of a building.

The counselor at the veteran's hospital called it a common reaction for soldiers returning from war. Then in what Chris supposed was the counselor's attempt to lighten the session, he had joked that a friend of his who taught high school in a small town used the same caution when dining out. The teacher claimed he always felt just a little paranoid that some of his alternative education kids—the ones who had behavior problems—would sneak up behind him.

A woman in Plain clothing walked over to take their orders. Chris had spied an open-faced roast beef sandwich, with a huge mound of mashed potatoes and gravy atop it, carried by a waitress on a tray. He'd debated about ordering it or the pile of crispy fried chicken that he saw served to a teen at the next table. He spent several minutes deliberating on his choices and decided on the roast beef. That and a big hunk of pie and the trip would be worth it.

By the time he worked through most of the sandwich, though, he realized he felt pleasantly full. When he glanced at a nearby table, the teen who looked like a football player had set down a piece of fried chicken and taken a break from eating.

"How can people eat like this—Plain people, I mean—and not have a weight problem?"

"Hard work," Hannah said simply.

He noticed that she hadn't chosen a salad and picked at it the way some women did. Yet the modest dress she wore didn't hide extra weight. It had been obvious when he'd lifted her up to the loft that day that she didn't weigh much.

Hannah had been suspicious that he'd come here to steal her sister-in-law, Jenny, but the more time he spent with her, the more attractive Hannah seemed to him.

If only she would stop trying to draw him out. He'd grown used to keeping his own counsel for years. After all, talking wasn't encouraged on the battlefield, and it was difficult to establish any kind of relationship in a hospital where patients came and went quickly.

Well, many of them did. Those who were forced to stay long-term sometimes found it difficult to hang out together. It became hard to keep their spirits up and not sound like

Pollyanna—harder still not to drag others down into depression when it covered him like a black cloud.

The place between his shoulders itched. Chris had felt it before on the battlefield but never in civilian life. Never in a restaurant. Had it happened because he'd been thinking about his counselor's teacher friend who didn't want to turn his back on his students?

Glancing around, Chris saw that several tourists stared in their direction. No, not in their direction, he corrected himself. They watched Hannah as though she were an exhibit in a zoo.

"It's all right," she said quietly.

He dragged his glance back to her. "What?"

"We're used to being stared at. Don't let it concern you."

"But it's not right that—"

"People are people," she told him and shrugged. "They're curious about the way we live. And you know, sometimes I'm curious about them. Besides, they're being respectful and not taking pictures."

She smiled as the waitress came to take her empty plates. "So, Fannie Mae, how is your mother doing?"

The two women chatted about their families while Chris resumed eating his meal.

But the itch wouldn't go away.

A surreptitious glance showed people sitting at tables around them, eating and talking with their friends and family. One man, who looked to be in his fifties or sixties, sat alone at a table eating and not looking up. Everything seemed very benign.

Chris told himself that what they called "situational awareness" might be in overdrive for some reason. Out on the battlefield you had to pay attention to your intuition, to play your hunches. Some of his buddies at the hospital told him the feeling of being watched became hard to shake stateside, maybe because at a hospital the staff watched you for symptoms—physical and mental.

But he was here on vacation. He needed to relax and enjoy himself.

Gradually, he became aware that Hannah and her friend had stopped talking and were watching him. "Sorry, what did you say?"

"Fannie Mae's mother made her famous peanut butter pie. Would you like a slice?"

"Can't. Peanut allergy. I saw some peach pie go past that looked really good. I'll take a piece of that."

"Warm, with ice cream?" Fannie Mae asked him.

He grinned. "Now you're talking."

The waitress left and Hannah frowned. "Maybe I shouldn't have ordered that pie."

"Too full?"

She shook her head. "I wouldn't want it to cause you a problem."

It took him a few moments to get her meaning. "We'll only have a problem if you kiss me."

Color flamed in her cheeks. "I assure you I won't be doing that."

Chris tried to school his features but failed miserably. He laughed, and her eyes shot daggers at him.

"Sorry, I couldn't resist," he said.

He stared at her mouth and his grin faded. Silence stretched between them, a charged moment in time where the people around them, the noise they created, faded.

"Here you go," announced Fannie Mae, as she placed their pie before them. "One peanut butter and one peach with ice cream."

"So what will you do after today?" she asked him. "How long will you stay in the area?"

"I'm not sure yet."

The pie tasted amazing: the fruit sweet and luscious, the ice cream rich and flavored with vanilla. He could die happy after eating his dessert.

A chill ran across his skin.

"You okay?"

She must have seen him shudder. "Yeah, I just got a brain freeze from the ice cream."

They ate in silence for a few minutes. Several more of her friends stopped to say hello and be introduced to Chris. He sensed their curiosity, but when they left the restaurant the itch between his shoulder blades stayed. Shrugging, he finished his pie and enjoyed his coffee.

Fannie Mae stopped back to refill their coffee cups and leave the check. To Chris's consternation, Hannah tried to reach for it. He snatched it first.

"This is my treat."

"But you're our guest. Matthew gave me the money."

"Give it back to him. It was nice of you all to put me up last night. Too bad he had to work today or he could have joined us."

"He'll be busy harvesting for the next couple of weeks."

"I missed it—working the farm—overseas," he admitted and saw her look at him in surprise. He guessed he deserved it after he hadn't wanted to talk much about himself.

They walked toward the cashier to pay the bill, and as they did, Chris swept the interior and noted the dwindling number of occupants. Just tourists. He wasn't a soldier any more, and he needed to remember that.

No one watched him. He'd left that worry behind him.

Phoebe looked up and laid aside the quilt she'd been stitching as Hannah walked into the house.

"Pretty," Hannah said, admiring the baby quilt.

"So how was your day?"

"Interesting," Hannah said after a moment. "Chris isn't like any man I've ever met. Plain or *Englisch*."

She sat down on the sofa and picked up her own quilting project.

"He has old eyes," Phoebe said. "Jenny had them when she first came to live here after she'd been hurt overseas."

"Old eyes?"

Phoebe nodded. "He's seen too much for someone so young."

"But he said he joined the military. No one made him go." She paused and thought about that.

"But I wonder if he knew what he was getting into. Can anyone? I don't know much about being a soldier but from what Jenny's shared with me, it's no wonder she came home with eyes that looked like they'd looked on too much suffering."

"But the *Englisch* spend so much time watching television, surfing the Internet, even using cell phones to stay up on things, not just talking. They seem to know everything about everything. You don't think he knew what the job of a soldier might involve?"

Phoebe shrugged. "I don't know. But it doesn't seem as though he's at peace with himself."

"Broody. That's what I called him today. Oh, not to his face," she rushed to say when Phoebe raised her eyebrows. "It's near impossible to get him to talk about himself. I sort of told him that."

"That's our Hannah. Never one to beat around the bush."

"Why waste time?" she asked lightly.

Phoebe's lips quirked. "If you say so."

"Oh, I know that's probably one reason why men haven't courted me." Hannah lifted her chin. "But I can't pretend to be something I'm not."

"Of course not." Phoebe lifted her needle and began stitching again.

"I'll probably become *en alt maedel*."

The needle fell from Phoebe's fingers. "That's the first time I've heard you talk like that. You will not be an old maid."

Hannah got up and paced around the room.

"Tell me what's troubling you, child."

Stopping, Hannah turned to face Phoebe. How she wished she could call back her words. This kind, wise woman who had invited her to stay in her home, to make it her home after Matthew and Jenny had married, shouldn't be privy to such blurted out admissions. Phoebe looked so frail and old these days. She'd insisted nothing was wrong when Hannah had questioned her several times but Hannah wondered.

"I'm sorry. You don't need to listen to me being so childish. I'm not a teenager anymore."

"Talk to me, Hannah."

Phoebe's voice sounded surprisingly firm. She patted the cushion next to her on the sofa.

"This is the first autumn I've felt like this," she confessed. Hannah dropped down on the sofa next to the older woman. "I guess I thought I'd be married by now and taking care of my own family."

"But you refused to have anything to do with the young men who were interested in you while you cared for Matthew's *kinner* and took care of his house."

"Don't make it sound like a sacrifice," she said, remembering how Matthew had said something similar back then. "I loved every minute of helping him. I love those *kinner* like they're my own."

She sighed. "But this time, this season with all the weddings . . . I don't know why, but this year it's affected me."

Phoebe's eyes were warm. "It had to happen, don't you think? You have so much love inside you, so much caring. It's only natural that you want to share that with a man and raise your own family."

Hannah laughed and shook her head. "Jenny and I talked about it once. She said I should make a list of what I wanted in a man. She called it a wish list, like I could just take it to God and ask for what I wanted. I told her that's not our way—that we feel God has someone set aside for us."

"There's nothing wrong with asking God for that man he's set aside for you, nor with telling him what you'd like in your husband. But since He knows what's best for you, He might not have the same timetable as you. And He'll surely send you someone better than you could even imagine. It's His promise to always be more than we expect, don't you think?"

"Yes," Hannah admitted. She shook her head. "He surely hasn't sent the right man yet. I *don't* believe anyone can say that Isaac is the right man for me."

"*Nee.* Even Isaac realized that." Phoebe pressed her lips together, and Hannah realized she was trying to stifle a smile.

She laughed. "Oh, Phoebe, he and I—" She paused as giggles overcame her. "We were like oil and water."

Her smile faded as she thought about how different the man she'd spent the day with was from her. And yet . . .

"What?"

"That phrase could describe the way Chris and I got along today. We're such opposites."

Shocked at what she'd just said, she blinked. "Not that I even thought about us being anything like a couple. I just showed him around. He's just here for a visit and will be gone soon."

Hannah jumped to her feet and paced the room again. When she turned, she felt disconcerted by Phoebe's expression.

"What? Why are you looking at me like that?"

"I don't know who's more surprised by what just came out of your mouth—you or me," Phoebe said finally. "If he's truly so opposite, then why would you even think about him?"

"I'm not!" Hannah grew more agitated.

Phoebe patted the cushion beside her again. "Come, *liebchen*. Sit before you wear out the floor."

Collapsing on the sofa, Hannah let Phoebe pull her into her arms. It felt so comforting to have her hair stroked, to have someone care for her like this. She'd always been the strong one, looking out for the needs of others.

"So why are you thinking about him?" Phoebe asked after a long moment had passed.

"I'm not sure I can put it into words. There's something about him that draws me."

She raised her head and her eyes searched Phoebe's for understanding. "I sense that he's a man who cares about people. You saw what he did last night to keep Mary from being burned. What you didn't see is how he kept me from falling from the loft ladder earlier that day. He could have fallen himself."

"No, I didn't hear all the details," Phoebe said, her mouth curving into a smile. Hannah felt her cheeks grow warm. She told Phoebe the story but left out the part where her eyes had met Chris's and she'd felt a connection deep in her soul.

Chris bent to scoop up a handful of the earth at his feet. He studied its rich brown color, squeezed it to see how it held moisture, and sniffed at it.

"Taking home a souvenir?"

Turning, he looked at his host, and then he laughed, shook his head, and opened his hand, letting the soil drift to the ground.

"No, we have dirt back home. It's a little different color and smell from this. Yours seems richer."

"Crop rotation."

Matthew walked over to where Chris stood near the fence that separated the front yard from the road. He leaned his forearms on it like Chris and propped his boot on the lower rung of the fence. They studied the nearby field, efficiently harvested and ready for its winter rest.

"Had a lot of arguments with my dad about crop rotation," Chris said after a long moment. "He owned the place so he won the arguments. My brother tells me he only listened the last few years while I served overseas."

"When's the last time you saw the place?"

"I headed there as soon as I got out of the hospital. Saw the family. Hung out with some friends. Then I decided to take a little time for myself and travel."

"Jenny's sorry she couldn't show you around," Matthew said, turning to look at him.

"I should have written or called and asked, not just come and hoped to find she had the time. But I haven't had much control over my life this past year. I just wanted to move when I wanted to move."

He stopped, surprised that he'd said so much.

"What?" Matthew asked.

"What do you mean?"

"You looked like you started to say something, then stopped."

"I was just thinking about something Hannah said."

Matthew winced. "I'm afraid to ask. Hannah speaks her mind."

Chris laughed. "I'll say. She said getting me to talk felt like pulling teeth."

Matthew laughed. "That's Hannah." He paused. "Actually, the same could be said about Jenny. She says she's naturally inquisitive because of her background as a reporter. But I think all women want us men to talk more."

"And listen more."

"*Ya.*"

"And be more sensitive."

Matthew stared at him, aghast. "*Englisch* women say that?"

"Jenny hasn't?"

"*Nee.* No."

"Maybe you've been more sensitive than me."

Their eyes met and Chris felt like they took the measure of each other. Then Matthew shocked him by laughing.

"I don't think anyone can accuse me of that," Matthew told him.

He didn't seem like the kind of man Chris had thought he'd be: stern, authoritarian, overbearing.

On the other hand, even though Chris didn't know Jenny all that well, he couldn't have visualized her married to such a man as that. He imagined few *Englisch* women would want a man to control them, especially a woman like Jenny who had traveled around the world.

Of course, sometimes the kind of men some of the women he knew picked surprised him.

"Chris?"

He realized he'd been lost in his thoughts. "Sorry, just thinking of something."

"How long do you plan to stay?"

"I hadn't thought about it. Maybe a week. I didn't make any firm plans when I set out."

"You have no set time you have to be back home?"

Home. It hadn't felt like home when he went back there. So he'd decided to hit the road so he could think.

"No," he said slowly. "No set time. My brother and my dad seem to have things working well without me. I needed some time to myself. Time that I wasn't stuck in a hospital, I mean."

Then he realized why Matthew might be wondering. Although the man appeared to be friendlier toward him today, maybe the suspicion lingered.

He hesitated for a moment, then decided to plunge in. "Look, Hannah seemed to think that I might have come here to steal Jenny from you."

Matthew burst out laughing. "I'm sorry," he said when he had to take a breath. His eyes were actually tearing from laughing so much.

Taking a handkerchief from the back pocket of his broadcloth pants, he wiped his eyes. "I guess she gave you a time today, didn't she?"

"She's not the quiet Amish miss I expected," Chris admitted. "That should teach me about stereotypes."

"Well, I can assure you that my sister didn't speak for me. I have no worries that Jenny can be stolen."

He tucked the handkerchief back in his pocket. "If there's no need to go back soon, I wondered if you'd like to help me here for a while. One of my part-time workers just told me he needs surgery."

Surprised at the question, Chris didn't know what to say.

"Why don't we go inside, have some coffee, and talk about it? I don't expect a man to just suddenly change his plans."

"I didn't really have anything as concrete as plans," Chris told him. "I only thought ahead as far as to find a room."

He looked out on one of the harvested fields again. This land pulled him. He couldn't deny it. "I've missed farm work."

"Let's have some coffee then and see if Phoebe brought over one of her pies. She always does when Jenny has to be away."

"Pie." Chris found his feet moving. "Pie sounds good."

He followed Matthew into the house.

"What do you mean, he's staying?" Hannah stared at her brother. "Chris is staying?"

"For a while. To help out while John recovers from his surgery."

He picked up the lid of the frying pan and peered inside. "Mmm. Pork chops. But there's no applesauce on top."

Hannah sank into a chair at the kitchen table. "Don't worry. I'll add it when it's time."

"It was nice of you to take him to see the area today. He said he had a good time."

"He did not."

"What? He said he had a good time."

"Really?"

"You sound surprised."

Hannah realized that her brother watched her. She got up and stirred the contents of one of the pots on the stove.

"He doesn't talk much," she said.

"I noticed that. He kind of reminds me of the way Jenny acted when she first came here."

Matthew couldn't have surprised her more.

"*Ya?*"

Matthew nodded. "They've both been through so much. It's affected them. Maybe it will all their lives."

"But Jenny seems fine now. She hardly has a limp—"

"I still catch a glimpse in her eyes sometimes," Matthew said quietly. "And every so often she has nightmares and she doesn't want to talk about them."

Stunned, Hannah stared at him. "I had no idea."

"She hides it well."

He hugged her. "Thank you for stepping in to help while Jenny's gone."

"You're changing the subject."

"Me? No."

He returned to the stove and checked the contents of another pan, then opened the oven. "Mmm, biscuits too?"

Huffing out a breath, she went to shut the oven. "Shoo!"

She waved her hands at him and he scooted out of range. "Out of my kitchen." She stopped. "Oh, I didn't mean to say that. It's not my kitchen."

"It *was* for a long time." His grin faded. "What would the *kinner* and I have done without you after Amelia died?"

She waved away his thanks. "I loved doing it. Sometimes I miss being around them so much."

"But you're right next door with Phoebe."

"I know. But they're growing so fast."

"I'd hoped—" he stopped and held up his hands. "Don't look at me that way."

"Don't start with the talk of maybe it's time to be looking for a husband."

She opened the jar of applesauce and poured the contents into a pan to warm. Then she grabbed a potholder and opened the oven door.

Pulling out the biscuits, she set the pan on top of the oven. "Call everyone to the table. Supper's almost ready."

"But—"

"Maybe those biscuits need to stay in the oven a little longer," she said thoughtfully.

Matthew backed away, holding up his hands. "Then they'll be like Jenny's. Please don't do that to us!"

Laughing, she set the potholder down. "Only because I wouldn't do that to innocent *kinner*. Now get away from the stove!"

"What a sharp tongue."

Poor Jenny, thought Hannah as she used a spatula to move the biscuits from the pan to a cloth-lined basket. All of them loved to tease her for her cooking. She tried so hard but she often got busy with her writing and let things burn. Hannah planned to get her a timer for a Christmas present. A nice loud one. That should keep her from forgetting something in the oven or on the stove.

❧

Footsteps were heard overhead.

"I'll go call the *kinner*," Matthew said.

"*Danki*," she said with a smile.

He left the room and she heard him walk to the stairs and bellow up, "Supper's ready!"

Thoughtful, Hannah forked the pork chops onto a serving platter and poured warmed applesauce over them. She placed the platter in the center of the table, scooped green beans into a dish, and then pulled a pan of scalloped potatoes from the oven.

The table had been set by Mary, the water poured by Annie. Joshua had helped by doing chores in the barn with Matthew.

There, she thought. Everything is ready.

She heard a knock on the front door and when she went to answer it, found Chris on the doorstep. "You're right on time."

"I'm always on time for work. And for a meal."

"Then you'll get along well with Matthew."

"So he told you."

She closed the door and turned to face him. "*Ya*, he told me."

6

If the morning hadn't been so quiet and if she hadn't been in the kitchen sipping her first cup of coffee, Hannah might not have heard it.

It began as a low moaning sound that had her wondering if she heard right, then it became a muffled hoarse scream.

At first, she thought one of the *kinner* was having a nightmare, but then she realized that the noise came from the door off the kitchen that led to the *dawdi haus*.

She walked over and pressed her ear to the door. Could Chris be in pain? What should she do?

She knocked at the door. "Chris?" When he didn't answer, she knocked again, louder this time, and got the same lack of response. She banged on it this time, hoping she'd get him to answer so that she didn't have to go wake up Matthew.

Taking a deep breath, she opened the door and called his name.

"I'm here," he said, appearing before her.

She turned just in case he wore pajamas . . . or less.

"It's okay. I'm dressed."

She turned back and saw that he looked rumpled and bleary-eyed.

"Yeah? What is it? Did I oversleep?"

"Are you all right? It sounded like you were in pain."

"I'm fine."

"It's early. Matthew won't expect you for another hour."

He nodded and shut the door.

"Well, and *guder mariye* to you too," she muttered and went back to her coffee. It had cooled a little so she topped it off with more and sat down again.

She'd heard the *Englisch* refer to themselves as "early birds" or "night owls." Only one type of bird lived in the Plain community: early. The day began before the sun came up.

This was Hannah's favorite time of the day, when she had some quiet time to pray and enjoy the dawn of another day He'd given her. Quiet time alone with her thoughts had been precious when she took care of her brother's *kinner* and his home.

Each morning she lived here, she saw Joshua, Mary, and Annie come downstairs in varying stages of wakefulness and readiness to start the day. She packed lunches while the *kinner* ate breakfast; and she watched the clock to make sure she shooed them out the door in time for *schul*.

Mornings were always quiet at Phoebe's. The two women moved about the kitchen quietly, talked without interruption of young voices, and ate their meal in peace.

Oh, how she missed the slightly chaotic mornings of this house, she thought, smiling. When Jenny had come here as Matthew's wife, Hannah had felt a moment's envy and sadness that her time as a temporary *mamm* ended. Phoebe had been so wonderful to ask her to live with her in the house next door. She seemed to understand the loss Hannah felt. She made her feel welcome and kept her busy getting settled.

Hannah knew she could go next door at any time to see her nieces and nephew, and they came over often to see her. But she'd missed being needed to help with an occasional home-work assignment—not that many were assigned since Plain *kinner* had chores once they came home.

And while Joshua, Mary, and Annie were usually well-behaved, she still occasionally needed to referee a mild disagreement or redistribute chores. Her favorite time with them came when she prepared their evening meals, and after-ward, read them stories.

She'd had a borrowed family who had given her someone—four someones—to love. However, it made her realize how much she wanted a family—a family of her own, not just a bor-rowed one.

And now that she no longer had them to focus on, she found it even harder not to yearn for her own family.

With a sigh, she got up and turned the gas oven on to pre-heat. She'd make something special, maybe her breakfast cas-serole, to send everyone off to *schul* and to work. She reached for the pan she used, then hesitated and glanced at the door to the *dawdi haus*. The pan she held in her hand wouldn't be large enough to hold a casserole for another man-sized appetite in the house. Best to use two smaller pans so they wouldn't be too heavy to lift or take too long to bake. The men who were helping Matthew with the harvest would be here soon.

She'd thought Chris would be gone by now and wondered what it would be like to have him here. He was a type of man she'd never known, one who drew her to want to understand him and yet one she knew she should hold at arm's length because he never could be part of her world.

☙

Chris shot straight up in bed, covered in a cold sweat, pant-ing as if he'd run a race. Groggy because he felt ripped from a deep, unsatisfying sleep.

Someone knocked on the door that separated the *dawdi haus* from the main one. He pulled on his jeans and dragged a t-shirt over his head as he padded barefoot to the door. Had he overslept on the first morning he'd said he'd work for Matthew?

When he opened the door, he stared into Hannah's concerned face. "Yeah?"

"Are you all right?" His heart sank. She'd obviously heard him having the nightmare. Feeling embarrassed, he frowned, assured her he felt fine, and shut the door as quickly as possible.

He walked back to the bed and threw himself down on it. After a while, he turned over. His glance went to his backpack and the gifts he'd bought yesterday that were piled on the wooden dresser. He looked at the doll's blank face and remembered another childish image.

The memory of a child's wide, tear-filled eyes flashed into his mind, painfully reminding him that he'd condemned the boy's father to be shut behind gray prison walls for years. He could still hear the child crying, hear the voice of the boy's mother accusing him of betrayal, cursing him for what he'd done.

It was no less than he'd done to himself then, and since.

Rising, he went to shower and dress for the day. One foot in front of the other, he told himself. That's how he got through most days. He'd come here just wanting to talk to Jenny about how she coped with what she'd gone through, and he hadn't been able to do so yet. That's what he got for coming without letting her know first. But he'd felt so compelled to come here, he wondered if there was some bigger reason for him to be here. He'd just been here for two days but it felt right somehow to be here. It didn't make sense but even logical types like his military instructors had told the soldiers to trust their instincts, to listen to their intuition. So he'd stay for a while longer, until he could talk to Jenny. Until he could figure things out.

He'd always enjoyed working on the farm. He found the sheer physical labor, the ability to work outdoors and think— really think—without the constant interruption of others, satisfied him. He'd found peace working the land. Here, harvesting what Matthew had planted and nurtured, he hoped to find peace again. Maybe he'd even find a way to forgive himself here among people who were known to demonstrate it so readily toward others.

He showered, shaved, got dressed, and then started for the back door. He hesitated, but then went out and closed it behind him. Perhaps he could have used the other entrance, the one that led directly into the kitchen. After all, Hannah had knocked at the door so that sort of implied he could use it.

But then he told himself that he wasn't related to the family and it seemed like an invasion of privacy. He didn't want to do anything to upset Matthew now that he seemed to be trusting him more.

So he walked around the home and knocked at the front door like a guest—well, actually, now he was an employee. But still, he wasn't part of the family.

He winced as he thought about his interaction with Hannah a little while ago. What man likes to have a woman know he isn't strong? He should be able to control how he sleeps—he shouldn't have nightmares.

Everything had been out of his control for too long.

❧

When Chris walked into the kitchen, accompanied by Annie who chattered a mile a minute, Hannah handed him a mug of coffee before turning back to the stove.

"Annie, tell Joshua and Mary breakfast is ready."

She scampered up the stairs.

"Good morning," he said.

Surprised, Hannah turned. "Good morning. I didn't think you wanted to talk after the way you were earlier."

He took a seat at the table and stared into his coffee. "Sorry."

Resting her hand on her hip, she regarded him. "I figured you're not an early bird."

"You don't get a choice about what kind of bird you are in the military," he told her. He stirred sugar into his coffee.

He didn't meet her eyes. He hadn't been that way yesterday. Frowning, she went to the refrigerator for milk for the *kinner* and set it on the table. Then understanding dawned.

"You're embarrassed," she said with surprise.

He looked up briefly, then away.

"I used to have nightmares," Joshua said as he came into the room.

She watched Chris turn toward him.

"Yeah?"

Joshua nodded. "After my *mamm* died."

"You never told me," Hannah said.

Shrugging, Joshua avoided her eyes much as Chris had done. "Abe called me a sissy when he found out."

"Oh, *liebschen*, that's not so." Hannah wrapped her arms around Joshua and her eyes met Chris's over his blond head. "It's not sissy to have nightmares."

Joshua fidgeted in her arms and she bit back a smile as she realized that he probably felt too old for her to be hugging him. He'd been doing that lately. Like people said, *kinner* grew up too quickly.

"No, Joshua," Chris said in a low voice. "It's not sissy." He looked at Hannah. "I'm not embarrassed. I just don't like to talk about personal stuff."

"Then you shouldn't," Hannah said slowly. She could tell by the way Chris's eyes widened that he was surprised by her words.

Footsteps pounded down the stairs and the girls came into the room. Matthew walked in just then too.

"Perfect timing," Hannah said, walking to open the oven. "I think the breakfast casserole is ready."

"Ready to start work?" Matthew asked him.

Chris got up but Matthew waved a hand at him and laughed. "I didn't mean this minute. Breakfast first."

He washed his hands at the sink, wiped them on a towel, and sat down. "Mmm, smells good."

"Food," Hannah said, setting the casserole down in the center of the table and turning to smile at Chris. "It's Matthew's favorite."

Chris grinned. "That's what my mother always said about me." He glanced at Joshua. "I know I ate a lot, but I was a growing boy."

"I grew two inches this year," Joshua told him.

Hannah served the casseroles of bacon, eggs, cheese, and potatoes, and after grace, everyone dug in. It was good, solid food on a cool autumn morning, one that would fuel the men for chores and the scholars for their studies. She ate a good portion, too, for the housework she'd be doing. There were always housekeeping chores in a home, and it did a body good to have work to keep hands busy.

After chores and dinner, she'd be teaching a quilting class, something she loved and did occasionally when they needed her at Stitches in Time, a shop run by a friend of hers in town.

They sold the quilts she made and offered courses to locals and tourists who wanted to learn the craft.

The day would be busy and long, but she liked days like that the best, especially lately. She'd have less time to think the way she had this past month. Good. She didn't like the way she had been thinking. When, and if, God wanted her to have a *mann* of her own, a family of her own, He'd make it happen. God's will, in God's time.

Not Hannah's, she reminded herself sternly.

☙

Horsepower.

In Chris's world, it meant the engine under the hood of a car or a tractor.

When it was used on the farm in this community, it meant the team of really large horses Matthew led out of the barn.

What had he gotten himself into?

This was farming the way it had been done back in his great-grandfather's time, he told himself as he helped Matthew hitch the horses up and lead them into the field.

A half-dozen Amish men approached, dressed in broad-cloth pants, jackets, and black felt hats. Matthew introduced him to Daniel, John, and David.

Although the day started out cool, just as the sun came up, Chris's shirt quickly soaked with sweat. It burned his chest where the hot coffee burned him two days ago. He had wanted an excuse to stay and he'd gotten it.

As he stood in the field of corn watching the green stalks with their golden tassels wave in the wind, Chris felt a sense of peace wash over him. He'd missed it so much.

Matthew came to stand beside him. "This is my favorite time of the year—when we harvest." He looked at Chris's boots. "Not sure how those'll hold up. Tomorrow maybe you can go into town and get some better ones. I'll advance you the money."

"I'm okay for money."

Nodding, Matthew looked up at the sky, then out at the field again. "Weather's holding. Thanks be to God."

He turned back to Chris. "You just let me know what you're able to do. I don't want you hurting yourself by overdoing."

Chris straightened. "I'll be fine."

Two hours later, every muscle in his body screamed in protest. Hard physical labor hadn't been part of his life for a long time, and farming this way . . . well, he had a new respect for Matthew who appeared to have superhuman energy and stamina. He'd never fully appreciated until now the modern farm machinery they used on the family farm.

The process was different, and Chris didn't know just how much he'd be helping. Farming could be dangerous work and while he didn't have to worry about a tractor turning over on him and the like, he had to keep his wits about him or he'd end up under a big plow horse instead.

But it was hard not to daydream and remember what it was like back home when they harvested the corn—he, his brothers, and his father. At the end of the day what could be better than gathering around a big kettle set over a blazing fire boiling shucked ears, slathering them with real butter, and eating them with hamburgers or barbecue until they were stuffed?

Hannah came out with coffee and hot chocolate and saucer-sized cookies.

Chris watched her serving the other men and found himself feeling jealous of the amount of attention they got. He reminded himself he'd known her only a short time and would be on his way soon. Besides, what woman would want him with the baggage he carried?

But there was no doubt he was attracted to her and he couldn't stop the unfamiliar emotions welling up in him.

"Don't forget Phoebe will be serving dinner," she reminded her brother.

Matthew took off his hat and wiped his face with a bandanna. "*Ach*, that's right. It's your day to teach . . . and enjoy the Amish grapevine."

She elbowed him. "Stop that! Like you men don't love to talk about the goings-on in the community. The difference is that men walk around talking on their cell phones like they're doing business but you're gossiping." Chris heard one of the men snort as they turned away and began walking back to their work.

"More *kaffi*?"

He nodded and held out his cup. "You and Mathew remind me of the way my older sister and I used to get along." When her eyes widened and she stared at him, surprised, he muttered, "What?"

"I think that's the most you've said about yourself since I met you."

He set his cup on the tray she held. "People talk too much about themselves."

"Not you," she said. "Not you."

She turned and walked away. Tearing his eyes from her retreating form, he saw that Matthew was watching him.

Chris couldn't blame him. He wouldn't be surprised if it took a while for the man to get over how things had looked in the barn that first day.

He was surprised when Matthew came over and laid his hand on his shoulder an hour later. "Can you go see if Phoebe has dinner ready?"

"Sure."

Chris was halfway across the field when he suddenly had a thought: was this just Matthew's attempt to go easy on him his first day? He wanted to protest that he was doing just fine, thank you. Too late now. He'd gotten halfway there, and if this was indeed Matthew's way to keep him from overdoing his first day, well, he'd fix that tomorrow.

He knocked at the front door and heard Phoebe call for him to come on in. When he walked into the kitchen, she moved a big platter of sandwiches from the counter to the table.

"Matthew wanted me to ask if dinner's ready."

"We always—" she stopped. "*Schur*," she said quickly. "I'll have you ring the bell in a moment."

"That soup smells good."

"My vegetable beef. I'm about to put it on the table."

She wrapped a potholder around the metal handle.

"Wait! Let me help you with that. It's too heavy for you."

"Young man, I've been lifting heavy pots like this for many years," she told him with a trace of tartness.

"Well, I'm here right now and my grandma would be very upset with me if I didn't help. Just let me wash my hands."

He glanced back as he left the room. "Don't you go picking that up while I'm gone."

She smiled. "I won't."

When he returned, he saw that she'd listened to him and hadn't moved the pot.

"Thanks for listening to me."

She regarded him with a slight smile. "It seemed a shame to have you losing a chance to use those good manners you learned from your grandmother."

Chris took the potholder she gave him and together they lifted the handle and carefully carried the pot to the table where she'd put a trivet.

"Do you want to ring the dinner bell?" When he nodded, Phoebe smiled. "*Kumm.*"

He followed her to the porch, grasped the metal bar, and began banging it against the inside of the triangular shape, producing that unique sound he remembered from his days on his farm.

Then he saw that the men were already halfway to the house. Chris turned and looked at Phoebe.

"Something tells me that Matthew didn't need to send me to ask if dinner was ready."

She patted his cheek and smiled at him, her eyes wise but shrewd. "No. We eat at the same time each day during harvest. I'm sure Matthew just didn't want you to overdo since he knew you'd been in the hospital recently."

"I'm fine now."

"You need a break. Come sit and keep me company while the men wash up."

He sank into a chair and watched her check something in the oven. It smelled of apples and cinnamon and sugar. He hoped she'd made it for dinner, not supper.

"My grandma used to lift me up to ring the bell on the farm," he told Phoebe. "When I got too big for her to lift, then I stood on a stool. But I had the most fun when she lifted me up, I think."

"That's a nice memory."

"I miss her. She died while I was serving overseas."

"I'm sorry," she said.

She patted his shoulder, touching him more by her gesture than her words.

"You know," she said, "I was a little concerned when I heard that one of Matthew's part-time workers couldn't help him. Then I remembered Matthew 9:35: 'Ask the Lord of the harvest, therefore, to send out workers into his harvest field.'"

She sat and folded her hands as she looked steadily at him. "God sent you at the right time."

Chris shifted uncomfortably. "It's just a coincidence that I came here and Matthew needed someone."

"Oh, so you believe in coincidences?"

Surprised, Chris nodded. "Doesn't everyone?"

"A friend of mine once said that she didn't believe in coincidence, that it was God working in her life, not a coincidence every time something unexpected worked out."

She tilted her head and studied him. "You know, you remind me of Jenny when she first came home."

"Jenny?"

Phoebe nodded. "She had old eyes. She'd seen so much. You seem troubled. I think you've seen too much, too, Chris. I hope you find the healing and peace Jenny has found here."

The front door opened and boots clomped inside.

She stood and greeted the men as they streamed into the kitchen and took their seats. They bent their heads to say a prayer over the meal and when Chris lifted his head, his eyes met Phoebe's. She'd given him a lot to think about.

Food made the rounds of the table. There was little conversation. The men were too hungry, time too precious. Before long, they were thanking Phoebe for the meal and heading back out the door.

Chris followed them. He wasn't sure how much he'd contributed that morning or how much longer he'd last, but the rest and the food had helped. He looked forward to being out under the vast blue bowl of a sky, harvesting the crops.

<del>

Hannah usually loved her time teaching quilting to the local *Englisch* and tourists who wanted to learn more about the craft.

But even though the small class appeared excited and eager, she found her attention wandering back home, back to the conversation she'd had with Chris that morning. She knew she'd been feeling a vague sense of . . . well, she didn't know the word for it because she usually felt in tune with her life, her work, her community.

But it became harder each year when autumn came and people started pairing off like they were invited to sail on Noah's Ark. Weddings were always planned for after harvest. Some days, there would be two, even three weddings.

She wasn't a romantic—she was quite practical, in fact. But just like the other day, at the *kinner's schul*, she found her thoughts returning to those niggling little uneasy areas that hovered like a gray cloud this time of year. She wasn't happy about her thoughts; she did her best to believe in God's will.

But sometimes it was just a little hard to be a single woman here. It wasn't that she was expected to marry young. Many Plain women waited to marry until they were in their middle twenties. She liked helping family and friends, but she wanted to be more than the young woman who had family obligations of her own. She wanted to nurture her own children and be held in the arms of a man who loved her—

"Hannah?"

"*Ya?*" She looked up at Jane, one of her students.

"Where did you go?"

"Go?"

"It was like you were on a different planet."

"Sorry."

Jane laughed and shook her head. "I've never seen you like that. What were you thinking about?"

Hannah felt color flooding into her cheeks. "Nothing special."

She glanced over at the woman sitting next to her who was stitching a quilt block. "Beautiful work, Betsy. That's coming along so quickly."

"I'm really enjoying this even more than I thought I would," the woman confessed. "It's really relaxing. I feel like I'm . . . I don't know, it'll probably sound silly, but like I'm connecting with my roots somehow. I remember how my mother and my grandmother used to quilt."

She knotted her thread, used scissors to clip the thread, then picked up a spool. "It's like I'm following in a family tradition."

Hannah smiled, "Quilts are more than something to keep you warm. They give women a way to express themselves creatively. I like the way that you're using pieces of your children's outgrown clothing to make this quilt. It already has memories built in it that way, don't you think?"

"Such a nice way to think about it," Betsy said. "This robin's egg blue material? Susie's party dress when she was five. This yellow came from scraps left from Marie's piano recital dress when she was ten. I think the quilt will look nice hanging in the family room."

She threaded her needle and knotted the ends of the thread. Looking down at her thimble, she laughed.

"What's so funny?" one of the other women sitting in a circle asked her. Others looked up.

"I was just remembering when I first came here and I didn't know which finger I was supposed to put my thimble on. So I put it on my thumb and then I couldn't get it off. Talk about embarrassing."

Hannah smiled. "Life helps keep us humble sometimes, doesn't it?"

"It's so interesting the way the Amish think about things," Lucy said. "I would never have thought about it that way."

Rising, Hannah walked around and looked at each quilt the women were working on. "We each have our own way of expressing ourselves. I just think that life gives us things, situations—people—to make us see how much we have to learn . . . how much we need to remember to stay humble and realize we are just like children. We don't know everything."

As she said it, she knew she was speaking to herself. She didn't know why God hadn't revealed the man He'd set aside for her yet. She didn't know what her purpose was here on earth. And she didn't know why she found herself thinking about Chris Matlock when she'd met him just days ago.

Hannah remembered how he had noticed the quilt she gave him that first night. He'd said he thought he might get one to take home when he left. Maybe she should make him one, she thought, as a way of thanking him for helping Matthew.

Oh, she knew Matthew would be paying him to help harvest, but still, Chris had come here for a vacation, not to work after spending so much time recuperating in the hospital. Chris's willingness to help Matthew out deserved a thank you, some kind of showing of gratitude, didn't it?

The Amish sewed two different types of quilts—the almost stark, vividly colored ones for their own homes, like the one Chris had admired, and the ones they created to sell to others. Those quilts were made from solid materials left over from clothing sewn for family—the blues, purples, greens, and burgundies of dresses for women and the black material used for capes, aprons, and men's clothing. Since nothing was wasted, the leftover material became quilts, kitchen aprons, craft projects for outside sale, and many other things.

Quilters cut bigger pieces for an Amish home quilt and used more creative designs. Often, Hannah and her fellow quilters favored patterns with some kind of subtle, often spiritual, meaning. Intricate stitching might form images of flowers and other things, but no patterned fabrics found their way into quilts for Amish homes. In simple houses where little of the fancy decoration of an *Englisch* home existed, the quilts made the homes brighter.

However, the quilts for purchase were more what the *Englisch* world expected in design—smaller pieces and a traditional design they were more familiar with, and more suited to the decorating needs of their homes.

Both types of quilts hung on display in the shop. Hannah thought about what type of quilt she would sew. Chris seemed to be enjoying his time here and acted appreciative and respectful of this way of life. He'd said this place reminded him of his childhood home. Apparently life there had been one of hard work and simple things too.

She decided it would be a quilt like those she designed and quilted for Matthew and Jenny and Phoebe and her friends. She thought about what pattern she wanted to use—should it be a diamond quilt based on an old Amish hymn? Quietly, she hummed the words: This is the light of the heights/This is my Jesus Christ,/The rock, on whom I stand/Who is the diamond.

A Cross Within a Cross Quilt . . . or the Friendship Quilt. *The Rules of a Godly Life* said that, "Finally, be friendly to all and a burden to no one. Live holy before God . . . your forgiveness willing, your promises true, your speech wise, and share gladly the bounties you receive."

Or, perhaps the Sunshine and Shadow design. The Amish *A Devoted Christian's Prayer Book* contained the prayer, "We pray, O Holy Father, that we might leave behind the night of sin and guilt and ever walk in the shining light of Thy wondrous grace, and cast off the works of darkness, put on the armor of light, and walk honestly as in the day."

That's it, she thought. He seemed to be so caught up in some inner struggle, to be carrying some sort of burden. Yet when he stayed in the present, like when he laughed over her letting him buy a tourist souvenir like the Amish doll made in China, his face lit up, his eyes sparkled, and he looked so happy and fun-loving. This was the quilt design she wanted for Chris.

This quilt was more pieced than the traditional ones used in Amish homes. Maybe that's why she judged it as a good choice for him—a sort of cross between her world and his. But she'd have to work quickly to have it done before he left. Perhaps she should ask her quilting circle to help her.

A student brought over her quilt block, complaining that she didn't like her stitching. Together, they pulled out the offending section of thread and Hannah showed her how to make it more even . . . all the while she reassured the woman that she should relax and enjoy herself. Perfection wasn't the goal, after all.

7

Hannah stood at the kitchen sink washing dishes as she looked out the window at the men working in the field.

Well, if she were honest, she watched one man—Chris.

Her eyes found him easily in the midst of the men in the field since he wore *Englisch* clothes. Although it was obvious that he didn't have the experience with this kind of farming that the other men did, she'd seen him working hard, taking a break only when the other men did.

Matthew had spoken of what being injured, being exposed to so much horror in war zones had done to Jenny. Hannah watched Chris stretch and bend to work again and wondered about the scars on his back, what had caused them. How he'd felt when he'd been hurt. If he suffered any long-term effects from his injuries as Jenny had.

He was a handsome man, this *Englischer* who seemed to come at just the right time when Matthew needed him. Helping Matthew had cut short his vacation, but he'd said he was taking some time for himself and he hadn't seemed in any hurry to leave.

And Paradise wasn't going anywhere. It had been here for a long time and would be here long after them. Some of the tourists said it seemed like a place out of time, like Brigadoon. Hannah didn't know what that meant. She'd never heard of the town.

She loved it here. Though she knew some of her friends had felt the need for a *rumschpringe*, she hadn't wanted a full-blown *rumschpringe*. She'd done some of the things they had—gone to a movie in town, experimented with *Englisch* clothes and makeup, but she felt as happy and content here as her brother did.

The only thing that ever gave her pause was a vague discontent with not having married yet or having *kinner* of her own. It had surfaced again this autumn at her nephew's birthday celebration at *schul*, a recent night when she was invited to supper at Matthew and Jenny's house, and at the thought of the weddings planned for after the harvest.

Determined to shove the troublesome thought aside, she wrung out the dishcloth with more force than necessary and vigorously swept it around the sink.

"*Ach*, that's quite a polish you're putting on the sink," Phoebe observed at her side.

Hannah stopped and stared at the sink. It was spotless. She rinsed the cloth, wrung it out again, and hung it to dry. "You know what they say about idle hands."

"Yours haven't been idle since you got out of the crib."

Laughing, Hannah turned and watched Phoebe set a basket of vegetables on the table. "Shall I make squash casserole tonight?" she asked, gesturing at the vegetables.

But Phoebe had walked over to look out the window over the sink. She turned back to Hannah and raised her brows.

"What?"

"Interesting view," Phoebe remarked as she moved back to the basket of vegetables and began choosing several squash. She took them to the sink, washed them, and then returned to the table with a wooden cutting board and began slicing them.

Hannah looked out the window. She saw the same thing she had for the past few minutes: Chris stood with the other men as they discussed their next task.

"Just men working," she said dismissively. "I think I'll take them some refreshments."

"Sure you don't want me to do that?" Phoebe asked.

She started to respond and then realized that Phoebe wore a puckish smile. "I can do it," she assured her.

Then she stopped. Phoebe had gone white and grasped at the edge of the table.

"Phoebe?"

The older woman blinked and stared at her. "What?"

"Are you all right?" Hannah rushed to her side and set the tray of refreshments down.

"I'm fine, fine." She straightened. "Just got tired there for a minute. I think I'll sit down and chop these."

"You did too much today, didn't you? I knew it would be too much for you to help Sadie."

"I'm not letting my body tell me what to do," Phoebe said firmly. "My spirit tells my body what to do, not the other way around. Why, if it had its way, my body would just stay in bed some days. I'm not taking it easy. That's not my way. It's not our way."

Hannah kissed her cheek. "Sit down before you fall down."

Phoebe gave her a sharp glance. "Don't you be treating me like I'm old."

"I wouldn't dream of it. You can do twice what I can in a day. I'm just saying that you should sit down. I'll be sitting down in a few minutes myself."

Tilting her head to the side to consider that, Phoebe nodded. "Then you go take that to the men and I'll fix us some coffee and we'll sit."

"Sounds good." Hannah picked up the tray.

"Since you need it."

Laughing and shaking her head, Hannah walked out of the room.

❧

He got that prickle at the back of his neck again.

Chris stopped working for a moment and spun on his heel to look around. Daniel and Isaac paused, too, and stared at him. He looked past them and saw a buggy parked down by the road. A man sat in it, his face hidden from view within its depths.

A hand touched Chris's shoulder and he jerked and saw that Matthew was standing beside him.

"What?"

"Are you okay?"

Chris cast a glance at the buggy. "Yeah. Sure. Why?"

Matthew looked in the same direction, then back at Chris. "Something bothering you?"

"Who is that? Why are they watching us?"

"It's just Josiah," Matthew said, squinting into the sun to see better. "He's probably just curious."

"Curious about what?"

"About what we're doing. He doesn't have much to do these days since he can't farm anymore." He bent his head and looked closely at Chris. "Do you need to take a break?"

"No. I'm fine." He turned back to the task he'd been doing, then remembered his manners. "But thanks."

A few minutes later, when he looked again, the buggy still sat there. Frowning, Chris forced his attention on his work. It's just some old, busy-body guy, he told himself. Let it go.

Working with the other men felt a little like being with his Army buddies. No need to do a lot of talking, especially with these men. At first he wasn't sure if it was because he was the outsider or because they'd all worked together for so long. In any case, they found a rhythm, he and these men, and when one needed something, it took just a look or a word or two and another man appeared to lead the wagon they were loading with hay or soybeans or with one of the vegetable fields that had been planted.

Later, he wondered if he lost it because he'd felt uncomfortable or had been thinking about his military buddies.

Hannah came out of the house with a tray and started toward them, but the buggy caught her attention. She turned and walked toward it and began talking with its occupant. It didn't look like a friendly conversation because she seemed to stiffen, stand up taller, and she shook her head.

Then, when she turned, a man's hand shot out and grasped her arm, stopping her from walking away.

A buzzing began in Chris's ears. He dropped the hay bale in his hands and walked swiftly toward them.

"Let her go!" he called and then he began running. He hadn't been able to stop it last time, but maybe this time he'd get a second chance to make it right. "I said let her go!"

He saw Hannah glance up and look surprised. "Chris? What's the matter?"

All he could see was her being restrained by the man, being pulled into the vehicle. She fought with the man, crying out and hitting him. Her clothes ripped as he relentlessly dragged her toward him, tossing her inside. Chris reached her and pulled her away, shoving her behind him so forcefully that she staggered and fell.

In a haze, he turned to grab the man in the Jeep, but it had turned into a buggy that rolled on down the road.

"Chris! What are you doing?" Hannah cried.

He turned, shaking his head, breathing hard, and saw that she lay on the ground, the contents of the tray she'd been carrying scattered on the ground around her.

"Hannah? Are you okay?" he asked slowly, feeling as though his veins were filled with molasses.

He bent and reached out a hand to her to help her up and frowned when she flinched. "What's the matter? I'm not going to hurt you. I saved you."

"Saved me?" She got to her feet on her own and brushed the pieces of grass from her skirt. "Look what you've done!"

A car approached and pulled into the drive. The passenger door opened and a woman emerged.

"Hannah? Are you all right?"

Chris turned and saw Jenny running toward them.

"He was taking her," he told her. "He was hurting her."

She stopped and stared at him. "Josiah?" Frowning, Jenny touched Hannah's arm. "Josiah was hurting you?"

Hannah stared at Chris. "No," she said. "He wasn't hurting me. Jenny, something's wrong with Chris."

"Chris?"

He shook his head, trying to clear it, and then his stomach sank. "Sorry," he mumbled and he started for the back of the house, toward the *dawdi haus*.

"Jenny—"

"Let me talk to him."

He felt Jenny's hand on his arm.

"Chris, wait a minute!"

"I'm all right."

"Talk to me."

"It was just a spell. I'm fine, I don't need to talk to anyone."

All he could think about was getting to his room, getting his things, getting out of there. He'd made a fool of himself, scared Hannah, and had everyone staring at him. They all probably thought he was a freak . . . or mentally ill.

She yanked on his arm with more force than he'd have thought she had in her petite form. He tried to continue but he realized he was half-dragging her and from the corner of his eye he saw Matthew running over.

He stopped, but he wouldn't look at her.

"Chris, I know what you're going through—"

"No you don't."

Matthew appeared at his side. "What's wrong?"

"I need to talk to Chris."

"But—"

"Please, I just need a minute."

"Okay," Matthew said finally. "I'll give you a minute. But I'm staying right here."

Jenny waited a moment and then she shook Chris's arm. "Look at me. Please?"

He raised his eyes and saw that she looked at him with compassion. "You had a flashback, didn't you?"

"How'd you know?"

"Because I've seen them. I've had them."

Sighing, he ran his hand through his hair. "Haven't had one in months." He glanced over his shoulder. Hannah stared at him and appeared confused. When he looked up at Matthew, he was surprised to see that he was wearing an expression much like his wife's.

"Post-traumatic stress syndrome?"

Surprised, Chris nodded. "You've heard of it? Here?"

Matthew nodded, touched Jenny's shoulder. "Jenny wasn't a soldier like you, but she's had some problems."

"I scared Hannah."

"Go talk to her. She'll understand."

"I don't know how," Chris said. "I don't understand it myself." He took a deep breath.

"Go talk to her."

"Later," Chris mumbled. He pulled open the door. "Later."

As he closed the door behind him, he heard Jenny exclaim, "Men!"

"Hey!" said Matthew.

The door shut out their exchange.

⁓

Hannah took a deep breath and then knocked at the door of the *dawdi haus*.

When no one answered, she knocked again, louder this time.

She heard a thud inside the house and then the door opened.

Chris glared at her, one hand on his hip. "What? Can't a man be left alone?"

"I wanted to make sure you're okay."

"I'm a soldier—was a soldier," he amended. "I can take care of myself."

Taken aback at what he'd said, she searched for something to say. "I'm sure you can," she said at last.

She knew about men who had to look strong, be strong. Matthew was one of them. He'd spent the year before his first wife died being strong for her and their *kinner* and then grieved so hard for three years after her death, before Jenny had come back into his life.

Since Chris had been a soldier, she supposed it was even more a part of him to be masculine, to be strong physically and emotionally, to not depend on anyone for anything. .

"I'm fine."

"Really?" She stared at him. "You don't look fine."

"Well, I am." He started to close the door, then hesitated. "Look, I'm sorry I scared you."

"I'm okay. Does that happen often?"

"No, thank God." He sighed. "I thought they were over. I hadn't had one for a long time."

"Come outside and let's talk about it."

"There's nothing to talk about."

"I want to understand, but I shouldn't come inside." She glanced around a little nervously.

He frowned, and then she saw his look of comprehension. "Oh, right."

Then he saw her glance go to the backpack on the floor behind him.

"You're leaving?"

He shrugged. "I originally came for just a few days, visiting."

"But Matthew needs your help."

"I don't think I was giving him much help."

He stepped outside and shut the door. She noticed that he looked everywhere but at her.

"There's no need to feel ashamed for what happened," she told him quietly.

His eyes, full of emotion, flashed at her. "Easy for you to say. You didn't lose control. You don't know what it's like to have these things just come out of nowhere."

"You're right."

Shaking his head, he shoved his hands in his pockets and stared at the ground. "I'm sorry, I shouldn't be taking it out on you. It's bad enough that I scared you."

"I can stand it. I'm hardly delicate."

He looked at her then, an intense look. "My mother always said a man's supposed to treat a woman right. That doesn't include scaring her."

"That's what this is all about, isn't it? What just happened out front. It's because you saw someone who wasn't treating a woman right. Who was she, Chris?"

The shuttered look came into his eyes again. He shrugged. "Doesn't matter."

"I think it must matter to have made that kind of impact." She waited but he wasn't forthcoming. "Look, I don't know much about this sort of thing but maybe you should talk about it with someone."

"I did. But no one understood like—" he stopped.

She stopped and frowned as a thought began forming. "Is that why you came here? To talk to Jenny about it?"

His head shot up. "You just have to keep at things, don't you?"

He shook his head. "I don't think I've ever met anyone like you before. You're sure not what I expected an Amish woman to be like—" He stopped. "Wait, that didn't come out the way I meant it to—"

Hannah felt herself stiffening. She knew she could be blunt sometimes. Matthew had told her so on more than one occasion when she offered him advice. But he'd never made it sound like a character flaw.

"I mean, I thought the women here—"

"Were meek and mild and never spoke up?"

"No, well, yes, I mean, no, I—"

"We're not all alike any more than you *Englischers* are," she told him and she heard a tart tone in her voice. "But I'll apologize if you feel I've intruded."

With that, she spun on her heel and walked away.

"Wait! Hannah! Wait!"

Though she was tall and so her strides were long, he caught up with her in a few steps. He grasped her arm and stopped her.

"I didn't mean to hurt your feelings," he said.

She stared at his hand on her arm, remembering how his touch a couple of days ago sent unexpected feelings coursing through her. "Let go."

He dropped his hand. "I'm sorry. But I can't chase you across the yard."

Her eyes swept his form as his words made her curious about his injuries. She wondered again how the skin on his back had been scarred. Jenny had said she'd met him in the veteran's hospital but that's all she knew. She had no idea of the extent of the injuries he'd suffered. Since he walked—and worked—she'd just assumed he'd been healed.

"That's not to be talked about either, is it?"

"What?"

"How you got injured."

His face closed up. "It's not important." He glanced over where the men were finishing up in the fields. "I need to get back to work."

She began walking toward the front yard again. The tray and the glasses and refreshments were still lying on the grass where they'd fallen when Chris pulled her away from Josiah. Hannah knelt and began picking up the glasses and placing them on the tray.

Unexpectedly, Chris appeared beside her. He picked up a glass and handed it to her. "I'm sorry."

She felt herself tremble a little as she remembered how he'd run at her, yelling and acting like a crazy person, pulling her away from Josiah and making the tray she'd carried tumble to the grass.

Looking up, she met his eyes. "It's okay." She put another glass on the tray. "Please tell me what happened."

He hesitated.

"Please? Maybe it might help you." When he didn't answer, she sighed. "This isn't about me being curious. I realize I'm not Jenny, that I haven't gone through the same thing, but I really do want to help."

"I had a flashback," he said finally. "It's like—"

She held up her hand. "Like Matthew told me Jenny had when she first came here?"

Nodding, he went back to picking up things from the tray.

"Does everyone who sees war get it?"

"I hope not," he said fervently. "Some do. I don't know how many. Sometimes people who've been victims of a crime or something traumatic get them. It isn't just from war."

When he continued to look away from her, she put her hand on his. "It makes you feel ashamed. Why?"

His hand tightened to a fist under hers, then relaxed when she refused to let his go.

"A man doesn't like to lose control."

"Ever?"

He stared at her. In her eyes he saw something . . . the same something he'd glimpsed that day in the loft when he caught her before she fell . . . an awareness of him as a man.

"Don't tease," he said and heard the roughness in his voice. He picked up the plate and began piling slices of pumpkin bread on it.

"Don't worry about that," she said. "No one can eat it now."

He popped a piece in his mouth and she waved her hands. "They're dirty!"

"You don't know what we had to eat in the field," he said. "There was this time they couldn't get any rations to us and we saw this rat—"

Her stomach turned. "Oh, stop!"

"I was just joking."

He stood and lifted the tray, then held out his hand and helped her to her feet. She was sorry when he let it go.

"I guess it's good you can joke now."

She watched his eyes darken as he looked at her. "There was nothing funny about what happened. I'm sorry I scared you."

"You apologized. You're forgiven."

"Already?" He smiled slightly. "I guess you're known for that, huh?"

"My community, you mean? Matthew will tell you I've never forgiven him for putting a big ugly toad in my bed one night."

His laughter was rich. "Typical boy."

"Yes, Matthew was definitely that when he was younger." She met her brother's eyes as she walked up the steps of the porch where he and Jenny stood talking.

"I was what when I was younger?"

"A brother who teased me unmercifully," she said tartly as Chris opened the door and waited for her to walk inside.

"What? How'd that come up?" he called after her, sounding indignant. "You were talking about me?"

Hannah turned and took the tray from Chris. "Of course. Thanks, Chris."

"What was she saying?" Matthew demanded, sounding indignant as Hannah started toward the kitchen. "Did she tell you what she did to me when she was twelve?"

8

If Chris had any thought of slipping away, matters were taken out of his hands.

Mary came over a few minutes after Hannah left. "*Mamm* says I'm to get your laundry."

"Laundry?"

Mary nodded. "She says she's doing laundry tomorrow and it's no trouble to do yours."

"I—"

She held out the basket. "If you put it in here, I'll take it to her. She says I'm to make sure I get it." The way she looked directly at him reminded him of her Aunt Hannah a little. "I know you've got dirty clothes. You've been helping *Daedi* in the fields."

"But—"

"And *Mamm* says supper's in half an hour and don't be late."

Chris blinked.

"It's a special occasion," she said, holding out the basket. "She just got back today, you know."

"Yes—"

"And she says she wants to talk to you."

Chris glanced at the backpack near the door. He shouldn't have. Her eyes followed his and then she looked at him, her eyes wide. "You aren't going anywhere, are you? I thought you were helping *Daedi* with the harvest since John's having surgery."

Yes, she definitely reminded him of her aunt with her directness, and it wasn't just because she'd used an adult's first name. He knew there was an attitude of complete equality here, that everyone called each other by their first names.

"No—"

"*Gut.* Now, can I have your clothes? I need to help *Mamm* in the kitchen."

Resigned, Chris unzipped the backpack and pulled out the plastic bag of dirty clothes he'd tucked inside just a short time ago. He wadded them up and placed them in the basket. It didn't seem right that Jenny should be doing his clothes. Surely she had enough of them to do.

"*Danki.* Remember, supper's in half an hour."

After she left, he took a shower and folded up the clothes he had been wearing and set them by the front door. Since laundry wasn't being done until tomorrow perhaps he could add them to those he'd given to Mary.

Midway through getting dressed, he stopped and frowned.

Exactly how did the Amish do laundry if they didn't have electricity?

The first chance he got at supper, he asked Jenny. To his surprise, she didn't blink at his question.

"I'll show you the machine later," Jenny told him. "Joshua, take those clothes and put them in the basket for me, will you?"

"*Schur,*" the boy said and he took them from Chris.

Jenny looked tired but radiant. When she refused his offer of help, Chris sat and watched as she moved around the kitchen taking food from the oven and the stovetop while listening to the children chatter about what they'd done while she was gone.

Chris glanced toward the front door.

"Hannah will be here in a few minutes," Jenny told him.

"I wasn't thinking—" he broke off when she just smiled.

Matthew walked in a few minutes later and Chris wondered if he'd say any more about what had happened that afternoon. But the other man excused himself to wash his hands and when he returned, Hannah and Phoebe were coming in the door. Phoebe hugged Jenny and the room became one big joy-filled space. The few days Jenny had been gone were pleasant, but it was obvious this woman was the heart of the home, and everyone was glad to have her back.

When Chris glanced over at Hannah, he was surprised at the expression on her face.

There was yearning in her eyes as she glanced around the table. When she realized he watched her, Hannah quickly schooled her expression and held out her hands to Joshua and Phoebe. The rest of the family joined hands for the blessing.

Mary took Chris's hand and he reached out his other to Phoebe. Her hand felt dry and frail in his, but her grip felt strong. The look on her lined face as she glanced around the table was so full of joy it was almost blissful.

Family. He watched a family connect in a way they were supposed to. His own family had been that close when he was growing up. They might still be. He'd stayed only a few weeks and couldn't seem to settle. He and his dad hadn't gotten along for years but there was a newer, bigger distance between them. Now he wished he'd given it a little more time.

Soon. He'd go back soon. His family worried about him while he was in the hospital. They'd called, visited, even sent him letters and "care" packages.

But he'd been so afraid of losing it the way he had earlier today to risk it. He didn't want to frighten them or cause them any more concern. Or, to be honest, shame himself. His father and his older brother had been in the military, as was the custom in his family, but neither had returned with any problems.

The psychiatrists at the veteran's hospital talked a lot about why more soldiers who served in overseas conflicts experienced problems like post-traumatic stress syndrome. What was different about these conflicts than the ones before them? No one seemed to have the answer yet.

But it wasn't so much the place he served that had been what had ultimately affected him, damaged him.

No, it had been what one of his fellow officers had done that set the course of his life, not that of the war enemy.

You were supposed to stand by the men in your platoon, your country. He knew that. Many of his comrades and commanding officers had tried to persuade him to look the other way if he saw them break a law.

But he hadn't been able to ignore what he'd seen. He couldn't go through the rest of his time in the military as if nothing had happened, so he set the wheels in motion to get justice.

Two weeks after the trial, just days before he was due to be discharged, a roadside bomb blew up while he was on a routine patrol.

"Payback," one officer told him as they carried him onto the plane to ship him back home.

Chris knew he was paying the price of betraying one of his own—

A loud noise jerked him from his thoughts. Glancing up, he saw Hannah staring at him with frown lines puckering her forehead.

Jenny jumped up and he realized the noise had been Annie dropping her glass of milk on the table. Milk rapidly spread across its surface, running in a sure path toward Chris. He grabbed his napkin and threw it down, mopping up the spill.

"Crisis averted," he said, smiling at Annie whose bottom lip trembled. "No harm done."

Hannah reached for the napkin and threw it into the sink. She walked over to the sideboard, pulled out another, and handed it to him.

"Thanks, Chris," Jenny told him. "Sorry, it's a little more chaotic here than usual."

"I think it's very nice."

"It's a zoo," she said cheerfully.

"But you love it."

She grinned as she reached for Matthew's hand and squeezed it. "You bet."

❧

"You were quiet at supper," Hannah said as she followed him out onto the porch after the meal. "You looked like you were a million miles away."

"At least a couple thousand," he muttered.

"What?"

"Nothing." Time to turn the tables on her, deflect her attention from him. "What were you thinking about before the prayer?"

He watched color flood her face. She opened her mouth, then shut it.

"I don't know what you mean."

"Sure you do. I think I saw jealousy."

"Who do you think I'm jealous of?" When he said nothing, her eyes widened with shock. "You think I'm jealous of Jenny?

Why, I love her like a sister. And she deserves every good thing she gets after all she's been through."

He rocked back on his heels. "Look who doesn't like personal questions."

"It's not a personal question. It's an accusation!" she shot back. Stomping over to the door, she opened it and then shot him a fulminating glance. "I'm not even going to justify such —such—"

"Baloney?"

She made a noise and went inside, letting the door slam behind her.

A moment later, Matthew came through the same door. His eyebrows went up in question.

"Problem?"

Chris hesitated. After all, the woman was Matthew's sister. "Hannah . . . she asks a lot of questions."

Taking a seat in a chair on the porch, Matthew nodded. "She's been like that since she was a child. She's very curious. And a little outspoken at times."

Rocking back on his heels, Chris grinned. Then he realized that Matthew's eyes had narrowed. "I don't mean to frustrate her by not answering them."

A laugh burst out of Matthew and he shook his head. "You're really a match for her, she—" he stopped.

Chris's grin faded.

The door opened again and this time Jenny walked out. "Matthew, I—what did I just interrupt?"

"Nothing," Chris said, uneasy with where his thoughts traveled after Matthew's words. "Nothing at all. I think I'll go on back to my room, have an early night. Nice to see you again, Jenny. See you tomorrow, Matthew."

He beat a hasty retreat to his room.

But as he lay in his bed a little while later, covered with one of Hannah's quilts, he thought about what Matthew had started to say. A match for Hannah? No way. It was obvious that the two of them were opposites in every way. And they could never be a match. The Amish and the *Englisch* didn't marry.

He closed his eyes and was nearly asleep. And then a thought struck him and his eyes shot open.

Jenny and Matthew had married. Was that what Matthew had been about to say? Couldn't be, he decided. What man would want his sister tied to a man like him?

And where had any thought of marriage come from, anyway? Like a lot of men he knew, he'd rather face a firing squad than think about marriage.

Sleep was a long time coming.

❧

Chris and Matthew walked to the barn after breakfast.

Matthew glanced up, studying the sky, sniffing at the air in the manner Chris had seen farmers do for years. "We'll have another good day harvesting tomorrow. Rain's holding off."

"My dad used to do that."

Reaching into his back pocket, Matthew pulled out a cell phone. "I checked the weather channel before I came out."

Chris chuckled. "Neat little gadgets, huh? Thought they weren't allowed."

"It's for business, not personal chatter."

"Ah, I see." Chris shoved his hands into his pockets and absorbed the quiet dusk settling down like an indigo cloak.

"You have any experience with gas engines?"

"I used to work on my car all the time."

"Maybe you can help me with the engine we were using on the conveyor belt yesterday."

"Be willing to try."

They walked to the barn and as Matthew started to pull the door open, Chris felt he had to say something.

"I'll make up that time I missed yesterday."

Matthew glanced at him. "I'm not docking you for that. When you were working you were doing twice the job I expected. I was beginning to worry that you were pushing yourself too hard." He hesitated for a moment.

"You got something to say, say it," Chris told him bluntly.

"I would. I will," Matthew amended. His eyes were direct on Chris. "Are you sure you didn't overdo and that's why you had the flashback?"

He shrugged. "I doubt it. It's more likely that . . ." he broke off.

"That you thought Hannah was in danger?"

"How'd you come to that conclusion?"

"I put two and two together." He smiled slightly. "And I talked to Hannah later. I know she can look out for herself, but I'll always be her big brother."

Buggies were pulling into the drive, filled with the men who would help that day. Chris wondered if anyone would say anything, but after an hour went by, he decided they'd been too far away yesterday to notice.

Working with horses instead of horsepower had felt strange at first but as the days passed, Chris became accustomed to a slower pace—more arduous, certainly, but with a lot of satisfaction as well. Chris liked partnering with another man to accomplish a task, but today he didn't mind working alone, tinkering with the engine. He thought it was interesting how the engine was prohibited in a tractor used for harvesting or in a car, but it could be used to help power a piece of machinery like a conveyor belt.

Matthew came into the barn to see how he was doing and to tell him dinner was ready. He appeared relieved to hear that the engine still had a lot of life in it. As they left the barn, Chris saw Hannah hanging laundry on the clothesline.

"Oh, you're doing the laundry," Matthew said as they stopped where she stood pinning up one of Annie's dresses.

"Some people would thank me for my help," she told him with some asperity as she bent down to pluck a pair of Joshua's pants from the basket of wet clothes.

"That means Jenny's doing the cooking."

Hannah stared at him, poker faced. Then she covered her mouth with her hand, but she couldn't stop the giggles.

"Oh, this is so wrong," she said. "We shouldn't poke fun at her. She tries so hard!"

Out of the corner of his eye, Chris saw someone approaching. Jenny. Should he tell them any second she'd hear them joking about her cooking?

Remembering how Hannah had behaved the last time he'd seen her, he decided to stay silent. He felt a little guilty that Matthew would take some heat. The guy had been good to him, especially after finding him in the loft with his sister. But it couldn't be helped.

"So, what's so funny?" Jenny asked brightly and Hannah jumped and spun around.

"Oh, nothing really."

"But you both were laughing so hard."

She looked from Hannah to Matthew and back again.

"Did you come out to tell us dinner is ready?" Matthew asked her.

Her eyes narrowed with suspicion. "You were talking about my cooking, weren't you?" She swatted him with the dish towel she carried in her hands.

"Oh, now why would we do that?" he said quickly, a little too quickly, for she looked even more suspicious.

Jenny turned to Chris. "That's what they were doing, right, Chris?"

He hadn't expected this. "Er, uh, now why would they do that?"

"Because my cooking's still not very good," she said honestly. "Now tell the truth. That's what they were doing."

"I—" He held out his hands and shrugged.

"Did I tell you that I'm the farm's bookkeeper?" she asked, giving him a sweet smile. "I sign the paychecks."

"You sign my paycheck?"

She folded her arms across her chest. "Yes."

"Sorry, I'm giving you up for that," Chris told Hannah and grinned when she glared at him. "Yes, Jenny, they were making fun of your cooking."

"I think you should have an extra slice of pie for dessert," Jenny told him.

"Pie?"

"Shoofly pie."

When he hesitated, she frowned. "Phoebe made it."

"Oh, okay."

She tossed the dish towel at him. "You're no better than those two," she complained.

But she was smiling at him, so Chris didn't figure he could be in too much trouble with her.

"Hmmm. Phoebe brought over the pie."

"That she did, dear husband."

"I still get a piece of it, don't I?"

Chris saw Jenny's lips twitch.

"I'll need some convincing," she told him, giving him a smile.

Chris exchanged a look with Hannah.

"See you inside," she said and she slanted her head in the direction of the house.

Chris nodded, showing he understood the silent message. Chris and Hannah walked to the front of the house and climbed the porch steps. He opened the door for her.

As he followed her inside, he turned and wondered where Matthew and Jenny were, then he saw them silhouetted behind a bed sheet. It was obvious they were kissing.

"Newlyweds," Hannah said with a smile.

≈⊘≈

The explosion caught them unaware as they sat at the table eating.

Matthew jumped up and looked out the kitchen window. "The barn's on fire! Jenny, go to the shed and call 911."

Chris shot out of his seat and followed Matthew out the door. Flames were licking up one side of the wooden barn. Before they got to the barn door, Eli came staggering out, waving his arms wildly, his shirt on fire.

Acting on instinct, Chris ran and tackled him, throwing him to the ground and using his hands to put out the flames. Groaning in pain, the man stared up at Chris, his eyes wide and terrified, his face blackened by the explosion.

"What happened?" he croaked.

"Lie still, help's on the way."

The shirt had burned off Eli and his skin was peeling, blistering, a burning bright red mass on his chest and arms.

"Are you okay?"

"*Ya*," he said. "I think so." He struggled to sit up. "I need to help."

Chris pushed him down, hoping he didn't hurt him further. "You stay here."

Hannah raced over and dropped to her knees beside him. "No, don't get up. Jenny's called for help."

"Got to—got to help them put out the fire," Eli gasped.

"Make him stay here," Chris told her. "The pain hasn't set in yet so he thinks he's okay but he's not."

He sprang to his feet and ran to help the other men throwing buckets of water from the water trough onto the fire. It seemed like hours, but only minutes later, Chris heard sirens heading toward the farmhouse. The local volunteer fire department arrived and began unfurling their hoses and spraying water on the blaze.

Paramedics grabbed their bags and ran to Eli. Relieved of his firefighting detail by those more experienced, Chris walked over to watch them check Eli's vitals, insert an IV, and do some preliminary treatment of the burns.

Though Eli protested, they placed him on a gurney and took him to a waiting ambulance. The vehicle pulled away, siren blaring, and raced down the road.

Chris stood with Matthew, Jenny, and Hannah and watched as the men extinguished the fire. A large gaping hole showed in the side of the barn, the edges of the wood blackened and smoking. The stench of smoke lingered on the air.

"Thank goodness the horses were out in the field," Hannah told Matthew as she rubbed his back with her hand.

Matthew had the look of a shell-shocked soldier in the field.

"I don't understand what happened," he said. "Did Eli say what happened?"

Jenny put her hand on her husband's arm. "He was in shock."

"I should go to the hospital and see how he is."

A man separated himself from the group of firemen who were talking and walked over to them.

"Are you the property owner?" he asked Matthew.

"Yes."

"I understand you heard some kind of loud noise before the barn caught on fire? Any idea what could have caused it?"

"No, I don't understand it, we're careful, all of us, with what we do and what we store in the barn."

The man nodded and looked at the barn. "They're always a problem. Wood structure, hay, equipment . . ."

He flipped open a pocket on his shirt, dug out a small notebook and pen and jotted something down. Then he glanced up at them.

"I'll be back tomorrow when things cool down to look around some more. Keep everyone out, okay? Don't want anyone messing with evidence, just in case."

The firefighters loaded their hoses onto the truck, climbed aboard, and drove away.

"Evidence?" Hannah said, frowning. "What does he mean by that?"

"I'm sure it's nothing," Jenny reassured her. "No one around here would deliberately set fire to our barn. Come on, Matthew, let's borrow my grandmother's buggy and go to the hospital to see about Eli."

They started to walk away and then Jenny stopped and clapped a hand to her mouth. "Oh, Hannah, the children will be home from school soon. Can you—"

"Don't worry about a thing," Hannah said quickly. "I'll take care of everything."

After they left, Chris walked over to the barn.

"He said not to go near it—"

Waving a hand at her, Chris moved a little closer and peered into the blackened barn. The family buggy had collapsed into a heap of burned rubble; the horse stalls still smoked. Farm tools were blistered by the heat of the fire. The table where

Chris had worked on the engine lay broken in many pieces on the dirt floor.

He wondered if the structure might be safe enough to repair it or if it would have to be torn down and rebuilt. Well, it would have to wait until they were finished harvesting. Getting the crops in had to be first. No matter what happened, the family depended on the money they would bring in.

Sighing, he shook his head. Something nagged at him, something he couldn't put his finger on.

"I'm making some *kaffi*," Hannah said. "Do you want some?"

"Huh? Oh, yeah, that would be great. Thanks."

He followed her back inside. The remains of their dinner lay on the table, sandwiches dropped on plates and cups on their side amidst a puddle of coffee.

"Oh," Hannah said, then she looked at him. "I should have thought to ask you . . . we'd barely started eating. You must still be hungry. I'll fix you something."

He shook his head. "I'm not hungry. Are you?"

She pressed a hand against her stomach. "No, I couldn't eat. Not after seeing what happened to Eli—" she shuddered.

Chris picked up a plate, scraped the contents into the trash can, and put it into the sink. He noticed that she didn't tell him that she'd do it and to sit down because he was a guest. Clearly, she'd been rattled by what had happened.

He watched her out of the corner of his eye as she dumped the cold coffee in the sink, filled up the percolator with fresh water, and measured out ground coffee. She set the percolator on the stove, turned on the flame, and sighed as she looked around the kitchen.

"You're sure you're not hungry? I can warm up the soup, make new sandwiches."

He shook his head. "Just the coffee."

The liquid heated and began to beat with a rhythmic music against the clear glass knob at the top of the pot. It was a familiar sound he remembered from sitting in his grandmother's kitchen. A soothing one. The newer electric coffee makers just didn't make the same sound or give the process a homey feel.

The rich aroma of it brewing took him back to sitting at the table in his grandmother's kitchen just before he deployed. She'd made him coffee and served him a plate of his favorite cookies—oatmeal raisin—and pressed a box of them to his chest as he left the house. Later, he'd known something had happened to her, even before the chaplain notified him. There hadn't been the usual weekly care package of cookies at mail call.

He shook his head, forcing the memory away, as Hannah set a cup of coffee before him.

Instead of sitting down to drink a cup herself, she started filling the sink with hot water.

"Sit down," he said. "I'll help you with them after you have a cup too."

She continued to stand at the sink and he saw her look out the window.

"Don't," he repeated. "We need to take a break first."

She started to argue and then she nodded. "Let me finish putting them in water. They'll be easier to clean that way."

But when she sat, he noticed that she just stirred and stirred the coffee without drinking it.

And his own coffee cooled as Chris stared into his own cup as he tried to figure out what had happened to Eli and the barn.

9

*H*annah walked down the road quite a distance from the farmhouse so she could talk to her nieces and nephew before they saw the barn.

They looked surprised when they saw her standing by the side of the road. They were old enough now that they usually walked home from *schul* by themselves.

"Something happened today," she told them. "Everyone's all right," she assured them quickly when she saw fear spring into their eyes. She didn't blame them—they had lost their mother and probably the first thing that came into their minds was that they were about to get bad news concerning their *daedi* or *mamm*.

"There was a fire in the barn today."

"The horses—" Joshua cried.

Hannah grabbed his arm as he started to run. "The horses were in the fields. They're fine."

"What caused the fire?" Mary wanted to know.

"The firemen don't know. They're going to find out."

Annie tugged on Hannah's apron. "*Daedi* and *Mamm* aren't hurt? You're sure?"

"Positive. You'll see for yourself when they get home. Eli was hurt but he'll be okay."

Annie stuck her thumb in her mouth, something Hannah had seen her do many times when she felt uncertain. She hadn't done it since Jenny came into her life. Hannah held out her hand and Annie took it as they walked to the barn.

She told them what happened, leaving out the part about the explosion and graphic details of how Eli had looked with his skin so burned. Instead she focused on how quickly the firemen had arrived so they'd be reassured that there were people who would help in such an emergency.

"We're not to go near it," she warned. "The man who's in charge of the firemen said that they want to come back tomorrow when it's not hot inside and see if they can figure out what caused the fire."

"Will the house catch on fire too?" Annie asked.

"No, no, *liebschen*," Hannah soothed. "Something in the barn caused it. Maybe some paint or something. We don't know but the fireman will find out."

"Where will our horses sleep?" Mary asked.

"Either at Phoebe's or the Lapps. They'll be fine."

Joshua glanced around. "Did the buggy burn up?"

Hannah nodded. "*Ya*, it wasn't safe to go in and get it. So your *mamm* and *daedi* are using Phoebe's to go see Eli. Your *daedi* will get a new buggy later."

"Maybe one with a radio?"

Laughing, Hannah shook her head. "I know that Leroy has one in his courting buggy, but he's in his *rumschpringe*."

"But why is it okay when he's in his *rumschpringe* but not later?" Joshua persisted.

"That's something you should ask your *daedi*. Just not today, *allrecht*? I'm sure he'll be too concerned about Eli and the barn."

Joshua nodded.

She ran her hand over his hair. "How about we go inside and have some *kichli* and milk before we start our chores?"

"Yes!" they chorused and the three of them raced to the kitchen. After oatmeal-raisin cookies and big glasses of milk, the children went about their assigned chores. Mary went to take down the laundry, Joshua ran to get the stalls in Phoebe's barn ready for the horses, and Annie started setting the table for supper.

Phoebe. Thank goodness she'd gone to help a friend today, thought Hannah. It would have been so upsetting for her to witness what had happened, to see Eli burned. Hannah didn't look forward to telling her later, but being there herself would have been too much for the older woman.

Hannah went into the pantry and thought about what to cook for supper. A roast had been left to thaw in the refrigerator. This must be what Jenny had planned to have for supper, she thought.

Pulling it out, she glanced at the clock and figured she had just enough time to cook it for supper. She'd put some carrots and potatoes in with it. Dessert would have to be something simple and quick to make.

Someone knocked at the front door. Hannah went to answer it. Chris stood on the doorstep, hands shoved in the pockets of his jeans, his expression unsmiling.

"Is there anything I can do? Chores that Matthew would do at this time of day that I can take care of for him? Animals to feed or whatever?"

"Joshua is fixing up some stalls in Phoebe's barn. The horses are out in the pasture," she said after a moment. "I'd thought about sending Joshua out to get them—"

"I'll take care of it."

She bit her lip, thinking hard. "Take Joshua with you since they know him. Phoebe's got room but I don't know if she has enough food. If not, let me know and I'll send Joshua over to get some from the Lapps."

He nodded and turned to leave.

"Chris?"

Turning again, he looked at her. "Yes?"

"I appreciate you thinking to offer this and I'm sure Matthew will too."

"I'm happy to help."

"And you've *been* a help too," she said. "You came here for a vacation and you've had little of it."

"I had a lot of time off before this," he said, shrugging.

"I'd hardly call being in the hospital time off."

"I'm not used to sitting around for any reason."

"Hannah, do you want me to peel the potatoes?" Annie called.

"No! Don't touch that knife!" she turned to respond. "Do you hear me?"

"I won't!"

"Anyway, I want to thank you," she told Chris.

She took a deep breath and said what she knew she should have said some time ago. "I know we got off on the wrong foot, and I haven't always been pleasant to you."

"Yeah, it was a surprise because we're so much alike," he said.

"Alike?" She stared at him. "How?"

He chuckled. "We're both stubborn, protective, and sure we're right."

She leaned back against the doorjamb. "Are you saying those things about yourself so that you can say them about me?"

"Oh, of course not," he said, but the twinkle in his eyes belied his words. "And then there's the fact that you're Amish and I'm *Englisch*, as you call it, so you can see we should have no differences in how we feel and act about things."

Hannah shook her head and grinned. Then she spotted a buggy turning into the drive. She straightened and her smile faded as she saw who had come to visit.

"That's the bishop. I wonder why he's here."

"Do you want me to stay or go get the horses?"

"Get the horses," she said quickly. "I'd rather he not think I'm entertaining *Englisch* men."

"I'd be happy to tell him otherwise." Chris stood straighter himself.

"No, there's Joshua now," she told him, spying the boy walking up to the bishop's buggy and helping the elderly man alight. "And thank you for—for—"

"For being sensitive?" he asked, struggling not to laugh.

"I'm sure you've never been accused of that," she said tartly.

"Now, now, let's play nice. We were actually getting along for a few minutes there."

"Joshua, Chris is waiting to help you bring in the horses," Hannah called to him.

The bishop and Joshua walked up the steps and the older man studied Chris.

"This is Chris Matlock, a friend of Jenny's," Hannah said as she introduced them. "Chris, this is Bishop Miller."

The two men shook hands. "I hear you're helping Matthew with the harvest."

Chris nodded. "My family owns a farm out in Kansas."

The bishop's glance went to the barn. "Heard there was some trouble here today."

"Joshua, why don't you and Chris go get the horses now and put them in Phoebe's barn? Be sure to feed them."

She waited until the two had left and then turned to the bishop. "Eli had some burns on his arms and chest but he's okay. They're keeping him at the hospital for observation tonight, but he should be out tomorrow."

The bishop descended the stairs and walked toward the barn. Hannah followed him.

"The fire chief doesn't want anyone to go near it."

He stopped and peered at her over wire-rimmed glasses. "Why?"

"Said he wants to send an investigator to look around tomorrow."

"Are you saying he thinks someone set the fire?"

"I think he's just making sure of what caused it," she said, frowning. "I don't think he suspects anyone set it. He said barns are a problem, being a wood structure, things stored it, that sort of thing."

The bishop folded his arms across his chest and stared at it. "It's not a good time for it to have happened," he said finally. "Matthew can't really afford the time to fix it while he's finishing up the harvest. We'll have to talk."

"He's not home. He and Jenny went to the hospital to see about Eli."

"I knew that," the man said mildly.

"Oh, of course." The Amish grapevine was working as usual.

"I also heard about the young man who's staying here. The one I just met that you said is a friend of Jenny's."

"Heard about him?"

"Josiah said he came running toward his buggy, waving his arms, fussing about him not taking you. Said he didn't know what all that was about."

Hannah sighed. "Chris just misunderstood something."

When the bishop continued to stare at her, she realized she'd have to give him some kind of explanation or things might look worse for Chris.

"He served overseas in the military and saw bad things. He had a kind of stress flashback."

"He was a soldier?" The bishop stroked his beard and looked thoughtful. "I hope he's not talking about it, glorifying what he did there with the *kinner*. They're at an impressionable age."

"No, of course not."

"*Gut.* We're a peaceful people. We don't believe in making war."

"Chris knows that. And I don't think Chris went into the military with the idea of making war."

She felt compelled somehow to defend him although she wasn't entirely sure why. "His family has a tradition of serving to defend the country."

"Seems like the two of you were being friendly just now."

Hannah felt her cheeks warm at what she felt was a mild rebuke. She hadn't done anything inappropriate. "He came to ask if there was anything else he could do since Matthew is at the hospital," she told him, trying to keep her voice level.

Don't be defensive, she told herself. If you do, it'll just seem as if you're feeling guilty. And she wasn't guilty of anything. Well, okay, if she was honest with herself she had to admit that she thought he was attractive but . . . "Matthew was lucky Chris was here when he needed someone, especially someone who's worked on a farm the way he has."

"*Gut.*" He scanned the bright blue, cloudless sky. "Well, let's hope the rain holds off until all the crops are in."

She walked him back to his buggy and watched it pull out of the drive and proceed down the road.

Annie came out onto the porch. "Hannah! The pan is making funny noises!"

Hannah's hand flew to her throat. "I forgot! I put it on to boil the green beans!"

Gathering up her skirt, she flew up the steps and ran inside, calling to Annie to stay on the porch. The pan on the stove had nearly boiled dry and was, indeed, making "funny" noises, sputtering as the last drops of water danced on the surface.

"I didn't go near it," Annie told her.

Hannah bent to kiss the top of her head. "*Danki, liebschen.* It's important to stay safe."

The safety games were paying off, thought Hannah as she took the pan to the sink and refilled it. Farm living could be dangerous for children, with farm equipment moving around, animals being raised, *kinner* doing chores alongside their *eldre*. During the time she'd come to live with Matthew after his wife died, she played the safety games that were taught to Plain children so they'd be more careful.

Today, she'd forgotten the pan of water, but Annie had stayed away from it. Annie had remembered what she'd taught her.

As Hannah stood at the sink refilling the pan with water, she looked out at the barn. The day had been sobering enough without something else happening.

⤨

Chris had seen the way the bishop looked at him when he walked up. The man had behaved much like a suspicious father—he knew there was a strict code of conduct, more propriety than in the *Englisch* world. Something called the *Ordnung*. He wasn't going to do anything that caused the family more problems.

Without Matthew and Jenny here, maybe he shouldn't expect to eat supper in the kitchen as usual.

When he and Joshua finished feeding the horses and they had returned to the house, he asked the boy to have Hannah come to the front door.

She wiped her hands on a dishtowel as she stepped outside. "Did you need something?"

"Is there any place to get something to eat around here?"

"You don't want to eat with us? I made pot roast. I know you'll like it."

"With the way the bishop was looking at me, I figured he was trying to tell me that I shouldn't be here without my hosts."

She smiled. "You were perceptive. I got that message too. But it wouldn't be right to tell you to go get supper elsewhere. Besides, I solved the problem—Phoebe will be joining us."

"Good," he said. "I like her."

"Me or the pie I'm bringing?" Phoebe asked.

Chris turned. "You, of course. But I'll be happy to carry in that pie for you."

"*Ya,* because it's sooo heavy," she said with a twinkle in her eye. She held out the pie. "I'm not sure which people like better, me or my pies."

"It's a tough choice when it's your apple cranberry," he told her seriously and then he grinned to show her he was teasing.

Matthew and Jenny came in midway through supper. They said Eli was doing well and would be home the next day. No one talked at the table. Matthew and Jenny appeared exhausted.

Afterward, Chris walked out to the barn with Matthew and they studied the scene, discussing how the fire might have started. Storing hay had always been dangerous—both of them had heard of the volatility of the dust it created.

They agreed there could be many things that might ignite, such as chemicals or the gasoline used for various equipment.

"Don't know when I can start repairs," Matthew said. "We still have to get in the rest of the crops."

Chris shook his head as he assessed the damage. "You think it can be repaired? It won't have to be pulled down?"

"I'll know more after the investigator comes."

"A farmer's life isn't an easy life."

"*Ya*," Matthew said simply. "But it's the life I love, with God walking alongside me helping things grow."

He bent to pick up a big flake of ash and study it.

"If God is walking alongside you, why did He let this happen?"

"I don't always understand why things happen," Matthew said after a long moment. "God's will is a mysterious thing sometimes. But I don't have to understand. It's enough for me to know that whether He reveals why He's done something or not, He is all-knowing."

Chris thought about that. How could anyone be so accepting of something bad like this happening? He'd been struggling with doing what he thought was right when he saw something bad happening, only to then have the men he saw as brothers in the military turn on him because of it.

He suddenly realized Matthew was saying something. "Sorry, I was thinking about something that happened sometime back. It's hard to accept it as God's will, to believe that it was somehow part of His plan for me. It just feels like it's caused me nothing but problems."

But as much as he wanted to talk to Matthew about his inner conflict, he felt the old reserve creep back. It wasn't good to share too much when you didn't know someone well, no matter how good a person he considered Matthew to be. And how much could the other man understand when he wasn't from the world Chris had experienced—not just *Englisch*, but military?

Besides, dusk was falling and they'd both had a long day.

"You okay?"

"Sure. Why do you ask?"

Matthew shook his head. "I thought you were about to say something. Guess I'll get the horses in."

"Done. Joshua and I took care of it—fed and watered them too."

"Well, *danki*. I appreciate it." He held out his hand. "And *danki* for grabbing Eli and saving him from hurting himself worse today. You have fast reflexes."

"You learn 'em on the battlefield," Chris said, shaking Matthew's hand.

Matthew started toward the house, to his wife and family, and Chris toward the *dawdi haus*.

Chris hesitated and turned back to look at Matthew.

Matthew stopped. "Did you say something?"

Shaking his head, Chris opened the back door and went inside. It was just that the day had been strange—an emotional roller coaster, he thought as he got a glass of water. He felt out of sorts.

No, if he was honest with himself, he suddenly felt lonely. He drained the glass and went into the bedroom to go to sleep.

But once again he lay awake for a long time.

❧

An investigator came the next morning and looked around the barn.

Hannah watched him as she hung out the laundry she'd helped Jenny re-wash because it smelled of the smoke from the fire.

Every so often, she glanced over to the fields where Matthew, Chris, and the other men worked. And often, she found Chris watching her.

Buggies and cars slowed and sometimes stopped as people gawked at the damage the fire had done to the barn.

"Wonder what he's finding," Jenny said as the man came out of the barn.

"What's that in his hands?"

"Evidence bags."

"Evidence? What kind?"

"I don't know. But if he wasn't finding something that made him suspicious, he wouldn't be bringing bags out."

Chills ran up and down Hannah's arms. "Jenny, you're not saying that someone would start a fire in the barn?"

Jenny bit her lip as she watched the investigator. "No, that can't be. He's just being careful. Why would anyone start a fire in our barn? No one's mad at us."

Then she frowned.

"What?"

"No, it's too ridiculous to think—"

"*What?*" Exasperated, Hannah stood with her hands on her hips, wanting to shake her sister-in-law.

"You don't suppose Josiah—"

"Josiah what?"

"I know he wasn't happy when I first moved back. He went to the bishop and the elders of the church, saying he was afraid of my influence on the community."

"But he got over it."

"Well, maybe. Maybe not. You said he looked really unhappy that Chris came rushing at him, thinking he was forcing you into his buggy. And you told me the bishop came the other day and said Josiah talked to him about Chris and how he had that flashback."

"Then wouldn't he be mad at Chris, not at you and Matthew?"

Jenny picked up a clothespin that had fallen in the grass. "I don't know. I'm probably just being paranoid thinking such a thing."

Realizing that her hands were suddenly clammy, Hannah rubbed them up and down her apron. "But you know how to figure out things like this—from your TV reporter days—when you lived in the *Englisch* world."

"I wasn't an investigative reporter, Hannah. I was a feature reporter, covering stories about how children were being affected by war."

"No, you know how people think—people who do bad things."

Jenny blinked. "Are you saying I have some insight into the criminal mind?"

"A lot more than me. Bad things don't happen here. Oh, Isaiah Lapp got a ticket for driving his courting buggy recklessly last month and Abe Miller had to apologize for trying to climb into Fannie Mae Yoder's window as a joke. But we hardly ever have any crime here.

"Barns have burned here in the community before. There could have been a spark that started it. Maybe one of the men was smoking a pipe out there and didn't want to admit it because Matthew would have a fit."

"But we heard an explosion."

"Could have been chemicals stored in the barn or gas for the engine—" she stopped when Jenny just gave her a disbelieving stare.

"Denial's not a river in Egypt," Jenny said.

"What?"

"Never mind. It's just a silly *Englisch* expression."

"Just when I think you've completely adapted to being Plain, you say something that makes you sound *Englisch*."

"Well, I guess it's because so far, I've spent more time being *Englisch* than Plain. Forget I said anything about Josiah. He's just an old man set in his ways, afraid that outsiders will ruin the community. I'm sure he's harmless."

She put her arm around Hannah's waist and they started toward the house. "Let's go inside and have some tea and talk about your job."

"It's just twenty hours a week. Not a real job. At least it doesn't feel like a job. It's fun teaching other women how to quilt."

"And admit it, you've been curious about the *Englisch* for a long time. Teaching them how to quilt should give you a chance to know more of them."

Hannah laughed. "*Ya.*"

They entered the kitchen, and Jenny filled the tea kettle and set it on the stove while Hannah dug some cookies out of the cookie jar and placed them on a plate. When the tea was ready, they sat down at the table to rest a few minutes.

"We sew a lot of quilts here for function, you know, because we need them to cover our beds so we can stay warm," Hannah told Jenny. "And it's a pleasure to make them because we love the person who will be warmed by something we made with our hands."

She stirred her tea and took a sip. "It's fun, too, to make something creative, using patterns and material pieces and colors. Some of the *Englisch* women come to learn how to quilt because they want to do the same thing, to make a quilt for a loved one. It's not a necessity for them like it is here. They can buy blankets. However, I like watching them get the same joy from experimenting with quilt making that we do."

"Because we're more alike than we're different, don't you think?"

"*Ya,* I suppose so. Except—"

"Except . . ." Jenny found her looking toward the kitchen window.

Her eyes followed Hannah's. "I guess I don't need to look out the window to see who you're talking about, do I?"

"He's different from the men I know."

"I remember that first night he came here you said he was attractive and I teased you," Jenny mused.

Hannah blushed. "You're not starting on that again, are you?"

"No, I just wonder if you're interested in him because he's someone different. Maybe you should visit another Plain community—" She stopped when Hannah held up her hand.

"I wish it were that easy." She sighed. "Phoebe and I have talked about it."

"You're sure it's not that you feel . . . sorry for him? Because of what he's been through?"

Hannah smiled and shook her head. "But I don't know how he feels about me. Sometimes I feel like he's looking at me . . . like there's something there, and then I wonder if I'm just imagining it. It's not like he's flirting . . ."

It was Jenny's turn to shake her head. "Chris doesn't strike me as the kind of man who plays with a woman's feelings."

"I'll get the door," Hannah said when someone knocked. "You relax."

The fire investigator stood on the front porch. His expression was grim. "Is Matthew Bontrager available?"

❧

Chris watched Jenny wave to get Matthew's attention as he stood on the edge of the field. Matthew acknowledged her wave and began walking toward her.

One of the first things a soldier learned was to study body language. If he didn't understand how to read a person's mood, his intent, it could cost him his life. A battlefield wasn't always marked; an enemy didn't always wear a uniform. Sometimes a person—even a child—could suddenly pull out a weapon, trigger a riot, or become a human bomb.

So he studied the way Jenny stood stiffly, wrapped her arms over her chest as if she were shivering—even though the day was still warm—and wore a worried frown as she talked to Matthew.

Matthew stood with his back to him so he wasn't able to see his expression, but he saw Matthew straighten and he put his hands on his hips as he listened to his wife. Then he touched her shoulder in a reassuring way and they began walking back to the farmhouse.

The fire investigator's truck was still parked in the drive. Had Jenny come to get Matthew because the investigator wanted to talk to him about the barn? If so, that couldn't be good.

Chris glanced out at the road and saw a buggy parked to one side. From where he stood, Chris couldn't see its occupant. He felt that odd sensation of being watched again. It had happened a number of times that day because so many buggies and cars had slowly gone by.

He shook his head, telling himself he didn't have time to let it concern him. There was too much to be done. He turned back to his work.

10

$\mathcal{M}$atthew walked into the kitchen where Hannah sat with Jenny at the kitchen table, mending some of the *kinner's* clothes.

"What did the fire investigator have to say?" Jenny asked him.

Matthew's glance slid to Hannah, then he looked at Jenny and shrugged. "Not much. He poked around the barn and said he'd get back to me when he knew something."

"That sounds like he thinks it wasn't an accident," Jenny said, putting down the mending. "Otherwise, he'd just say he didn't see anything out of the ordinary."

When her brother glanced her way again, Hannah stood. "I think I'll go see if Phoebe needs anything in town."

"You don't have to leave."

Hannah looked at Matthew. "I think you need to talk to Jenny privately."

"Why would he need to do that?" Jenny made a knot and clipped the thread. "We're not talking about anything personal."

"He just said that he'd prefer it if I didn't say anything about the investigation," Matthew said.

"Hannah is your sister, not an outsider."

Matthew nodded. "I know." He sighed. "You know how it is when something happens. People talk. Rumors get started. I think the investigator is just saying the less anything is said about it, the better, regardless of whether the fire was an accident or something more."

He got a glass, filled it with water, and drank it down. "I need to get back outside. We'll talk later."

Hannah picked up her mending when he left. After a few minutes, she put it down again. "Do you want some more tea?"

"No, but have some if you like."

She fixed the tea, brought it to the table, and let it cool while she tried to concentrate on fixing a rip in one of Annie's dresses. The child was harder on her clothing than anyone Hannah knew.

Getting up, Hannah checked on a casserole she'd brought over for dinner. Jenny had been grateful for it, although Hannah didn't think it took any special effort on her part to make a second when she was already making one for herself and Phoebe.

She found herself wandering to the kitchen window, looking to see what the men were doing out in the fields. *Allrecht*, maybe she looked to see what one particular man was doing.

When she turned to walk back to the table, she saw that Jenny watched her, a faint smile on her lips.

"Feeling restless?"

"No, of course not." Hannah took her seat again. Then, after a long moment, she gave up. "Would you mind if I took this home to finish later?"

Jenny looked up. "Of course not. Why would I mind? It was nice enough of you to offer to help to begin with."

"I think I'll ask Phoebe if she'd like to go into town."

"I thought you looked restless," Jenny said sympathetically.

"A bit."

"I know the feeling."

"You're feeling restless too? Would you like to go?"

Jenny laughed and shook her head. "No, I meant I know the feeling but I'm not feeling it now. I'm actually quite content to sit here and do something domestic. But then again, I was just out of town days ago. It feels good to be here now." She put the sock she'd been mending down. "We've all been so busy and then there's been this . . . tension since the fire."

Hannah sighed. "You've felt it too?"

"How could I not? Every time I look at the barn I get this uncomfortable feeling. I think it's bothering Matthew as well. He hasn't been sleeping well. It's a shame. Harvest time is always exhausting enough."

Hannah tucked her needle and thread into her sewing basket, stood up, and reached down to give Jenny a hug. "Anything you need from town?"

"I'm fine." Then she looked at the socks in the basket. "But next week, let's you and I consider a trip to get some new socks for the kids. It just seems to me that mending isn't worth the time as cheap as socks are. I know that's probably sacrilegious to say here because nothing's to be wasted but . . ."

Hannah laughed. "I understand how you hate it."

When Hannah returned home, she found Phoebe had a visitor who'd just arrived. With just a little sigh of disappointment, she went on out to hitch up Daisy to the buggy.

Within a block or so of the house, the vague restlessness faded. She didn't often feel such a thing; she loved being at home, doing things in and around it.

A man walked on the right-hand side of the road. Although all she could see was the back of him, he looked familiar. When she pulled alongside, she saw that it was Chris.

"Going somewhere?" she asked and then found herself holding her breath. Why did she hope he wasn't going to say that he was leaving?

"Matthew told me to take a couple of hours off."

"Really?"

"Really. Thought I'd take a walk into town, go to the library."

He kept walking and Daisy plodded along next to him.

"Would you like a ride?"

When he didn't answer for some time, Hannah wondered if he'd heard her. Then he turned and looked at her. "You're not afraid of me?"

"You know I'm not."

"I don't know anything," he muttered. "Josiah just went past. I got the distinct impression he wishes I'd just keep traveling on down the road."

"I'm sure. He's not the friendliest man. Come on, get in, I'll give you a ride." She stopped the buggy, watched him hesitate and then climb inside.

"Where are you headed?" he asked her.

"I'm getting some supplies at the quilt store. I wouldn't mind looking in the library too. My nieces and nephew always love it when I get books for them. Annie loves a good book, especially when I read it to her."

"Okay. You decide which one to visit first." He leaned back against the seat and watched the passing scenery.

"You'd go into the quilt shop with me?"

He shrugged. "Sure. Why not?" Then he looked at her. "Oh, so the men here can't do that sort of thing?"

"It's not that they can't, but they're not really interested in what they view as a woman thing."

"I don't mind going in with you. My grandmother took me a few times when she ran errands."

Hannah found herself laughing. "Bet you were a little boy then."

He grinned, his teeth bright white against skin turning tan from being out in the fields. "Yeah, but I'm not afraid to be in a woman's enclave. I was in the military."

When she looked blank, he held up his arm and flexed the muscle. "I'm a manly man. I can take it. That's *Englisch* guy humor," he explained when she stared at him.

"I see," she said dryly. Then she smiled to show him that she "got" it, as the *Englisch* said.

They fell silent as they traveled.

"What do you like to read?"

"A little of everything," he said noncommittally. "I want to poke around. But ladies first. Let's go to the quilt store, then the library."

"Okay. I hope you won't be sorry."

"Looks like a little store. How long can it take?"

Famous last words, thought Chris.

Stitches in Time turned out to be a tiny store with spaces in front for just four cars or buggies to park. But the minute Chris opened the door for Hannah, he realized that the room inside stretched for far more than the usual length of a store.

It was interesting to watch Hannah as she walked through the shop. Her fingers touched a fabric here, another there, and she got a faraway look in her eyes, as if she were already planning out a design for a quilt.

The clerk, dressed in Plain clothing, stood at the counter cutting fabric. She glanced up and greeted Hannah. "Hi, didn't expect to see you today. You don't have a lesson until Thursday, do you?"

"No, I decided not to wait until then to get some fabric to start a new quilt."

"Can I help you with something?" the clerk asked Chris.

"He's with me. Chris, this is Naomi, one of the owners of the store. Naomi, this is Chris, a friend of Jenny's."

She turned to Chris. "Naomi, Anna, and Mary Katherine are sisters. They and their *grossmudder* own the shop."

"Hi, Chris. So, are you interested in quilting too?" she asked, tucking her tongue in her cheek.

He grinned at her. "Nope. Thought I'd try knitting."

"Knitting? Did someone say knitting?" Another young woman, who looked a lot like Naomi and dressed like her, approached.

Hannah laughed. "Chris, meet Anna. She can help you with any knitting supplies."

Another young woman joined them, looking similar to the other two and dressed the same. "Hi, I'm Mary Katherine. Maybe you'd like to look at our weaving section?"

"Now, now, don't tease the poor man," an older woman said as she walked up. She turned to Chris. "I'm sure he's here to learn how to make the little Amish dolls I'm known for."

Chris backed up. "I think I'll just wait in the buggy for you, Hannah."

Feminine laughter followed him and he slunk off to the buggy. Geez, he'd faced down men with guns, but surrounded by a bunch of Amish women teasing him about making crafts he'd turned tail.

Outside, he became the subject of curious stares from passing tourists who obviously wondered why he was dressed in *Englisch* clothes but sitting in an Amish buggy.

Yes, it is an interesting time, this trip to Paradise, he thought.

The minutes ticked by and he became aware that he was being watched, the itch between his shoulders was back. He glanced around but didn't see anything out of the ordinary. Tourists walked around dressed in logo T-shirts, food in hand, looking in shop windows and carrying bags of things they'd already bought.

None passing by gave him any cause for concern. He wasn't sure if that meant they truly didn't warrant concern, or if it was because he was getting soft.

Surely there was no need for him to be thinking about watching his back now that he wasn't a soldier—now that he was in a place called Paradise.

When Hannah returned to the buggy, she was carrying a big bag with the store name imprinted on it. Chris got out to put it in the buggy for her and she looked surprised.

"What? Is there no chivalry among the Amish men?"

"I don't know this 'chivalry' but I'm capable of carrying a shopping bag."

Chris pretended to heft the bag with great effort. "I don't know about that. I think you bought a piece of every bolt of fabric in the store."

Hannah put her hands on her hips. "I did not!"

"And spent all your salary from teaching there last week." He could tell his words hit home when she blushed.

"Not all," she said primly.

"Because you got an employee discount."

Her eyes widened and she opened her mouth to protest until she saw him grin and hold out his hand to help her into the buggy.

"How do you know about employee discounts?" she asked him as she climbed in by herself.

"My first job was at a store, and I spent most of my pay-checks buying things," he said, chuckling at the memory. "I only stopped when my dad refused to pay for my car insurance."

He glanced at her as she called to Daisy to get the buggy moving. "No sixteen-year-old boy can go without his wheels."

"It's much the same here," she said with a smile. "Our young men have courting buggies and some of them deck them out with radios and such."

Her smile faded. "Some of them leave before being baptized because they want the cars. And the music. Well, what some of the young people call music. It sounds like—"

She stopped and shook her head. "Well, it doesn't sound like any music I remember listening to during my *rumschpringe*."

"Caterwauling," Chris told her. "My dad always called it caterwauling. Now I think it's just blasphemous calling heavy metal that kind of name."

He stretched out his long legs as best as he could within the confines of the buggy. "So anyway, I stopped buying this and that so I could keep my wheels." He chuckled again. "Of course, the car was one big rust heap and held together with duct tape. And prayer. I did a lot of praying when I drove, that's for sure.

"Prayer stood me in good stead when I went into battle," he said, looking inward. "I don't know of anyone who doesn't do it on the front lines." He fell silent. "I remember doing a lot of prayer there. But I know now I was trying to bargain with God, asking him to keep me alive. And later, after my friend was killed in front of me and when I was hurt, I was just so angry at Him."

"I think everyone's had a time when they're angry with God. Or at the very least disappointed?"

He was silent for so long that she wondered if she'd come across as preaching. The Amish didn't believe in doing that, but he still could think that. Neither of them spoke for several blocks.

"I doubt you've ever told God you're angry with Him."

"Well, disappointed might be more accurate," she agreed.

"Anyway, I didn't mean to take us down that path. This was supposed to be a pleasant hour or two away from home."

"I'm happy to listen if it helps."

He glanced at her. "You're a nice woman, Hannah."

"I don't think you thought that when you first came here."

"You were just being protective of your family. I don't blame you."

Another buggy passed, and its occupant leaned out the side and studied them. Chris saw it was Josiah coming back from his errand.

"Now I *know* he doesn't like me."

Hannah waved at Josiah. "He's just protective of the community. Doesn't like outsiders. And someone told me he's always been a little grumpy. His wife kept him from being that way when she was alive, but now that she's passed, well, there's no one to temper that, I suppose."

The clip-clopping of Daisy's hooves was the only sound for a while.

"Who's going to do that for me?" he heard her mutter.

"What?"

But she wouldn't answer him. He'd caught glimpses that all wasn't placid beneath her surface. He wondered why.

She was the most interesting woman he'd ever met. But she was also probably the most different woman from any he'd known in his life. Their worlds didn't mix.

Besides, he'd felt like he had the worst luck with women. He'd dated just like any other guy in high school, just not very often before he'd gone off to do his military service. He'd worked up the nerve to ask Bobbie Joe to be his steady and had even given her a promise ring. She'd written him overseas a number of times but abruptly dropped him over "the trouble" as she called it.

Now, of course, he was glad she had. Who knew how much worse it might have been if she'd done it after he was injured.

✧

The library was their next stop.

Hannah decided to look for some books for her nieces and nephew and maybe a book on quilt patterns. They agreed to meet back at the front door in twenty minutes.

Chris headed straight for the computers available for public use. He sat beside an elderly woman who was looking at photos of children. "My grandchildren," she told him proudly as she scrolled through the shots.

A teen sat on the other side of him, casting nervous glances around. Chris didn't know if he was looking at something he shouldn't or if he was playing truant from school.

Chris logged on and pulled up his e-mail account. There were just a few that had been sent in the last couple weeks: one from his brother, Steve; one a reminder about a bill; and two from the buddies that had stuck by him through The Trouble.

He opened the one from his brother first. It was the usual—a mild complaint that he hadn't written for weeks and asking if he was enjoying his travels. It ended, as most e-mails from his brother did, with a request that Chris give him a call when he could. So he wrote an apology, explained that he was having a great time in Lancaster, and that he would call soon.

Of course, if he really intended to do that, he'd have to do something about his cell phone. When the battery on his cell had first run down, Matthew offered to charge it for him in the barn. Since so many of the Plain people ran businesses, he'd told Chris that cell phones were allowed for such. But Chris got few calls and really didn't care. So time passed and it lay in his backpack.

Taking care of some bills was next. And then Chris clicked on the first of the two messages from buddies. Jokester Brian told a joke so raw it made Chris glance around like the nervous teen next to him to make sure no one was reading it over his shoulder.

The next e-mail was from Jack, a rambling litany of complaints about life in the "private sector" by a former soldier buddy who'd complained nonstop during his time in the military. Chris had thought he'd be happier getting out, but now he wondered if Jack was the type of person who wasn't happy anywhere.

His hands stilled on the keyboard. He wondered if he was like Jack. He'd been so eager to get out of the hospital—get back to normal, everyday life. And the farm. He'd been so looking forward to being back on the farm.

And then, when he got there, the farm was much as it had been for years, but it felt different. No longer familiar. No longer home.

His family hadn't changed. He supposed he should be happy about that; all of them were just the way they'd been when he went overseas, just a little older. His brother, Steve, still talked about finding a good woman to help him run the farm. Aunt Bess still kept Uncle Joe in line. And his dad claimed it was time for Steve to do some work, so he went fishing when he could.

They hadn't changed, but he had—in ways they couldn't possibly understand. He tried to talk to his father and to Steve, but they had no frame of reference at all for what he tried to communicate to them. His father had served in Germany, his brother one tour during the early days of Desert Storm.

They looked away from his injuries and their discomfort when the pain he'd suffered caused *them* pain. They couldn't understand why he'd put himself through the *trouble*. Sure, one of the men who served under his command had done something wrong, but couldn't he have looked the other way? Hadn't he considered the consequences to himself?

"Young man? Young man?"

Chris blinked and came back to the present. The older woman sitting beside him was staring at him curiously.

"Can you show me how to print these out?"

"Sure." He explained the steps and the printer hummed and spit out picture after picture of smiling plump-cheeked children.

Returning to the computer, Chris logged out of his e-mail account and did a Google search. After inputting the name "Malcolm Kraft," he saw several hundred results come up. Clicking on the first one, he read about the event he was so familiar with, an event that had forever changed his life.

Funny thing, he thought darkly, how bad things could turn so quickly, how they could go so differently from how you thought they would. How what you did in the name of morality could turn so many people against you, including the most important.

Why had God let so many bad things rain down on him when he thought he was doing the right thing?

The story was more than a year old, so he skipped ahead since the events were etched on his brain. What he was hoping to find was that Kraft was still safely tucked away where he should be—prison. He'd felt he had to do this every few months. Too often there were stories of people being released from prison early. Kraft had promised at the sentencing that things weren't over between them. It wasn't wise to ignore the threat.

Tapping the keyboard, he searched the library system for the book that had been recommended to him by his buddy. Relieved to find they had two copies, he glanced up to see where Hannah was and saw her over in the children's section, looking like she'd be a while.

He clicked back to his Google search for Kraft and went from one story to the next when he realized Hannah was standing next to him. Quickly he hit the back button and the screen for the book he wanted came up.

She held out a book called *Learn a New Word Every Day.* "I think Annie will like this one."

Sitting down in a chair next to him, she searched her purse for her wallet and pulled out her library card. "I thought you wanted to get a book."

Chris jumped up. "Sorry, I'll get it and we can be on our way."

"There's no rush—" she called after him.

～⌘～

"Nice young man," the woman beside her said. "Helped me print out photos of my grandkids."

"I see."

She glanced at the computer Chris had been using and wondered why he'd hit the back button so quickly when he looked up and saw her standing there.

Repeating his action, she glanced curiously at the list of articles about some man serving time in a military prison. Her heart in her throat, she skimmed the contents of the article quickly, hoping Chris wasn't involved somehow.

Something moved in the periphery of her vision and when she looked up, she saw him crossing the library, a book in his hand.

"You said Chris showed you how to print something?" she said to the woman. "Can you show me?"

"Oh, sure, hon."

The woman leaned over and used the mouse to click on a bar on the top of the screen and there was a whirring noise from the printer beside Hannah. She looked for Chris and saw him searching a shelf, his back to her. Keeping her eyes on him, Hannah reached for the page printing out and quickly folded it into a square that she tucked into her pocket.

"Thank you for the help," she told the woman.

"I didn't think the Amish were allowed to use computers." The woman gathered up her sheets of paper and slid them into a manila envelope and stood.

"They're allowed for business," she said with a smile. "As long as we don't bring electricity into the home for them."

Jenny used a laptop for her writing and she had to take it to the barn to recharge it. She'd told Hannah she loved writing in longhand best and then typed her work on the computer. Sometimes when she needed to do research she came to this library; several times she'd brought Hannah and shown her how to look up quilt patterns on the computer.

Hannah chatted with the woman at the next computer for a few minutes. The woman was clearly enjoying working on the computer since she said she didn't have one at home. That news surprised Hannah. She thought every *Englisch* person had a computer.

"Ready to go?" Chris said as he walked up.

"Yes, sure." She gave his book a curious glance. It was a book that looked to be about a soldier, with unforgiving in the title.

They walked to the circulation desk and Chris waved at Hannah to go first. She checked out her books and then waited for him to get his.

But the clerk frowned when Chris asked if he could apply for a card to check out his book. "If you could please step over here so other people can check out their books, sir."

He did as she asked and Hannah moved out of the way also. The librarian handed him an application. Chris dutifully filled it out and handed it over. When she asked for identification he pulled out his driver's license.

"This isn't local."

"No. I'm from Kansas."

"Are you living here? Can you supply me with some proof of residence here?"

"He's staying with us."

"Can you give me proof of that?"

Hannah shook her head.

Chris pushed the book toward the librarian. "Thanks anyway."

"No, here," Hannah said, holding out her card. "I'll check it out."

"You do realize that you're responsible for the book should it not be returned, ma'am?"

"Of course."

The book was duly checked out and Hannah accepted her card back. She and Chris walked out and climbed into the buggy.

"Maybe I should go buy the book at the bookstore," Chris told her as Hannah called to Daisy to get them moving.

"Why should you do that when we have the book now?"

"'You do realize that you're responsible for the book should it not be returned, ma'am?'" he mimicked the librarian.

She smiled slightly. "She was just doing her job. It's her responsibility to make sure the rules are followed. You'd understand since you're a keeper of the rules, too, wouldn't you? As someone who'd served in the military?"

He eyed her oddly. "That's an interesting way to put it. You mean, like I'm used to following the rules, obeying authority?"

Her left hand slipped inside her pocket to feel the folded paper there.

"Yeah, I guess so. Where's this going?"

"Nowhere," she said. "Nowhere at all. Thanks for going with me today."

"It was fun. Really."

"You didn't enjoy the visit to the quilt shop."

"Sure I did. Well, until all of you ganged up on me."

She grinned. "You mustn't mind them. They love to tease."

"It's a nice shop. You really enjoy making quilts and teaching there, don't you? I could tell from the time we walked inside."

She nodded. "At first, I did it to help out—"

"Because you always help when someone needs you."

Frowning, she looked at him. "Of course, that's not a bad thing."

"No, it's not," he said slowly. "You're a good person. But I wonder how much you do for yourself."

"And what about you?"

"Me?"

"You're a good man," she said. "You could be having a vacation instead of helping Matthew."

Their glances locked and something passed between them, unspoken but powerful. When Hannah looked away, she saw that they had traveled several blocks. Good thing Daisy knew her way, she thought. If she'd been driving a car, Hannah knew she'd have gone off the road.

"You've already thanked me. Everyone has. It's no big deal. I had plenty of time off when I was in the hospital."

That shuttered look came down over his face again and he was silent for the rest of the journey home. When they alighted from the buggy, she gathered the library books in her arms and he carried the package of quilting material to the front door for her.

When he went to turn away, she stopped him, her hand on his arm. "You forgot your book."

"Oh yeah, thanks."

Their hands touched and she quickly pulled hers back, causing him to bobble but catch the book.

11

$\mathcal{H}$annah approached the library computer with some trepidation.

Her computer skills weren't the best. She'd learned what little she knew from Jenny. She supposed she could have asked Jenny for help in looking up more on the article. But what she was looking for was information on Chris and talking to Jenny about it felt like a violation of his privacy. And computers and such were just supposed to be used for work . . .

She shook her head at the thoughts, especially the privacy issue. The fact was, it felt like a violation of privacy for *her* to do it. It was a failing of hers that she wanted to know about him, wasn't it? If he wanted her to know this about him, he would tell her. She didn't know why she was so intrigued by him. When she'd seen him walking to town, she'd been upset, thinking he was leaving town. But he'd stayed longer than he'd probably intended to as it was.

And when he *did* leave, she wouldn't hear from him again. They weren't friends now. He wouldn't call. He wouldn't write. It was doubtful he'd ever come here again.

Nonetheless, she couldn't seem to stop herself from typing the website from the bottom of the printed page into the address bar and calling it up. She began reading the article—the part after the first page. Apparently there was a trial of U.S. serviceman Malcolm Kraft in Afghanistan. He'd been charged with a crime against a citizen of that country. Kraft said he wasn't guilty, that he'd never been anywhere near the crime scene even though there were witnesses. Kraft claimed Chris had it in it for him and that the witnesses were Afghans who hated the Americans who were there.

However, after evidence of something called DNA, Kraft admitted he'd been with her. He claimed he'd been drunk and had smoked pot, insisted the relations he'd had with the woman had been consensual. A military court found him guilty.

Hannah studied the photo of the man who appeared to be in his early thirties. He didn't look like a bad person to her, just like any other young *Englisch* man dressed in his military uniform and standing with his wife at his side. She looked closer at the little boy Kraft held. He appeared to be around three years old, and he sucked on his thumb as he stared, his expression confused, into the camera.

Another article followed, telling how a week later, there'd been a fire in the barracks. Everyone had gotten out but Chris, who was supposedly determined to make sure none of his men remained. A support beam fell on him and he sustained burns on his back, an injury that would have sent him stateside for treatment, but he'd refused. He insisted he would stay and complete his tour. Questions had been raised about whether the fire had been intentionally set—an investigation found no proof.

Then in a third article, a month later, just days before Chris was to finish his tour of duty and fly home, his armored truck was hit by a roadside bomb and he and another soldier were severely injured. He was sent home for treatment and to recover from injuries and related infections.

There the articles ended. Apparently Kraft was still in prison, serving ten years for his crime.

Poor Chris, Hannah thought as she printed out the remainder of the articles. He must have felt—maybe even still feels—like Job with his many trials and tribulations. It must have been devastating to feel compelled to pursue prosecution of one of his own men and then to have his superiors refuse to back him up. How awful it was to wake and find your sleeping quarters on fire, fear for the lives of others, then find out the blaze may have been deliberately set.

And how horrible to get so close to finally getting sent home only to get injured and have to spend so much time recovering in a hospital? No wonder he was taking some time now to travel, to do as he pleased.

Now she understood that brooding air about him sometimes . . . that look of vulnerability in his eyes when she'd asked him if she could give him a lift to town and when he'd seemed hurt that Josiah was being unfriendly.

She didn't want to assume too much from just these articles—Jenny had talked to her about how people in her old world were so influenced by newspapers and television—but she wondered how Chris had been affected by how others had turned a cold shoulder, had shunned him at the trial. Had it felt like that was continuing here, with Josiah?

And she herself had been unfriendly, suspicious of him when he'd first arrived. She felt shamed at the memory. While she'd since behaved differently and had thanked him for helping Matthew, she wondered if it was enough to make up for her earlier behavior.

A teenager came to sit in front of the computer next to her. He typed some keys on the keyboard and started playing with a video game. He leaned over and looked at her screen.

"I thought you people weren't interested in war," he said and popped his gum.

"We don't participate in it," she said, clicking the back button to look at other articles related to the case Chris had been involved in.

"Oh," he said, and he turned to play the video game on the computer.

Hannah knew that wasn't allowed on the library's public computer, but it wasn't her way or that of the Plain community to tell others how to behave.

She glanced through some of the articles and printed another and then, glancing at the clock, saw that she should be leaving to teach at the store. Logging off, she gathered up the printouts and left the library.

ை

Hannah woke instantly when she heard the creaking of the stair step.

Slipping into her robe, she found her slippers—the nights were getting cooler—and walked to Phoebe's room. The door was ajar and the bed empty. Going downstairs, she made certain to make plenty of noise so she didn't startle the older woman.

"Did I wake you?" Phoebe asked, turning from the stove. "Sorry, I tried to be quiet."

"It's that creaky fifth step."

Phoebe sighed and took the kettle to the sink to fill it. "I don't even hear it these days."

"Maybe we should take you into town for another hearing test."

"Doc says I don't need a hearing aid. At least, not yet. It's just certain sounds I don't hear."

Hannah sat at the table and propped her chin in her hand. "So what's keeping you awake tonight?"

Shrugging, Phoebe sat down while the water heated up. "Sleeping through the night just gets a little harder each year."

When she started to rise, Hannah motioned her to remain seated and went to fix the tea herself, a soothing chamomile should help Phoebe sleep.

They sat, drinking the tea, talking quietly.

Phoebe glanced at the kitchen window. "A harvest moon," she said, tilting her head to study it. "My favorite. It's my favorite time of the year, really."

Hannah stirred her tea. "Did you used to go for hay rides with your husband, John?"

Smiling, Phoebe nodded. "He was such a sweet *mann*. And, may I say, a romantic one. He wrote me a poem on each anniversary."

Hannah's eyes widened. "I didn't know that."

"I'll show them to you sometime."

"I'd like that."

She watched Phoebe's smile fade and reached out to grasp her hand. It felt frail, like bird bones.

"What's wrong? What's made you look so sad?"

"Sometimes I think all people remember is how stern he was with our *sohn*, Luke. They were two hard-headed men."

"Jenny's *daed* was hard-headed too?"

Nodding, Phoebe sipped her tea. "They disagreed about most everything but especially about Luke being baptized. I kept telling John that Luke needed to find his own way and the Plain life might not be for him. In the end, Luke left and—and—"

"You felt like part of your heart went with him?"

Tears welled up in Phoebe's eyes. Some things still hurt even though much time has passed, Hannah thought as she hugged Phoebe.

"You're a sweet *kind*," Phoebe told her after a moment. "I missed him, but when he came to visit a little while later, he was so happy. I couldn't feel sorry for myself any longer. And when he brought Jenny . . . oh, my, what a gift he gave me each time he left her to visit for the summer."

"I remember the last time she was here, when she and Matthew had a crush on each other," Hannah said, resuming her seat.

She tasted her tea and found it had cooled, but she didn't care. "It was so wonderful to see her come back again and find out that she and Matthew had never forgotten each other, that they were still in love."

"I know. And now they're married and living right next door."

Hannah found her thoughts traveling next door, but not to Matthew and Jenny. She got up and put her cup in the sink and saw that a light shone from the bedroom in the *dawdi haus*. As she watched, the back door opened and Chris came out and sat down in the chair on the back porch.

So, he couldn't sleep, either.

"Phoebe?" She turned and sat again at the table. "What would you do if you knew something about somebody, but you were afraid to tell because it made someone look bad?"

Was it her imagination that the older woman turned pale? She grasped her hand and found it trembling. "Are you *allrecht*?"

"*Ya*, of course. What do you mean?"

"You'll think badly of me."

"No, I wouldn't," Phoebe said.

"See, you're already looking at me like I've done a bad thing."

Phoebe took her cup to the sink and stood looking out at the night. Hannah wondered if she saw Chris. Phoebe's eyesight wasn't the best these days and she'd left her wire-rimmed glasses upstairs.

"I was at the library the other day and I looked up something about Chris."

"Oh." She turned and faced Hannah.

Was that relief on her face? Hannah told herself she was being fanciful. "It's nothing bad. It's just that he hasn't told anyone—"

"So you wonder if he'd want you to say anything to him or anyone else."

"Yes."

"Chris is a proud man." Phoebe paused and smiled slightly. "Most men are." She sat again at the table. "He's strong but he's carrying a lot of pain in him."

"You think he's injured more than he wants to show? Should he be helping with the harvest?"

"I'm talking about pain in here," Phoebe said, pointing to her temple. "I'm talking about here," she said, gesturing at her heart.

She sighed and stood. "And speaking of pain. I think I'll take these old bones back to bed and give them a rest. My knees have been a little arthritic lately."

"Maybe we should think about moving you to the downstairs bedroom."

Phoebe gave her a look.

Hannah threw up her hands. "Never mind! Forget I suggested it! Me? Did I say something?"

"Say goodnight, Hannah."

"'Goodnight, Hannah.'"

Laughing and shaking her head, Phoebe started for the stairs. "See you in the morning."

Hannah put the cream in the refrigerator, made certain the propane stove had been turned off, and extinguished the kerosene lamp.

Just as she was about to turn away, she saw that Chris was no longer sitting in the chair but was pacing back and forth, back and forth, on the porch next door.

Was no one sleeping tonight?

Her gaze traveled upstairs, to the window that was Matthew and Jenny's room, and saw that it was dark. So, too, were the rooms where the *kinner* slept.

Chris's movement on the back porch drew her gaze again. There was something agitated about his form. She wondered if he were in pain or distressed for some reason. It was none of her business, but she worried about him. What if he was having one of his spells, his PSDT—no, that wasn't it. His PDST . . . whatever. The stress thing he had.

She gathered her robe more closely around her and slipped out the back door.

❧

It felt a little like his days in the barracks to be lying in a bed, reading by the light of a battery-powered lantern, but Chris had to admit the glow was a pleasant one at the end of the day.

Reaching for the book Hannah had checked out for him at the library, he opened it to the place he'd marked with the due date slip. He fingered the slip and found himself remembering how he hadn't been able to check out the book himself. The librarian hadn't been able to give him his own card because he wasn't a local resident.

Not a big deal in the grand scheme of things, he supposed. But while he had a physical address back in Kansas, it hadn't felt like home. And here, in Paradise, a place that increasingly felt like home, well, he didn't have roots here. He was staying in a part of someone else's home, their *dawdi haus*, a place that was designed to shelter family when they could no longer take care of themselves.

He remembered the counseling session he had to endure before he left the hospital. It was a rough transition for some veterans to move back into civilian life, the counselor had said. Sometimes they found it hard to reconnect with family, deal with the reality of the lasting effects of an injury, or find a job.

The counselor said about a quarter of the people sleeping on the streets in America had once worn a military uniform—and they weren't all from the Vietnam era. Many of those in attendance at the counseling session had been sobered by that fact, but only for a few minutes. It couldn't—wouldn't—happen to them.

Technically, Chris supposed, he could be labeled as not having a home right now. The librarian had implied that, and he didn't fault her for that.

But it had made him think.

He read a page of his book and the due date slip fell from his fingers and landed on the quilt covering him. Without taking his eyes from the page he was reading, he felt around on the quilt for the slip. His fingers traced the pattern of the sunburst on the quilt and he took his eyes from the page and studied it. He wondered how much time Hannah had spent on the quilt and whether she had sewn it alone or with the quilting circle ladies he'd seen visit her.

There was such closeness here. It wasn't just that so many people were related to each other—there were large families here and they stayed in the same area. They didn't spread out all over the country the way those he knew did—he hadn't even met some of his cousins. Families had church together in their homes, helped each other harvest crops, raised barns, and funded medical care and prayed during times of illness and death.

Lives were stitched together here, like the fabric pieces on the quilt. Family was bigger, community-sized. Paradise had been in existence for generations and generations. Maybe the phrase "It takes a village to raise a child" had originated because of places like this.

He'd had the same closeness with his men. A band of brothers was what he'd had in the military; it wasn't just the title of a PBS television series. They shared good times and bad—talked about births, deaths, and loves back home; loaned each other money; drunk the occasional beer together; and covered each other's backs. Well, until the end, they'd covered each other's backs. At the end, Chris felt they'd deserted him.

Troubled by the direction his thoughts had taken, he closed the book he'd started reading and reached for the Bible he kept beside his bed.

He was tempted to read Job again. When he'd first read through it he'd felt a kinship to the poor man. But then he'd felt he had to move on, that he had to see he couldn't go around feeling like he was walking around with a big cloud over his head.

He still had his moments—but hopefully they were getting fewer. What had the chaplain advised? Let go and let God? It was a snappy phrase, he said, and he admitted that he often said he would let go and let God. However, the chaplain's wife had told him he'd then try to take back a small part of it and tell God he could handle it—to no good result!

On a whim, Chris let the Bible fall open and give him direction. It was something he'd seen his late buddy Vince do with this same Bible. The pages parted and he saw Psalms 28:7: "The Lord is my strength and my shield; my heart trusts in him, and I am helped."

With a deep sigh, he closed the book and placed it with the other one on the nightstand. He clicked off the battery-operated lantern, turned on his side, and lay in the dark watching moonlight filter in through the window.

His hand stroked the quilt again, and he thought about Hannah and then felt himself dosing off . . .

Her cheek was like the petals of a rose. He couldn't stop stroking it. Her eyes were dark, dreamy, half-closed with pleasure from his hand touching hers as she stood with the moonlight behind her.

Standing close to her, he inhaled her clean scent, part of it the mild soap Phoebe made for the family, part of it the light scent of lavender.

Her hair was down, a rich, dark mass that waved and flowed down over her shoulders. His hands stroked it and it felt like silk.

"Chris?"

"Hmm?" He'd never thought he'd get this close to her, be able to touch her.

"Chris! Are you all right?"

"More than all right," he said, smiling, and he bent to kiss her.

Her lips were so soft, so warm, moving against his in a way that took his breath away.

Then she was pulling away from him, taking the sweetness, the hope, the promise—

Her voice became sharper, not at all dreamy and romantic the way it was. "Chris! Are you all right?"

He blinked and found that she was standing there in front of him, looking concerned.

"What—what happened?" He realized he'd just awoken from a very delicious dream.

"You were pacing around. I saw you from the kitchen window. Then you were standing here, looking odd, your hands moving like—like—" she stopped. "I got worried that you were having one of those stress episodes so I ran over. Then you were—you were—"

His face burned. "Kissing you," he said hoarsely. He watched her pull her robe closer, push her hair behind her back.

"Were you sleepwalking?"

Chris glanced around him. He didn't remember coming outside but he must have. "I guess so. It happened a couple of times when I was in the hospital."

She reached out to touch his arm. "Are you okay now?"

He shook his head. "I wish you hadn't woken me up," he said softly and he reached out to stroke a lock of her hair that the wind caressed in a way he wanted to do. "Some things you only get to do in your dreams."

He could tell he'd shocked her and he withdrew his hand and straightened. "Go home."

"But—"

"Go home before I show you how I'd like to touch you."

Her mouth fell open at his words and then she spun around and ran from him, her steps soundless on the ground between the houses. He waited until she disappeared into Phoebe's house.

He let himself back into the house, threw himself down on the bed, and prayed he'd dream that dream again.

12

Chris heard the soft footsteps sneaking up on him as he sat on the porch of the *dawdi haus* reading his Bible.

Pretending to yawn and then turn the page of his book, he cast a surreptitious glance around, pretty certain he knew who was sneaking up on him. Yes, it was just as he thought.

He waited until the last minute and then jumped up, dropping his book and grabbing her around the waist and swinging her around and around out over the edge of the porch.

"I'll teach you to sneak up on me!" he growled.

She squealed as her feet flew into the air and her skirts fluttered. "Stop, Chris, stop!" she cried.

But when he slowed, she shook her head. "No! No! More! More!"

He felt his heart lift as she giggled. What a delight to hear pure joy, he couldn't help thinking.

"Annie!"

Chris recognized Hannah's voice.

He set Annie on her feet and steadied her when she laughed and lurched, dizzy from being spun around. How could one little girl wrap him so completely around her little finger, he wondered.

What would it be like to have a child like this? Not just the woman you wanted, but a child? Annie wasn't just a beautiful little girl in looks, with her blond hair, big blue eyes, and a dimpled smile. She had such a sunny disposition and endless curiosity.

"Annie!"

"She's back here," he called and saw Hannah round the side of the house and spot them.

He couldn't take his eyes off her. She wore a dress in a deep blue color, like dusk, and when she saw him her cheeks pinked up in embarrassment and she looked prettier than he'd ever seen her.

Her hair was tucked so neatly under that demure-looking covering she wore like all the other Amish women. Now he knew what her hair looked like streaming down over her shoulders and her back. He knew what it felt like to touch its softness, to smell the flowery sweetness of it.

His stomach tightened.

Deliberately he dragged his attention back to the present.

"I snuck up on Chris!" Annie told her proudly. "I 'sprised him."

Hannah smiled at her. "Time to go, *liebschen*."

Annie's bottom lip jutted out and she grabbed Chris's hand. "I want to stay with Chris."

"No, we need to go." Hannah's tone was firm.

"Chris can come with us." She gave him a winsome grin.

"Annie, maybe Chris has plans."

He laughed and waved his hand at the books lying on the chaise lounge. "Yeah, I was reading my Bible since I hadn't checked out a church. I figured after I did that, I'd have a heavy date with my library book. And then maybe a nice little snooze on the lounge."

"I should have thought to invite you. I wasn't sure you'd be interested."

She was avoiding his eyes. He wondered what to say about last night. What *could* he say?

"Ah—where is it?" he managed to ask "I didn't see an Amish church when we were in town."

"We don't have a formal building. Church is every other Sunday in someone's home. You'd be very welcome if you'd like to come."

Chris weighed what she was saying as he looked at her. He didn't want her to ask just out of courtesy.

"Are you sure it would be okay?"

"*Schur.* We have *Englisch* guests sometimes."

Annie jumped up and down. "*Kumm* with us, Chris."

Chris glanced down at his jeans and T-shirt. "But—"

"You're fine," Hannah told him. "We're Plain, not Fancy, remember."

"Give me one minute. I'll put on a better shirt."

"Hurry, hurry, hurry," Annie sing-songed. "We gotta go."

"Be right back!" Chris jogged into the house and changed his shirt.

When he came out, Annie was gone.

"Hey, where's my date?"

Hannah smiled. "It'll be Phoebe. Annie went to ride with her family."

He started walking with her across the field to the other house. "Phoebe, huh?"

Slanting a glance at him, she smiled. "I think Annie's a little young for dating."

Chris glanced around to make sure no one was in hearing range. "Phoebe isn't a little too old? You'd be . . ." he trailed off.

Just right lingered in the air.

"Yes, well, uh—look!" she said quickly, pointing at the buggy approaching. "Here she comes now."

Phoebe pulled up.

"I invited Chris to come with us."

"I see," the older woman said with a smile. "So nice to have you with us to worship, Chris."

"Thank you."

He turned to Hannah. "Ladies first."

"I'll take the backseat," she told him and her eyes twinkled with mischief. "That way you can sit up front with Phoebe."

Resigned, not knowing what to do, he watched as she climbed into the back and he got in the front. Phoebe, unaware of the electrical current between Hannah and him, got the buggy moving.

When they arrived at the home where the service was held, Chris found the church was just as Hannah had said it would be. He was warmly welcomed by the older couple who were the hosts, and the men he'd worked with shook his hand and invited him to sit in their row. Matthew and Joshua joined them a little later, and Chris saw Jenny with Annie and Mary. Annie brightened when she saw him and waved and grinned at him. He waved back.

At first it felt a little strange to be seated on a bench in a home instead of in a church, but the way that things were set up showed that the home had clearly been built with the intent to accommodate a large number of people. One wall was a sort of partition that folded back so that the benches could be brought in for seating.

Chris was surprised when the men and women sat on different sides of the room, and he didn't understand when Pennsylvania German was spoken. He was surprised when there was no musical accompaniment to the hymns. But he felt right at home because the lay ministers were so genuine when they spoke about a message they got from the Bible.

And when one of them began talking about a passage in Matthew, quoting, "Blessed are they who are persecuted for righteousness' sake: for theirs is the kingdom of heaven," he found himself sitting up straight and listening hard.

⁓⥾⁓

"You didn't tell him, did you?"

Hannah shrugged. "I don't know what you mean."

"You do, too," Phoebe whispered. "That poor man has no idea how long our services last."

"He didn't ask."

Phoebe made a tsk-tsk-ing sound. "Shame on you," she chided.

But Hannah could see that Phoebe was trying to hide a smile. Her own lips twitched as she tried to do the same. She'd looked over to where the men sat and listened to the service and seen that for the first hour and a half or so, he seemed absorbed in what the ministers said. Especially when John B. talked about Matthew 5:10. Chris was particularly absorbed in what he was saying.

When voices were lifted in song, Chris stood and joined in. He had to look at the hymnal but he seemed earnest and interested, acting as if he enjoyed himself, she saw.

She wondered how he sounded when he sang and wished he wasn't so far away that she couldn't hear. His voice was always low and measured when he spoke. He probably had a nice singing voice.

But as the service went on, she saw him shift a little, and he appeared surprised when he surreptitiously looked at his watch and saw the time.

When he glanced over at her, raising his eyebrows in question, she had to bite her lip to keep from smiling. Understanding dawned and when she saw the glint in his eyes, the knowing nod and the slight smile, she wondered if she'd hear about this later.

Phoebe leaned over. "I think you should apologize to him later."

"He doesn't have to go to another one if he doesn't want to."

An older woman in front of them turned and frowned at Hannah.

Hannah whispered, *"Er dutt mir leed"*—"I'm sorry."

Looking somewhat mollified, the woman turned back around.

More time passed. Phoebe got up once to walk outside and relieve the stiffness she'd been experiencing lately. Annie needed a bathroom break so Mary took her.

When the service was over, the men began turning the benches into tables and the women went to the kitchen to fix the light meal that was served.

Once, when Hannah was walking around refilling coffee cups, she saw Chris staring at her. There was something dark and intense in his eyes, something she'd never seen when a man looked at her. Something mysterious and yet known, so desired and yet feared.

She looked away and felt her cheeks warm as she remembered *that kiss.*

"You okay?" Jenny whispered as she came to stand next to Hannah.

"I'm just a little warm. Lots of people in the house."

But Jenny was looking at Chris. "Oh yeah? It's not just one man who's making you feel that way?"

"Why is it you can't get off that topic?"

Jenny patted her shoulder. "Just want to see you as happy as me."

"Did you ever think—" she broke off.

"Did I ever think what?"

She glanced around. "Not here."

Jenny took her hand and drew her outside, to a corner of the porch where no one could hear. "Did I ever think what?"

Hannah watched the children running and playing in the yard. Some of the men were filtering out of the house now and congregating in front of the barn, talking business and horses and who knew what.

"Did you ever think maybe I'm just not meant to marry?"

Shocked, Jenny stared at her. "No way. Look, we talked about how you feel a little down this time of year, but you have to keep your spirits up. I wondered if I was ever going to get married, too, but look what happened."

Mary came out and brightened when she saw her mother. "*Mamm*, Joshua isn't feeling well. *Daedi* thinks we should go home now."

"Is he complaining about his stomach again?"

"*Ya.*"

Jenny sighed. "We should have stayed home. I think he has a touch of the stomach flu that's gone around the community. Tell your dad I'll be right in. No, tell him to go get the buggy and bring it around."

Nodding, Mary went back inside.

"So, did Chris enjoy the service?"

Hannah brushed a nonexistent piece of lint from her dress. "I don't know. I haven't had a chance to ask him."

"Well, it was nice of you to ask him to attend. I didn't think of it."

"I didn't," she told her, a stickler for honesty. "Annie did."

"That Annie," Jenny said with a laugh. "She really likes him, doesn't she?"

"I don't think there's anyone Annie's ever met who she didn't like."

Jenny gave her a hug. "Are you okay?"

Hannah absorbed the love and then she pulled back. "*Ya. Danki.*"

❧

Chris told himself that the funny feeling in his stomach was from overeating.

But he really hadn't eaten any more than usual—well, maybe a little, but that was because he had been doing manual labor.

When his chest started feeling funny and his breathing got a bit raspy, he felt a trace of anxiety.

He walked outside for a breath of air and passed Jenny coming inside. Hannah was standing to one side of the porch and when she saw him approach she looked like she was going to go inside too.

"Don't leave on my account," he told her. "I just came out to get some fresh air. I—" he stopped.

"Chris? What is it?"

He turned away, not wanting her to see he was struggling for air. "Nothing."

"It's something," she insisted, pulling on his arm and making him turn.

"Just having—just having a little trouble breathing. Weird."

It was more than a little trouble, he realized. He had asthma, but he seldom had trouble with it except when—

"Something's wrong. I can hear your lungs wheezing. Here, sit down."

He rubbed a hand over his chest. "Must have—must have eaten something wrong—" Reaching into his pocket, he found the inhaler he carried in case of emergency.

"What did you eat? Chris?" She knelt before him.

He took a quick couple of puffs on the inhaler and leaned back in the chair. "I don't know. A little of everything."

"You didn't have any of the peanut butter spread, did you?"

"Hey, give me some credit," he said a little irritably. "I know not to eat peanuts."

Uh oh, he thought. Crankiness often came first when he was about to have an asthma attack.

"Did you have some of those little cookie balls made of chocolate?"

"Yeah. Why?"

"Because I think Sadie uses ground nuts in her recipe."

"Didn't taste nuts in them."

But he'd been so occupied with talking to John B. that he hadn't paid attention to what he put in his mouth, he remembered.

"I'll be right back," Hannah said.

"No need to—"

He was talking to thin air. She was going to make a fuss. He just knew it. He was all right. Or he would be in a few minutes. He hadn't eaten many of the cookie balls . . . just one or two, he thought. And he'd used his inhaler. Some water might help. In a minute he'd go inside and get some water.

In a minute . . . when he caught his breath.

◆

Hannah jumped up, ran into the house, and found Sadie in the kitchen with the other women.

"Did you put nuts in the cookie balls?"

"*Ya*, why?"

"Someone who ate them is allergic."

Sadie clapped a hand to her mouth. "Oh, no! Who?"

"A friend of ours. Chris."

"The *Englischer* I met a little while ago? Is he *allrecht*?"

Hannah bit her lip and tried to think of what to do. She could probably find someone who had a cell phone or send them to the phone shanty to call 911, but there had to be a faster way to help Chris.

Then she remembered. "Sadie! Sarah said her little boy is having a lot of allergy problems. Grab her from the kitchen and bring her out to the porch for me."

Rushing back outside, Hannah found Chris leaning over the railing of the porch. He looked ill, really ill.

"This is just intolerable."

Hannah glanced back at the familiar male voice. Josiah stood there, stern and disapproving.

"How dare he come to church drunk?" he said, sounding angry.

Chris turned from the railing, wiping his mouth with a handkerchief. "Not—not drunk."

Sarah rushed out carrying a diaper bag. "Hannah, Sadie said you need help."

She looked at Chris. "Oh, my, you look like my poor Levi after he's eaten something he's allergic to. Don't worry, I have something to make you feel better."

She unzipped the bag, rooted around in a pocket, and pulled out a package of Benadryl. "Here, take these."

Uncapping a plastic bottle of water, she handed it to him with the pills.

"Glad—glad I don't have to drink from a sippy cup," he said, taking the pills and washing them down with gulps of water. He wiped his arm across his sweaty forehead.

Sarah set the bag on the porch and pushed Chris down into the chair. "Sssh, just sit and let it work. Catch your breath."

"Do you think we need to call for help?" Sarah asked Hannah.

Chris shook his head. "Be—fine. Minute."

Sarah studied him and then she nodded. "I think he's right." She pulled out a little plastic baggie, put several of the pills into it, and handed it to Hannah. "Here, hold onto these just in case."

A few minutes later, Sarah nodded at Chris. "Feeling better?"

"Yeah. Thanks. Thanks a lot."

She picked up the diaper bag. "*Gem gschehn*. You are welcome."

Hannah glanced around. Josiah had disappeared. Thank goodness. She had enough on her hands without him causing problems.

"Thanks for helping," Chris said.

She breathed a sigh of relief. "Are you really feeling better?"

He nodded. "But you didn't need to make a fuss. I'd have been okay."

"You don't think someone should make a fuss when someone else is having trouble breathing?"

Shrugging, he looked away. "I'd have been fine in a minute."

"I see." She handed him the pills. "I'll leave you now. It's evident you don't need me anymore."

"You'll make someone a wonderful wife one day," he told her, finally meeting her eyes. "That was really amazing the way you took care of me."

She folded her arms across her chest and regarded him. "But you don't really want or need someone to do that for you, do you?"

"They have this phrase they use to recruit soldiers in my world," he said slowly. "They say they'll teach you how to be 'an Army of one.' They did."

He got up and walked away, going over to the barn to talk to the other men, leaving Hannah to stand there and stare after him.

⊷❧

"So you had an interesting time today, *ya?*" Phoebe asked Chris as she drove them home a little while later.

"You could say that," Chris agreed.

"I am so sorry," Phoebe told him. "I'm sure Sadie feels terrible that she made you sick. She'll know to tell people what's in the cookies next time."

"It happens."

"What did you think of the service?"

"It was long." He glanced at her. "Sorry, I shouldn't have said that."

She pulled the buggy to the side of the road to let an impatient automobile driver pass them.

"There's nothing wrong with the truth," she said, guiding Daisy to pull them back onto the road. "The services are long. But they're every other week."

"Really?"

She chuckled. "*Ya.*"

"So what do you do on the alternate Sundays?"

"Visit friends. Read. Take a nap."

"Sounds good," he said, stretching out his legs. He didn't know if it was the meal, the Benadryl, or the peaceful ride in a buggy, but he was nodding off.

"Especially the nap right now, eh?"

"Yes."

"Don't go to sleep!" Hannah spoke up from the backseat.

Chris blinked awake. He glanced back over the seat and found her watching him with some apprehension.

"Why not?" he asked, deliberately teasing her.

Hannah glared at him but when Phoebe looked over her shoulder, she quickly schooled her features.

"If you fall asleep, we'll just have to wake you up in a few minutes when we get home. Or try to drag you out of the buggy."

He gave Hannah a careless grin before he turned back in his seat.

13

"*Aenti* Hannah? You need to come see Daisy."

Hannah turned and looked at Joshua. "Why?"

"I think she's sick."

"Let's go take a look." Hannah wiped her hands on a dish cloth and followed Joshua out of the house. She'd been so busy canning she hadn't noticed the time.

Daisy, indeed, did not look well. She was stumbling and bumping against her stall, and her eyes were wide and unfocused. Her skin looked clammy too.

"Daisy? Poor thing, you're not feeling well?"

One look in her stall and Hannah saw that Daisy hadn't touched her food or water last night.

"Joshua, go get your *daedi*," Hannah said quietly.

Her nephew went flying from the stall and ran smack into Chris.

"Daisy's sick," Joshua told him. "I have to get *daedi*."

"Matthew's gone to town." Chris moved closer. "Is there anything I can do? We had horses on the farm."

Hannah walked closer to the horse and raised her hand to touch her to check for fever. The horse, normally a placid mare, reacted with wide rolling eyes and reared back, showing her teeth.

An arm wrapped around Hannah's waist and she was swept up and off her feet, away from the horse. The world spun.

"What—" she sputtered as she realized Chris had lifted her as if she weighed as little as her niece Annie.

"You were about to get hurt!"

"Daisy wouldn't hurt me!" she protested. "We've had her for years."

He set her down, safely away from the horse.

"Sssh, there, girl," he said to the horse as he moved closer slowly, very slowly. "You wouldn't have meant to hurt Hannah, but you're feeling very sick, aren't you?"

Hannah pressed a hand to her heart and felt it racing at the sudden protective movement Chris had made. She didn't want to admit it, but he was probably right. Daisy wasn't acting like herself at all, and she'd known a momentary fear when the horse reared back like that.

It was the second time he'd reacted with such speed and strength to protect her.

"I don't think Matthew's intending to be back for a couple of hours."

Hannah looked at Daisy and bit her lip. "Joshua, go get Phoebe. Be quick."

The boy ran. Chris walked forward. "Something's definitely wrong with her."

Hannah studied Daisy. The horse had moved a step closer to Chris when he approached. Hannah had noticed the horse really seemed to like Chris.

But when he tried to stroke the horse's nose, Daisy wasn't having any of it. She whinnied and backed away.

"Something's definitely wrong with her," he agreed as he glanced around inside the stall. "Might be colic."

"She had colic once and she didn't behave like this."

Chris stepped closer and talked soothingly to the horse. She shied from him the way she had with Hannah, curled back her lips, and showed her teeth. But he persisted quietly, soothing her, and she let him reach out and touch her jawbone under her cheek. Hannah remembered how his touch had felt the night before.

"Be careful, she could bite you," Hannah warned.

"You won't bite me, will you, girl?" He felt around and gently pressed the vein on the inside of the jawbone, his mouth moving as he counted and watched the second hand moving on the dial of his watch.

"Her pulse is very fast," Chris told Hannah. "Since Matthew will be gone a while, I don't think you should wait. Go call your vet now. I'll stay with her."

Hannah hurried from the stall and met Phoebe halfway to the house.

"Joshua says Daisy is sick? This came on suddenly. She was fine yesterday."

"Chris says we need to call the vet right away."

Phoebe nodded. "You go call. I'll sit with her until he gets here."

The number for the vet was in an address book inside the telephone shanty. With shaking fingers, Hannah dialed the number and told the vet what symptoms Daisy was experiencing.

She returned to the barn and they waited for the vet to arrive.

Daisy seemed to grow worse by the minute. For the first time since she'd lived with them, she lay down in the stall and wouldn't get up. Her breathing grew labored.

The three of them knelt on the hay. Chris wiped Daisy's damp skin with a towel while Hannah and Phoebe prayed.

Hannah began to wonder if the vet would be able to get there in time. She felt tears sliding down her cheeks as she tried to comfort Phoebe.

It felt like hours before the vet got there, but it was no more than half an hour. The man strode in, did a quick exam, and looked around her stall. Then he pulled out a huge syringe and gave Daisy an injection.

"That should make her feel better," he said, pulling out a plastic IV bag filled with clear liquid. "I'm giving her some fluid since she's dehydrated."

"What's the matter with her?"

"I'm not sure. I think she may have eaten something that didn't agree with her."

He pulled a plastic zip-lock bag and a lab tube from his medical case and scooped up some of the feed in her stall. He put it in the bag and filled the tube with some of Daisy's water, then put both into his bag.

"Why did you do that?" Phoebe wanted to know.

"It's rare, but occasionally something will get into an animal's food or water. The lab'll check it out and I should have the test results in a day or so. In the meantime, get rid of that food and water and put in new feed from another bag. Are the other horses okay?"

"They're fine," Phoebe told him.

The vet frowned and then he nodded. "That's what makes me think she ate something that didn't agree with her, that it isn't the food she and the other horses were eating."

He gave Daisy a final look. "Someone should keep an eye on her until she's better. You have my number if she should turn worse. Otherwise, I'll be back tomorrow morning."

Hannah could see the worry written on Phoebe's face. Daisy had been a gift from Phoebe's *mann* years ago, and she wasn't just a horse but a member of the family.

"Why don't you sit with her for a few hours while I finish the canning?" Hannah suggested. "She seems calmer with you here."

Hannah suspected that Daisy would probably need watching tonight; she could spare Phoebe from spending the cool night hours there.

"Are you sure?"

"Absolutely. I'll call you when supper's ready."

Chris had been standing back while the vet took care of the horse and now he backed away. "If you don't need me I'll see what else I can do outside. If Matthew's back I'll send him over to talk to you about Daisy."

Phoebe touched Chris's arm. "*Danki* for helping, Chris."

"I was happy to do so," he told her, taking her hand and squeezing it gently. "Try not to worry."

Phoebe nodded. "I don't. I believe—"

"Worrying is arrogant because God knows what He's doing," Hannah finished with a smile.

Chuckling, Phoebe smiled. "I guess I say that a lot."

Hannah bent to kiss her head. "I don't know about that. But it's a wonderful way to live. I'll finish the canning and start supper. You call me if you need anything."

"Uh, not to worry but—" Chris started.

"*Ya?*"

"I'd feel better if you don't get too close to Daisy. She was acting pretty wild earlier, almost lashed out at Hannah."

He glanced back at Hannah and gave her a slight smile. "Not that Daisy wanted to hurt her, but she isn't feeling well."

"Is there something else you can sit on—" he began and then he spotted an old beat-up chair in the corner of the barn. He dragged it over.

Phoebe had been sitting on a bale of hay. She started to get to her feet and her movements were so stiff and jerky Chris that reacted immediately, taking her arm and helping her up.

"Old bones," she said self-deprecatingly. "*Danki*."

"My pleasure, ma'am."

Hannah saw her frown and she thought about how much harder it seemed to be for the older woman to get around these days. She wondered, as she had several times recently, if she should try seriously broaching the subject of their moving Phoebe's things to a first-floor bedroom again. Phoebe was looking so tired and pale now.

Distracted, Hannah looked at Chris when she realized that he was saying something to her. "I'm sorry, what did you say?"

"I'm going back to work. Yell if you need anything. I'll check in later."

She nodded. "*Danki*."

Once she saw that Phoebe was safely settled, Hannah hurried back to the kitchen. As quickly as she could, she finished up the canning, lined up her day's work on the counter, and turned to prepare supper. The sooner she got Phoebe to come in and eat, the sooner she'd get her to rest.

Daisy had to get better. She just had to.

❦

Chris stood under the shower and let the water beat on his sore back.

Farming the Amish way was definitely harder work. But in some strange way, it was more satisfying. He shook his head at that, scattering droplets of water. Funny thought. He loved technology—or so he'd thought.

But the fact was, he hadn't really missed anything from his modern world so far. Well, maybe television, just a little. After all, he'd watched a lot of it at the hospital. What else could you do when patients came and went; it had been hard to make friends and keep them.

Except for the long-termers—the patients who were there for an extended time recovering from serious conditions and doing physical therapy. Trouble was, sometimes it made it seem like you'd been there even longer when you heard them say something about *their* length of stay. Keeping spirits up became a daily struggle.

He saw a smaller circle of people here in Paradise. Funny, he'd used the word circle. But that's what it seemed like, a circle. People were closely bound here, eager to help with the harvest—the way his men had bonded over a task.

Well, except for one. One man had never seemed part of them, and he'd ended up bringing them all down.

Chris turned off the shower, toweled dry, and dressed. He kept a close eye on the time. It wouldn't do to be late for supper. Jenny ran a tight ship with the meal on the table, dishes washed, and children in bed by a certain time. Bedtime came early here.

He made it to the table with time to spare, his offer of help turned down, as usual. They treated him like family, but he was still a guest who wasn't supposed to set the table or wash the dishes.

Supper was a noisy gathering of the children sharing events of their day, what Chris had always thought of as "chowing down" on big bowls and platters of home-cooked and home-grown food, and then good coffee and conversation with adults afterward.

Chris stood on the porch of the *dawdi haus* later, watching the sun set over fields that were nearly harvested. His time here was coming to an end, and he was strangely reluctant to leave. Somehow it felt more like home than home had felt when he was there after being in the hospital.

He didn't mind the early bedtime here. It was enjoyable to lie on the big soft mattress, under sheets and a quilt that smelled of the sun, and read a book by the gentle glow of the battery lantern. Sometimes he read the Bible, sometimes the library book or a farming book Matthew loaned him. The window was always cracked open to let in the breeze and nature's music instead of the radio or recorded music he'd always listened to in the evenings.

A sense of peace, something he'd craved with an urgency akin to the worst hunger he'd ever experienced, had begun to steal over him. He was healing here in a way that didn't happen in a hospital. His restlessness and inner conflict was fading.

Except for the inner conflict he felt whenever he thought about the woman who lived next door.

He got up and looked out the window. There was a gentle glow of a lantern in the barn. Someone was obviously up with Daisy. He thought about how he'd promised Hannah that he'd look in later, but had decided against it when Matthew said he'd check in on her.

Joshua had begged to go along too. He worried that he'd done something wrong when he helped Chris take care of her the night before she'd fallen sick. Matthew pointed out to his son that people and animals often got sick while those around them didn't.

Chris went over and over what he'd done to feed and water her but there hadn't been anything out of the ordinary. And the other horses were healthy, so he suspected she'd just eaten something when she'd been out in the pasture.

He dressed, pulled on sneakers, and let himself out of the house.

As he walked the distance between the two farms, he thought about how nice it was that the two families lived so close together. He wondered if it was a case of Jenny falling in love with the boy next door all those years ago.

Funny thing, Hannah was the girl next door right now. She was so different from the girls he'd dated before he went into the Army: outspoken, unaffected, loving.

And so not someone even remotely in his league.

He pushed open the barn door, and she turned around and looked at him. The lantern light cast a soft glow on her as she sat on the old chair near Daisy.

She touched her forefinger to her lips as he approached. "She's sleeping. I think she's doing a little better," she said quietly.

He approached and looked down at the horse. She *did* look a little better.

"The vet stopped by on his way home and he gave her a shot," Hannah told him. "Phoebe was worried, so I told her I'd stay up with Daisy for a little while."

Chris pulled a bale of hay over and sat on it. "Mind if I keep you company for a little while?"

He saw her eyes shift to the barn door.

"Problem?"

She shrugged. "Single men and women aren't supposed to be alone together like this."

"Sorry, I didn't realize," he said. "Should I open the barn door for propriety's sake?"

Her eyes narrowed. "Are you laughing at me?"

"No, of course not! How could you think that?"

She folded her arms across her chest. "I suppose it sounds . . . quaint to you."

"Hannah, I wouldn't dream of being critical of you or anyone here," he said quietly. "Everyone's been very welcoming to me."

"Except for Josiah."

"Well, yeah, except for Josiah," he acknowledged. "Do you want me to open the barn door?"

She sighed. "No, it's all right."

It was quiet for a long time except for the soft noises of horses shifting in their stalls and settling in to rest for the night.

Chris glanced at Hannah and she blushed and looked away. A few moments later, when she thought he wasn't looking, he saw her glancing at him.

Neither of them mentioned the kiss the night before.

Then Chris broke the silence by telling Hannah about Annie's adventure at school that day.

"That Annie," she said, laughing and shaking her head. "She has such a colorful way of telling a story, doesn't she? I have no doubt she'll be a writer just like her *mamm*."

"They make quite a family, don't they?" he mused. "Jenny talked about how she was engaged to Matthew and going to be a stepmother when we met at the veteran's hospital. "

"*Kinner* respond to love," Hannah said simply. "They can tell Jenny truly loves them."

An easy silence fell between them for a time.

"Why did you become a soldier?"

His eyes widened. "Where did that come from?"

She shrugged. "Just wondered."

"It's a tradition in our family," he told her slowly. "Goes back to my great-grandfather's time. The men volunteer for a tour of duty. My parents actually met when my mother was a nurse in the veteran's hospital where he was sent."

"Was he injured the same way as you?"

"No, thank goodness."

Chris fell silent for a moment. Then again, if his father had experienced the same things he had in his military service, he might have understood what Chris had gone through. Nothing about his duty or his injuries had been within the scope of his father's understanding.

But he wouldn't wish that on anyone anyway. Even if it made for better rapport.

"Did they come to see you in the hospital?"

"Sure."

She nodded. "That's what families do."

He stretched out his legs and crossed them at the ankles. "Well, that's what a lot of families do, but not all. There were a lot of patients there who never got a visit. Sometimes it was because their families were too far away, but sometimes it was because they didn't get along."

"People aren't perfect. Families aren't perfect—even here."

"You're right. I've been around you and your family and none of you pretend to be perfect, or to be saints."

She laughed and Daisy moved her head and snorted in her sleep. Clapping her hand over her mouth, Hannah's eyes danced above her hand as she waited for the horse to settle again.

"Saints we're not," she whispered when Daisy settled again.

"Not even you?"

"Especially not me. You know I'm nosy and impatient—"

"No!" he said sharply. "That's not true."

Her eyebrows shot up at his vehemence.

"I might have thought that in the beginning. But you're just inquisitive . . . eager to understand. And you're one of the kindest people I know. So don't go putting yourself down."

He got to his feet, avoiding her startled glance, and took a closer look at Daisy. Then he met her eyes. "I'll go if you want me to."

She hesitated for a moment. "Like I said, we shouldn't be alone together."

Now it was his turn to raise his brows. "Surely it's not right to leave a woman alone in a barn all night."

She lifted her shoulders and then let them fall. "No. Matthew offered to come over, but I didn't want him to. He needs his sleep during a busy time like this." She sighed. "Stay for a while. It's nice to have company."

He sat again and after a moment, they began talking again, only this time, they talked about the horses, the harvest, the weather. Everyday stuff. Nothing deep and personal.

The long day under the sun, the physical work, and the big dinner Jenny had served him finally took its toll. Chris felt himself doing what his buddies called "chicken pecking"—falling asleep and the minute the chin touches the chest you jerk awake. He told himself he should just give in and go to bed, but it didn't seem fair to leave a woman alone in the barn in the middle of the night caring for a sick horse.

So he joked and apologized and accepted the coffee she made and brought out for them.

She'd said she was just staying up a little while longer but clearly she wasn't leaving, too worried about the horse. He was convinced he could pull an all-nighter. After all, he'd done it during his military duty. Hannah was keeping her eyes open. He became determined to do so too.

<hr />

He dreamed.

It was one of those dreams where you knew you were sleeping. Where you tried to wake yourself up. But you kept on dreaming because it was so pleasant where you were.

Chris walked through the field of corn, the sun warm on his shoulders, the sky a bright blue overhead.

If there was any place he felt at home, this was it. And this was his home at last. He'd plowed the fields in the way it had been done for so many years, here in Lancaster County. Planted the seed. Nurtured and prayed over it. Then given to God the glory of the bountiful harvest.

His feet sank a little into the soft soil as he walked down a row of cornstalks, healthy and tall and green, topped by golden tassels. He pulled down an ear, shucked its green covering to reveal the kernels within, and smiled and nodded with satisfaction.

He grew several crops, as did Matthew on the adjoining farm, but corn was his favorite. It reminded him of all the happy years he'd enjoyed growing up on the family farm in Kansas. He couldn't wait to harvest the corn and try out the first ears, boiling them in a huge metal pot right out in the fields the way his father had always done. They'd be served with real butter slathered on them and be almost enough to eat all by themselves.

But of course Hannah wouldn't allow that. She'd insist that they had to have something else: some fried or baked chicken and her special potato salad. And, of course, some pie. She'd become quite a baker since she'd lived with Phoebe. She was considered one of the top bakers in the community, and that was saying something with all the fabulous cooks here.

A flock of birds flew up suddenly, and he saw Hannah walking toward him, smiling. The fall breeze fluttered the strings to her *kapp* and molded the fabric of her dress against her body, outlining her shape. Her lips were parted in a smile that reached all the way to her blue eyes.

The ear of corn fell from his hands and he began walking toward her, meeting her halfway.

He cupped her cheeks in his hands, marveling at the softness of her skin. She gazed at him with such love. What had he ever done to deserve her? When he'd first come here, he thought life had dealt him a really rough deal, that somehow he'd been punished for doing what he thought was the right thing.

But now? Well, now he had everything he could ever hope for: a healing of his spirit, and the *true* peace that came with knowing God loved him, not just this woman.

Everything else was better than he could have ever imagined . . . he and Hannah owned this farmhouse and land since Phoebe had offered to sell it to them after they were married and move into the *dawdi haus* at the back of Matthew and Jenny's farmhouse. He had friends and family who loved him, who welcomed him into their church, their lives, their community.

Hannah kissed him fervently, surprising him. They'd exchanged kisses, of course, since they had become engaged. But she'd never shown him quite so powerfully how much she had missed him that day.

"Sweetheart, I love you, too, but we shouldn't stand out here kissing like this," he said as she continued to kiss him. It was torture, but he tried to pull away. He was trying hard to fit into the community and such passionate displays of affection—even between those who were engaged—was considered unseemly. He didn't want to get in bad graces with the bishop.

"Please, darling, I—"

There were giggles. It sounded like more than one person. He opened his eyes and stared up into pink rubbery lips, a big wet tongue, and breath that smelled like it could knock a tree over.

Daisy!

Not only did she look like she was feeling better, she was giving him big, sloppy, horsey kisses as Hannah and Phoebe looked on and laughed uproariously.

Chris struggled to sit up on the hay bale and carefully pushed Daisy away. "Well, look who's feeling better," he said, feeling his cheeks redden.

"Who were you talking to?" Hannah asked, trying but failing to look innocent.

Chris couldn't help it. He shook his head and then gave in and laughed with them.

14

*T*here's something different about you today," Jenny said to Hannah the next day.

Hannah bobbled the plate in her hands but managed not to drop it. "Don't know what you're talking about."

"No?" Jenny grinned. "It wouldn't have anything to do with a certain young man by the name of Chris, would it?"

She'd spent a lot of time thinking about that night he'd kissed her, and when he'd been talking in his sleep about kissing her.

"He's passing through," she reminded Jenny. "You haven't forgotten that, have you? He came for vacation, and he's stayed to help Matthew. That's all."

"I don't know," Jenny said slowly, glancing out the kitchen window as they got dinner on the table. "He seems happy here. He looks more peaceful than when he first came."

"But he—" Hannah stopped, appalled that she'd nearly mentioned Chris's episode of sleepwalking.

She didn't know much about sleepwalking—she'd only heard of someone doing that once here in her community, and that was Leroy Esh who'd done it after he'd had a traumatic experience.

"He what?"

"Nothing."

It didn't feel right to tell Jenny about it. She cast about for something to say to change the subject. But the only thing she could think of was to tell Jenny about her grandmother, and that didn't feel right either. She knew Phoebe didn't want anyone fussing over her and so far, there wasn't enough reason to do so.

"I think there IS something."

Hannah gave her a look. "Now you're trying to interrogate me."

Jenny laughed. "Old habits die hard." She shook her head and her smile faded. "You can't deny you're attracted to him. And I've never seen that happen with any man from this community."

Going to the refrigerator for the pitcher of iced tea, Hannah thought about how to maneuver Jenny away from the topic. When Jenny wanted to know about something, she was like a bulldog. She returned to the table with the pitcher and began pouring its contents into glasses, setting one before Jenny.

"We've talked about how I'm not interested in anyone here."

"I remember how you disappeared during my wedding reception when it came to the courtship games," Jenny said with a nod. "And there's something you're not considering. I stayed, remember? How do we know Chris isn't thinking about doing that?"

Hannah blinked. "He's said nothing about that to me. Has he talked to you or Matthew about it?"

Jenny shook her head. "But it's not outside of the realm of possibilities."

"I thought you wrote nonfiction, not fiction."

Laughing, Jenny got out a bowl for the vegetables.

Hannah finished pouring the tea and set the pitcher on the table. Trying to act casual, she looked at Jenny. "I know you said you met Chris at the veteran's hospital and you had a lot in common. But what do you really know about him?"

"Not much," she said as she started slicing a loaf of bread. "Well, this turned out very nice if I do say so myself," she said, looking at the bread.

She couldn't help it. Hannah started laughing and couldn't seem to stop.

"What's so funny?" Jenny demanded.

"'If I do say so myself,'" Hannah said, wiping away a tear. "I'm sorry, you said it again, just like that time you cooked artichokes."

"Hey, I did everything I was supposed to do," Jenny insisted, looking indignant. "I even cooked them a little longer than the recipe called for."

"So you sat there and when you realized they were barely edible, you could have just told us that they weren't fit to eat. But you just smacked your lips and said, 'Oh, these are very good if I do say so myself.' And the *kinner* and Matthew just chimed in with, 'And you do say so yourself!'"

Jenny put her hands on her hips and glared at Hannah. "I'm so glad I provide you with such a source of amusement! When are you people going to stop ragging on me about my cooking?"

Hannah wrapped her arms around her sister-in-law and hugged her. "I'm sorry, it's just that you do so many other things well!"

"Well, that's not true," Jenny said, but when Hannah released her and she stood back, she shrugged her shoulders. "It's taking so much longer to get good at cooking. And the Bontrager family is so interested in filling their stomachs."

"That we are," Matthew said, walking into the kitchen. He sniffed. "What are we having for dinner?"

"Oh, you!" Jenny waved her potholder at him. "Your mind is always on your stomach!"

"Not always," he said with a smile and they exchanged a look that was so warm and intimate that Hannah glanced away.

"I'll go wash my hands," he said and left the room.

"Hannah?"

"*Ya?*"

"What's on your mind?"

Jenny walked over to touch Hannah's arm and looked into her face with such concern that Hannah sighed. "We've talked about how this time of year I get a little moody."

Now it was Jenny's turn to wrap her arm around Hannah. "I know. It's not easy to watch so many of your friends and cousins getting married and you're thinking it's not going to happen. I thought that myself a number of times, especially after I was such a mess from being hit by the car bomb."

She shuddered at the memory. "But I found when I came here that Matthew was the man God set aside for me, and I couldn't be happier."

"There were those who said it wouldn't work."

"I know. I can't blame them. Matthew and I came from two different worlds. But when God plans something, He works everything out."

He'd have a lot to work out, thought Hannah. There was no denying she was very attracted to Chris. And she knew he was attracted to her.

But that's all it was—attraction.

Chris became aware that someone was staring at him.

He looked up and saw that Joshua was standing a few feet away, studying him with that quiet intense air that reminded him of the boy's father.

"Hi."

"Hi. What are you reading?"

Chris showed him the cover of the book.

"Do you like to read about soldiers?"

"A friend told me it was a good book."

"Is it?"

"Yeah."

"Can I read it after you?"

"I don't think so."

"I'm a really good reader."

Chris realized that he'd offended him. "It's not that," he said carefully. "I'm not sure your father would want you to read it. Since it's about being a soldier and war and all."

"But I like to know stuff."

Nodding, Chris marked his place in the book. "Me too. Tell you what. I'll ask your father and if he says it's okay, you can read it after I'm finished."

Joshua's face cleared. "Okay. See you at supper."

Annie opened the front door after his knock. "Chris is here! Chris is here!"

"I hear," Jenny said dryly as Chris walked into the kitchen. "I told you that you don't need to walk around the house to come inside, Chris."

He shrugged. "Doesn't feel right to come waltzing into your home through that connecting door," he said, indicating the door to his space with a wave of his hand. "That's for family."

She gave him what Chris could only describe as "the look," the one women brought out when they wanted to make a point. In this case, it meant, "don't be foolish." His mother had been particularly good at the look. Jenny was pretty good at it. Hannah hadn't given many of them. Maybe it was something you learned when you were a mom, he reflected.

He knew Amish families were pretty traditional and the husband and father made the decisions. But he was certain, having been around Jenny, that she would have some say in whether Joshua read the book.

While Joshua's solemn and friendly personality reminded Chris of Matthew, his inquisitiveness was obviously learned from Jenny.

"More meatloaf?"

Chris took the platter from Matthew. "I'll miss these meals."

Jenny smiled. "So nice to hear that you like my cooking." She slanted a look at her husband.

"Hey, I love your cooking," Matthew told her.

"You and Hannah are always teasing me about it. Even the children tease me."

He patted her hand. "Hannah learned to cook at our *mamm's* knee from the time she was little. You didn't. But you've done a fine job catching up." He studied her for a long moment. "Are we making you feel badly? We'll stop if it bothers you."

She smiled and shook her head. "No. It's okay. I know you're all just teasing."

After dinner, as Chris worked behind the horses doing the harvesting, he reflected on the path his thoughts had gone down.

Hours later, he unhooked the horses and took them to the barn, feeding and watering them before heading back to the *dawdi haus* to get cleaned up for supper.

The door opened just as he went to insert his key.

Chris frowned. Had he forgotten to lock it that morning? It wasn't a big deal. Doors didn't get locked a lot around here and with so many people moving around on the farm working, it was doubtful anyone could have deliberately broken in. And it wasn't like he had a lot—just a backpack with some clothes, a little cash, and his Bible.

Still, he pushed the door open slowly and was watchful as he moved inside. Because the place was so small, it took just a quick glance to see that he was alone.

After showering and dressing, he realized he had a little time before supper so he decided to read for a few minutes. But when he went looking for his library book, he couldn't find it. His Bible lay on the bedside table where he'd placed it the night before. The library book wasn't there or in the living room or on the table by the front door. He hadn't read it out on the porch that morning because it had still been dark outside, but he rummaged through the cushions of the porch furniture just in case.

Had Joshua taken it? No, he wouldn't do that, would he? Not after Chris had told him he'd need permission from his parents first.

Lost in thought as he left for supper, he didn't see Joshua approaching him until he nearly ran into him.

"Hi, Chris!"

"Hi." Chris paused. "Joshua, you know I said you may be able to read the book after I asked your father."

"*Ya*, I remember."

"I haven't talked to him yet."

"That's *allrecht*. You're not finished reading it yet anyway."

"No." They walked a few more steps. "Joshua?"

"*Ya?*"

"I can't finish the book if I can't read it."

"Why can't you read it?"

Chris stopped and put his hands on Joshua's shoulders. "Son, are you sure you didn't take the book?"

"Take it?" Joshua's eyes grew big. "I didn't take your book, Chris!"

"The book is gone, Joshua. I couldn't find it anywhere."

"But I didn't take it!"

"What could have happened to it, then?"

Tears were forming in Joshua's eyes. "I don't know. But I didn't take it."

"Is something wrong?"

Chris saw Hannah hurrying toward them.

"Tell him I wouldn't take anything of his!" Joshua cried.

Hannah gathered him in her arms and looked at Chris over his head. "Of course you wouldn't. What's this about?"

"He wanted to read that library book, and I told him I couldn't let him unless his father said it was okay." Chris ran his hands through his hair and then shoved them into the pockets of his jeans. "Then I couldn't find the book when I came home today. I just asked him about it, that's all."

"You looked everywhere?"

"Of course."

"Well then, we'll look again. Come, Joshua, you can help us."

Chris followed them back to the *dawdi haus* and the three of them looked through the place.

"It must be somewhere," Hannah said at last.

"I didn't take it!"

"Shh, *nee*, of course you didn't," Hannah said, rubbing his back with her hand. "Chris isn't saying you did."

She looked at him over Joshua's head. "Are you?"

Her eyes were clear and steady on him but he saw no blame in them.

Chris shook his head. "Of course not. I just asked him about it when I couldn't find it. I thought maybe he borrowed it."

"Go on in the house," Hannah told Joshua.

"Are you going to tell *Daed*?" he asked Chris.

"There isn't anything to tell, is there?" Hannah said quickly. Her eyes begged Chris to agree. "All we have right now is a missing book."

Chris nodded. "I'm not saying anything."

Joshua ran ahead of them and let himself into the house.

"Come on, let's go on inside."

He touched her arm. "Hannah, I asked him if he had it but I didn't mean it to sound like I was accusing him—"

"I know."

She sounded so sure. Surprised, he stared at her. "You say that like you know me so well."

"I do. And I know Joshua. He takes things seriously. Just asking him if he knew where it was would have sounded like an accusation."

"I don't want Matthew and Jenny upset with me."

She touched his hand on her arm. "They won't be. We'll find the book and besides, even if you had given the book to Joshua without asking first, Matthew wouldn't jump to conclusions."

Chris glanced at her hand on his and grinned. "No? I remember how he jumped to some the first time we met."

He watched a blush creep up her cheeks. It was like watching a rose bloom, he thought. She had the most amazing skin. Shaking his head to clear his thoughts, he dropped his hand and began walking toward the house. "Why are you here anyway? Were you invited for supper?"

"*Nee*. I promised to come over and help Jenny with something. I'm early."

Joshua was quiet at the table, but he tended to be sometimes. Jenny asked him something quietly and touched his forehead with the back of her hand, and he shook his head. Illness was a mother's universal answer for why a boy was being quiet or not eating much, he thought.

Chris felt guilty as he watched Joshua pushing the food around on his plate with his fork. He decided he should apologize when he got a chance and when he wouldn't be overheard. He hadn't expected that even asking him if he'd seen the book would upset him—but he should have remembered how sensitive he was.

Then, too, he hadn't thought about how different a child here might be from the ones he knew in the *Englisch* world. He doubted any of them would have reacted in the same way.

After supper, the children asked to be excused to play a game upstairs and Jenny nodded. The four adults were enjoying a second cup of coffee when there was a knock on the front door.

Matthew answered it, and when he returned, he looked at Hannah. "Bishop Miller's here to see you."

"Me?" Surprised, she got to her feet and followed him into the other room.

Jenny looked at Chris and shrugged. "Another slice of pie?" she asked him.

Chris shook his head. The piece he'd eaten was lying in his stomach like a cold stone.

"I don't believe this!" Hannah cried.

Jenny and Chris exchanged a look.

"Since when do you pay attention to anonymous notes? It's probably that old busybody Josiah and you know it! I did nothing wrong!"

There was a murmur of voices, Matthew soothing her and Bishop Miller saying something Chris couldn't distinguish.

Then Hannah stomped into the kitchen, her arms folded across her chest. Her eyes were flashing and two bright spots of color bloomed on her cheeks.

"I'm sorry, Jenny, but I can't stay. Can I help you with that proofreading tomorrow?"

"Sure, but what's the matter?"

Hannah glanced at the doorway. "Matthew can tell you later."

He came back into the room. "He's gone."

"Good!"

"Hannah! He wasn't trying to upset you."

"Well, imagine the job he'd do if he were trying," she said with a sniff.

"He just wanted you to be aware that your actions could be misconstrued, that's all."

"That's all? You wouldn't have appreciated that sort of thing and you know it."

Their eyes locked and Chris wondered who'd back down first. Hannah was one strong-willed woman.

"He's just trying to protect your reputation."

"I can protect my own reputation."

Matthew glanced at Chris, then back at his sister. He sighed. "Well, I'm sure we won't be hearing any more about this."

Chris put down his coffee. "Matthew, does this have something to do with me?"

When the other man reddened, Chris figured he'd correctly interpreted his look.

"Someone wrote the bishop a note saying Hannah had behaved inappropriately with you the other night."

Hannah threw herself into a chair. "It's absurd paying attention to an anonymous note. It's just cowardly. A person should have the courage to confront me or be quiet."

Chris realized that Matthew and Jenny were watching him.

"I'm sorry for causing you any embarrassment," he said, getting up. "I truly didn't think when I came over to check on Daisy."

"It's *allrecht*," Hannah muttered. "You were just trying to be helpful. I'm the one who should have insisted that you go." She looked up at him. "But I enjoyed the company."

He sat again. "I don't understand why it's okay for a woman to sit by herself at night in a barn. What about her safety? I don't care what anyone says about some place being safe, you just never know what could happen."

He stopped. No one knew better than he what bad things could happen to a woman . . . he reminded himself that this wasn't that situation. And Hannah was staring at him strangely.

"The thing is, if a man's sitting there talking to her and nothing inappropriate is going on—well, suddenly it's some-one else's business?" He blew out a frustrated breath.

Chris couldn't help but notice that Matthew and Jenny exchanged a look.

"It's just so insulting," Hannah said, still upset. "If I haven't proven that I'm a woman who knows how to behave by now, what is the point?"

"She's right," Jenny said. "I know I'm new to the commu-nity, but it seems to me that the reputation of being a woman of virtue should protect you from spurious letters from anony-mous senders."

"Spurious?" Matthew questioned.

When she opened her mouth to explain, he laughed and held up his hands.

"I'm sorry, I couldn't help teasing. You have an amazing vocabulary."

She swatted him with the dish towel. "Well, I should, con-sidering my occupation."

Hannah stood and hugged Jenny, then her brother. "I'm going home. I'll see you tomorrow to help you with the proof-reading, Jenny."

"Of course."

"I'll walk you home," Chris said.

"There's no need—" Hannah began.

Chris gave her "the look" and she subsided.

After all, women weren't the only ones who could use it.

⁂

"Does this sort of thing happen often?"

Hannah glanced at Chris as they walked to her house, the flashlight she carried beaming a path for them. "The visit from the bishop?"

She shrugged. "Not often. After all, we know the *Ordnung*, the rules of conduct. We've been taught it since we were children. Mostly, our church leaders are there for us when we seek spiritual advice."

"It's awfully dark out tonight."

"I believe that's why they call it night," she told him.

"Very funny."

"Don't worry, I'll protect you if anything jumps out of the woods," Hannah teased.

"Maybe it's easier not to fear if you don't know of all the bad things in the world."

"We are a community that wishes to be apart, but it doesn't mean that we're not aware of the 'bad things' as you call them. We're not immune to accidents or—what is the expression? Things that go bump in the night."

He chuckled. "Yes, that's the expression."

They reached the steps leading up to her house.

"Wait," he said when she started to ascend the steps.

She turned and looked at him.

"I'm sorry if my actions caused a problem for you," he told her quietly.

"Don't worry about it. It's probably just cranky Josiah who sent it. He had a fuss when Jenny came here."

"He did?"

She nodded. "He eventually changed his mind. Well, that's actually going a little too far. He's . . . come to accept that she's not here to draw media attention to the community just because she is a journalist."

"Then why make a fuss about you?" Chris said suddenly. "I'm the outsider. Why didn't the letter-writer complain about me?"

"I'm sorry, I'm not following you."

He repeated what he'd said and she shook her head. "I don't know. But it's not worth spending any more time or emotion on it. Don't *you* worry about it, either."

"Here," she said, handing him the flashlight "You can borrow this so you can walk back."

She stood on the porch watching the shining beam light his way and wished that she could take them back to the evening when they sat up talking all night.

15

Several days after the fire, Chris looked up from his work to see Jenny waving at Matthew to come in from the field.

Out of curiosity, he watched them talking in the distance, and it seemed to be about something serious. Then the two of them went into the house.

The next time Chris looked up, Matthew was approaching him. He looked even more serious than usual and he glanced briefly at Chris, then away as he called to one of the men nearby.

"He'll take over for you. I need to talk to you for a minute."

Chris turned over the reins of the horses to Sam. He could tell something big was bothering Matthew.

"I didn't give him the book."

Matthew stopped and turned to look at him. "Book?"

Chris realized that he didn't know. Now what could he say?

"Joshua," he said finally. "He wanted to read a book I'm reading, and I said I'd have to ask you because it's about soldiers. When the book disappeared I thought he'd borrowed it."

Matthew frowned. "Joshua wouldn't take something without permission."

"I don't think so either," Chris said quickly. "When it went missing, I asked him if he borrowed it because I was concerned that you and Jenny might get mad at me if he read it without permission. I know that such things are against your beliefs."

"Jenny and I don't try to hide things that are *Englisch* from our *kinner*. But no, I'd rather he didn't get exposed to adult books about such subjects until he was older."

He began walking again. "But that's not why I came to get you in the middle of our workday."

They rounded the house and Chris saw a car parked in the drive, one with the official county insignia. A man sat on the porch, one who looked familiar. Jenny was serving him coffee and a plate of cookies. She left a carafe of coffee and cups for Matthew and Chris.

It took a little while but Chris remembered when he'd seen the man—he was the fire investigator. Who could forget anything or anyone from the day the barn had burst into flames and a man had been hurt. Eli was still recovering from his burns and not back to work.

They acknowledged each other and the three men sat down in chairs on the porch.

"I'll get right to the point," the investigator said. "Preliminary reports show that the fire in Mr. Bontrager's barn was deliberately set."

Chris stared at him, then Matthew. "You're kidding!"

"I wish I was kidding," said the man whose ID badge identified him as Jim Killinger. "The engine you worked on that day had an accelerant in it."

"It would have had some gas to make it run—" Chris began.

"This was an unusual type of accelerant, not gas."

"Unusual how?"

Killinger looked at Matthew, then at Chris. "It's used by the military."

"I see," Chris said slowly. His heart started beating faster, and he felt sweat trickle down his back despite the coolness of the day. "So that's why you wanted to talk to me . . . because I'm former military?"

The fire marshal just looked at him.

Chris raised his hands. "I don't know where you think I'd get something like that. I've been in a veteran's hospital for the past year. You can verify that."

"Already done."

"I wouldn't do this to you," Chris told Matthew. "Why would I do this to you?"

"He told me that," Killinger said. "And after I did some of my own research on you, I'm inclined to believe he's right."

"Research? What kind of research?"

"I just looked up your military record."

Killinger stood. "I'll take another look around the barn. You haven't let anyone poke around in there, have you?"

Matthew shook his head. "We've just done some boarding up until we're finished harvesting. We're using Phoebe's barn to board the horses."

"I'll be in touch." With a nod, the other man left them.

Jenny opened the door and stuck her head out. "Finished out here? Why not break for dinner before you go back out there?"

Matthew hesitated, and then he nodded. "Sounds good. It'll give me a chance to settle down."

Chris stood. "I think I'll skip it if you don't mind."

"I knew you'd be upset," she told him. "But Matthew and I told him there's no way you'd do something like that."

"Thanks. I appreciate that. But I'm not hungry. I'll see you after dinner, Matthew."

As he walked down the stairs, he heard Jenny sigh. "I knew he'd be upset."

But she was wrong, Chris thought.

He went straight to the *dawdi haus* and pulled out his backpack, throwing in his Bible and the neatly folded stack of laundry Mary had brought him last night. Fishing in his pocket, he took out the key to the front door and left it on the table near it. Then, after an inner debate, he wrote a quick note thanking them for their friendship and telling them that he needed to get back home. He wasn't sure that was where he was going, but they didn't really need to know any more than that.

Opening the back door, he gave a surreptitious glance to the right, then the left, before slipping outside. When he didn't spy anyone around, he quickly crossed the fields to Hannah and Phoebe's house, hoping that Jenny and Matthew wouldn't look out their window and see him.

Phoebe came to the door and looked surprised to see him. "Is Hannah home?"

She shook her head. "It's her day to teach quilting classes in town. She borrowed Matthew's buggy."

Holding the door open, she invited him inside.

"I can't stay."

Phoebe eyed the backpack. "Going somewhere?"

He shook his head, looking away from the kindness in her eyes.

"That backpack looks like it's holding everything you've got," she said. "And those shoulders look like they're carrying the weight of the world. Come into the *kich* for just a few minutes and let me make a sandwich for you to take on the road. And you can sit down and write Hannah a note to tell her what you came to say to her."

How she knew he was leaving he didn't know. But he went inside and sat at the kitchen table and let her make him a sandwich. And while she made it, he took a piece of paper and a pencil out of the backpack and wrote a note to Hannah.

He couldn't tell her the real reason he was leaving, so he just told her that he had to leave and he was sorry he hadn't been able to say goodbye. Pausing, he tried to find the words to tell her how much he'd come to care for her.

Then he decided that it wouldn't do any good. He had a pretty good idea that she was as attracted to him as he was to her, that she'd come to care for him, but it wouldn't have worked anyway, he told himself.

Phoebe walked over to hand him the sandwich and a plastic baggie of cookies, and he tucked them into his backpack. Before he could rise, she laid her hand on his shoulder.

"I saw the fire marshal's car over at the house a little while ago."

He stiffened. "Yeah. I didn't start the fire."

"Of course you didn't. Any more than you poisoned Daisy's food."

Surprised, he turned to face her. "What?"

She nodded. "The vet called a little while ago. I was out returning his call in the phone shanty, and that's when I saw the fire marshal's car."

"I didn't—"

"Of course you didn't poison Daisy. I saw how much you love my horse. How much you love these friends you've made here—and Hannah."

"I—"

"My old eyes work just fine, young man. Don't tell me you don't have feelings for Hannah."

She sat heavily in the chair beside him, seeming to have run out of breath.

He looked at her swollen ankles, then into her eyes. "When are you going to tell them that your heart is giving you trouble?"

Startled, she stared at him. "How do you know? Hannah didn't tell you because she doesn't know."

"My grandmother had congestive heart failure. She'd get swollen ankles and she got breathless when she did too much."

Sighing, Phoebe sat back. "No one needs to know. They'd just worry and make an invalid of me, fuss over me, do so much for me I wouldn't feel I had a life."

She took a deep breath and let it out, then shook her head. "And don't try to distract me. You shouldn't be leaving. Not the way you're doing it—so quickly, without seeing Hannah and Matthew and Jenny."

He didn't know how she knew he had left a note for Matthew and Jenny. "I have to." Phoebe reached over and took his hand. "Tell me what's wrong. Please? I want to understand what's making you leave when you love it here."

"All the bad things will stop when I leave."

"But you're not doing them." She squeezed his hand. "I know you're not doing them. So don't even try to tell me you did."

"No," he said at last. "A man who wants to hurt me is. He was put in prison because I testified against him, and he said he'd get me when he got out. I don't know how, but he's gotten out of prison and he's doing these things. I just know it. The barn fire. Daisy. The note to the bishop. The only way to keep everyone safe is to leave."

"Why do you think you'll keep everyone safe if you leave?"

Chris sighed. "If I leave he'll follow me."

"But Chris, he could hurt you. We'll call the police. Matthew and Jenny and Hannah wouldn't want you to go if they knew. They'd want to stand with you."

He looked up at her. "I can't risk anyone else getting hurt."

Her eyes were sad. "So you'll draw him away and take him on yourself? You remind me of David taking on Goliath."

"The man who hates me isn't a giant, but he's had a powerful effect on my life."

Phoebe considered that. "Well, the giants of Gath were felled by David and his fellow kinsmen and servants. Why not this devil too?"

She tried to argue with him but he was resolute. He was nearly undone when she stood and hugged him. He'd come here and fallen in love not just with Hannah but with so many people.

There was no changing his mind, though.

When he stepped outside, he didn't see anything out of the ordinary.

But it was almost as if the air was charged as he stepped off the porch.

He walked toward town, knowing that he was putting himself right out in the open. There were other ways to get there without exposing himself, but this way it would be very clear that he was leaving and he'd keep the people he'd come to care for safe.

Several buggies passed on the opposite side of the road and some of their occupants who'd met him waved.

And then he saw the oncoming buggy driven by Hannah. He bent his head, hoping that she wouldn't recognize him.

"Chris!" She pulled the buggy over to the side of the road. "Where are you going?"

"Just into town for a while."

He hated the lie but didn't know how else to get rid of her. His eyes swept the area to see if he was being followed.

"No you're not."

"Yeah, I'm just on my way to town."

She climbed out of the buggy. "You're leaving and you weren't going to tell me."

He lifted his hands. "Okay, you caught me. Yeah, I'm leaving. It's time to move on, babe."

"*Babe?*"

"Yeah. Hey, it's not like we were an item or something. We didn't even have sex, so it's not like I'm gonna have to worry about you showing up in nine months with some brat."

She looked like she'd bit hit by a two-by-four. His stomach turned over at the way he had to hurt her, but he needed to move her along just in case they were being watched.

"So, I'll be hitting the road now, if you don't mind," he said. "It's looking like it's going to rain. Gotta make some time so I don't get wet, you know?"

"You're being deliberately cruel," she said, her lips trembling. "Why? Something's wrong. You wouldn't do that unless something was wrong."

"Nothing's wrong," he said. "It's just time for me to go."

He started walking, and from the corner of his eye he saw her climb back into the buggy. After a moment it began moving down the road. He breathed a sigh of relief.

But the relief was short-lived.

Several minutes later, a car slowed and then stopped. A man with a ball cap pulled low over his sunglasses leaned out the open window.

"Hey, Pretty Boy."

Only one man had ever called him that, the nickname a sarcastic comment on what he thought was Chris's boy-next-door looks.

Chris's blood froze.

It was Malcolm Kraft.

Babe!

How dare he talk to her like that! Hannah fumed. Like she was some—some—well, she didn't know what word to use.

And talking about how he felt relieved that they hadn't had sex so he didn't have to worry about her showing up to make him claim a "brat"! That was just plain crude—even more unlike Chris. She realized that she hadn't known him long, but she couldn't be that wrong about a person. Could she?

Was he really like that and he'd just covered it up all this time? No, she didn't believe that. She'd always been a good judge of character, even if she didn't spend a lot of time out in the *Englisch* world.

It took another half mile of thinking hard, trying to puzzle out his behavior. Why would he drive her away? Why? He seemed to be trying to put distance between them. Like he wanted to get her to leave for some reason. She didn't know the reason, but she remembered that he'd been looking around so carefully, as if he expected someone.

Well, she didn't intend to just go away. He owed her some answers.

∼✑⌒

She slowed the horse and then guided it to make a U-turn. Then she yanked on the reins, urging Pilot to go faster in Chris's direction.

He had some explaining to do.

But as she drew closer, she saw that he stood not far from where she'd left him and he was talking to someone in a car. *What was going on?* she wondered as she slowed the horse to a stop and waited.

Chris raised his hands, the way she'd seen a man do once when a police officer arrested him. Glancing over, she saw the sun glint off something shiny in the hand of the driver of the car.

He had a gun, and he was pointing it at Chris!

Her heart skipped a beat, and she felt nauseous for a moment. Then she forced herself to take a deep breath and calm down. She glanced up and down the road, hoping someone would be around.

But the road, usually busy at this time, was empty. There were no homes or businesses close enough to go to, and she didn't have a cell phone.

But there was God.

She sent up a quick prayer to Him and then got the buggy rolling.

Both men turned to look at her as she approached. Her eyes were on Chris and she saw his widen with fear. He mouthed a word she knew, even if she'd never used it. She wiped one clammy hand, then the other, on the skirt of her dress.

Pulling up beside Chris, she waved to him. "Hi, need a ride?"

"He's coming with me," the other man said.

She glanced at the man and gave him a bright smile. "It's okay, I can give him a ride."

"No, really, he's coming with me."

"It's okay. You can go now."

"I know who you are," said the man in the car. "Your name's Hannah."

"She's just passing by," Chris said. "Let her go."

"I know who she is," the man repeated. "Don't try to pull something over on me."

Hannah studied the man. His photo had been printed with the article. "And I know you too."

"Don't," Chris hissed at her. Turning to Kraft, he held out his hands, palms up. "C'mon, man, I'll go with you. Just leave her out of it."

"Why? You didn't care what it did to my wife when you accused me."

"You talk like he's the one who did the bad thing. But you did it. You're the one who should have been thinking of your wife when you took that girl and raped her. I read that her parents turned her out saying she'd been dishonored."

"The sex was consensual. I can't help that they have weird religious customs there." He gave her a disparaging glance. "So, Chris, you been crying to little Pilgrim girl here?"

Hannah merely looked at him. "No. I looked it up on the Internet. You raped her. Why are you blaming Chris for what you did? Why can't you leave him alone?"

Malcolm told her furiously. "Shut up!" he yelled. "You don't know what you're talking about! He ruined my life!"

"It's time to stop blaming others, Malcolm," she said, her tone quiet and reasonable. "Ask God to put you on a better path. It's not too late to start new."

Chris walked over to Hannah's side of the buggy. "Let it be," he said, looking at her intently. "You don't know who you're dealing with."

"I thought Amish chicks knew how to keep their mouths shut," Malcolm muttered.

Malcolm pulled his cap lower as a car approached. "Don't try anything stupid."

The car stopped and a man leaned out the window. "You folks need some help?"

"We're good," Malcolm told them. "Thanks."

The man nodded and drove on.

"Let her go, and I'll go anywhere you want."

"Chris—"

Malcolm nodded. "Get in the car."

"Chris!"

"Turn the buggy around, Hannah. Now."

When she hesitated, Chris leaned in, his voice low and intense. "Trust me. I was a soldier. I know how to get out of a tight spot. Now don't do anything stupid."

"But—"

"Don't you understand?" He grasped her arm with a grip so tight it hurt. "I'd never forgive myself if anything happened to you. Promise me you'll go straight home and be safe."

Without waiting to see that she did what he told her to do, he got in the passenger side of the car.

He just didn't know her. She'd always been a little rebellious. Matthew could tell him story after story about that. Torn, she stared at him sitting in the car for a long moment.

Then, inspiration struck. She pulled the buggy into a U-turn.

And stopped directly in front of Malcolm's car.

She turned and saw the two men struggling. She prayed and prayed as Chris fought to grasp the gun. But Malcolm slammed it against his head and got out of the car.

Chris was right behind him, clutching his head. "Hannah, get out of here!" Chris yelled.

But Malcolm already stood beside the buggy. "What, are you nuts?" He raised his gun. "I've had enough of you!" He pulled her from the buggy and shook her.

Chris came up behind him and grabbed at the gun, and the two men tussled for it again. Malcolm slammed the weapon against Chris's head again, and he sagged from the pain.

Malcolm turned and aimed the gun at Chris.

Hannah didn't think. "No!" she cried, flinging herself between the men.

She heard the shot, felt the burning pain in her arm and her side.

She stared down at the blood pouring out, then at Chris grappling with Malcolm, slamming his fist into the other man's face. Malcolm collapsed onto the road and lay still. Chris pulled off his belt, dragged Malcolm's arms behind his back and secured them.

The scene reminded her of the movie she'd seen once during her *rumschpringe*—not real. She watched Chris finish tying Malcolm's arms and held out her own injured one, staring at it as if it didn't belong to her. It dripped blood, dark red blood. Her head felt light and things were going gray.

She watched Chris jump to his feet and rush toward her, then everything went dark, as if it turned from day to night.

∾

The second Chris made sure he'd subdued Malcolm, he jumped up and rushed to Hannah's side.

She lay on the road, so still. Her eyes were closed, and the color had drained from her face. Blood pooled around her side and her arm. Everyone who'd served in the field had been taught basic first aid. The pumping of blood from her arm meant the brachial artery had been nicked or severed. If he didn't stop it right away, death would come in a matter of minutes. There was no time to wait for paramedics.

Forcing himself to stay calm, he checked her arm and guessed that the bullet had only nicked the artery. He yanked at the sleeve of her dress and it tore away at the shoulder seam. Wrapping the sleeve around her arm just above the wound, he tied it tightly, and the bleeding slowed to a trickle.

The wound in her side wasn't as bad as he feared. The bullet had torn through her arm, exited, and traveled through her side. If she was lucky—and so far she was because she was still alive—it might have missed vital organs. He prayed that it had.

Shrugging off his jacket, he folded it and pressed it against her side to stem the bleeding. When his shaking fingers touched her throat, he found her pulse was thready but still beating against his fingers.

When he looked up to scan the road, he saw that Matthew's horse and buggy Hannah had borrowed were barreling down the road, the horse terrorized by the sound of the gun firing.

Malcolm's car was parked behind him, but even if he managed to pick Hannah up and move her into it without her losing too much blood, he didn't have any idea where the nearest hospital was.

He pulled out his cell phone, but it was dead. He hadn't charged the battery in days. Getting up, he pulled Malcolm's cell from the holder on his pants, dialed 911, and tersely requested help.

That done, he knelt at Hannah's side and checked on her wounds again. The tourniquet still held firm, and the bleeding had slowed tremendously. The wound in her side seeped a little, but continuing to press on it helped slow the bleeding.

So much blood. She'd lost so much blood.

Tires screeched on the road and a car came to a stop. A man and a woman got out and rushed over. "What happened?"

"He shot her," Chris told them quickly, waving his hand at Malcolm who hadn't stirred. "Have you got a blanket or something in your car? She's going into shock."

The woman ran back to the car.

"Did you call 911?" the man asked even as he pulled his cell phone out.

"Yeah."

Other cars stopped by the road and people gathered. "Can you get them to move?" Chris asked. "The ambulance'll never get in here if they're in the way."

"Sure thing, mister."

The woman returned and helped Chris tuck the blanket around Hannah.

"Poor thing," she said. "Why would someone shoot an Amish woman?"

Chris heard a siren, then another. Emergency vehicles parked and paramedics ran over.

"He got off one shot," he told them. "It went through her arm, nicking her artery and passing through her side." He pulled the jacket away to reveal the wound. "She's lost so much blood."

They went into action, one paramedic doing his own compression on the side wound, another taking vitals and setting up an IV.

"Sir? Sir?"

Chris looked up to see a police officer.

"I need to ask you some questions."

"We'll take good care of her," one of the paramedics told him.

Another officer escorted a now-conscious Malcolm to a patrol car. Malcolm looked scared now, not filled with rage.

"What happened here?"

As briefly as he could, Chris filled the officer in with what Malcolm had done. Over the policewoman's shoulder, he watched as the paramedics placed Hannah on a gurney and pushed it toward the ambulance.

Chris glanced over at the road as he heard the pounding of hooves. A buggy came into view. The horse's mouth dripped foam from the exertion.

Chris felt a mixture of relief and trepidation as he saw Matthew and Jenny in the buggy. Matthew pulled the buggy beside the road and he and Jenny got out and ran over.

"What happened?" Matthew cried as a police officer held him back. "Let me through, I'm her *bruder*."

Chris nodded and the officer let him and Jenny rush toward Hannah.

Matthew spoke with the paramedics and then he climbed into the ambulance and sat beside Hannah. The ambulance doors were shut and the vehicle pulled out onto the road and sped off, siren blaring.

Jenny stood by, watching and waiting. When the officer left Chris, she rushed to his side. "What happened? Phoebe came over to tell us about you leaving and why she thought we should call the police. Then Matthew's horse came back with the buggy but no Hannah, and we knew something was wrong."

Chris ran his hands through his hair. "It's all my fault." He told her what had happened and Jenny's eyes widened.

"I remember reading about that when I was in the hospital. I never connected your name to the case."

"Well, Kraft's never forgotten. He blames me. Hannah got into the middle, trying to keep him from shooting me."

When Jenny pulled a handkerchief from her pocket and reached up to wipe his cheeks, he realized that he was crying.

"You love her, don't you?" she whispered, her eyes wide.

"Look what good my love was for her."

She hugged him. "Stop that. Let's get a ride to the hospital and find out how she's doing."

Jenny walked over to the officer who'd questioned Chris and spoke with her. The policewoman glanced at Chris and nodded. Jenny waved to Chris and they got into the police car.

The ride to the hospital wasn't the most comfortable for Chris. It was his first-ever ride in the backseat of a police car. Through the metal screen that separated the front and back seats he watched as Jenny chatted with the officer driving them to the hospital.

And he noticed how often the officer met his eyes in the rearview mirror.

He felt trapped and anxious, wondering if Kraft was weaving some story to extricate himself from his troubles on his way to the police station.

But he wanted to see Hannah, and he didn't know how to get there quickly except to go with the officer. And then maybe it would be best if he kept on going. He'd been responsible for her getting seriously hurt—almost killed. She didn't need a man like him in her life. Trouble had just followed him and caused her pain.

16

"I'm sure she'll be okay."

Jenny glanced at Chris as they entered the hospital. "She's *got* to be okay."

Chris looked at her, then away, unable to stand the hope he saw in her eyes. "You didn't see how much blood she lost," he blurted out.

And wished he could yank the words back when she paled.

"Look, there's Matthew!"

Amish or not, the other man would probably kill him. When Chris slowed his steps, Jenny slipped her arm through his and propelled him forward.

"How is she?" Jenny asked.

"They've got her in surgery. She's lost a lot of blood." He ran his hands through his hair and then turned to Chris. "I don't understand. What happened? Did someone try to rob the two of you?"

"I—"

"There you are!" Phoebe cried as she rushed toward them. Then, just as she got a foot away, her face went white and she stopped and fought for breath.

Chris reached her first and helped her sit down in a chair. "I'll get someone—"

She clutched his arm. "No, I'm all right. I'm all right," she repeated as Jenny hovered over her. "I just rushed too much, that's all. It was a shock hearing what happened."

Her eyes met Chris's and silently begged him not to say anything. He hesitated. Keeping secrets had only resulted in tragedy for him. They wouldn't be here in the hospital with Hannah lying wounded if he'd told everyone about himself.

He stayed silent. But if she showed another sign that she didn't feel well, he'd speak up and speak up loudly. He'd carry her into an exam room himself and that would be that.

"You're sure? Maybe I should get you some water."

"Later. I want to know about Hannah."

"Chris? What happened?"

He dragged his gaze from Phoebe and faced Hannah's brother.

"We weren't being robbed. The barn fire, the poisoned food Daisy ate, the missing book—I figured out it's a man who has a grudge against me and followed me here. As soon as I realized it, I tried to leave."

Matthew's fists clenched at his sides. "You brought him here?"

Jenny grabbed his arm. "Matthew, think. He wouldn't do that deliberately."

"The last time I checked, he was still in prison. I don't understand what happened."

"Probably won an appeal or got out early for good behavior," Jenny said absently.

She looked up when she realized she'd spoken aloud and the others were staring at her.

"Things like this happen all the time. How could you know that he'd been released? You've been here, helping us with the harvesting."

"I haven't done anything to help," he said bitterly. "I've just caused someone else to be hurt. I wish I'd never come. I don't know how any of you can even stand to be in the same room with me."

He turned on his heel and walked out.

He walked right into a police officer, the same one who'd interviewed him at the scene of the shooting.

"How's Ms. Bontrager doing?"

"We don't know anything yet."

The policewoman nodded. "I could use a cup of coffee. How about you?"

"If you've come to ask me more questions, you don't need to sugarcoat it with a polite cup of coffee."

She raised her brows and merely looked at him. "I don't sugarcoat anything. I could just stand to have a cup of coffee and get off my feet for a few minutes while I talk to you and confirm a few things. I'm on the long side of a twelve-hour shift."

He sighed and turned to go into the building. "Sorry."

"I understand. You've had a tough day." She walked beside him to the elevator. "Stay positive. I've seen people pull through worse. Maybe you have too."

"Yeah."

He glanced at her and then away. Although she appeared to be only a few years older than him, Officer K. Lang carried herself with a subtle authority.

They got their coffee and went to sit in a booth away from other diners.

She picked up a packet of Sweet N Low from a ceramic container of artificial sweeteners and, smiling slightly, pushed another with sugar packets toward him. Taking out a small notebook, she flipped it open and scanned a page.

"Kraft's saying Ms. Bontrager got in the way when he tried to defend himself against your attack."

"What?" Chris shot to his feet, bumping the table and almost knocking over his coffee.

The officer reached over and steadied the cup, then looked at him. "Have a seat. I had to tell you what he said."

"You can't believe him."

"Of course not," she said calmly, lifting her own cup and blowing on the surface to cool it before she took a sip. "I looked both of you up."

Chris sat again and stared at his coffee. Here it comes, he thought, feeling that old wariness come over him. A lot of police officers were former military. Many of them believed that you didn't air dirty laundry.

"He says he came here to forgive you."

Chris nearly blew out a mouthful of coffee. "You're kidding?"

"No. But you didn't expect him to say he came here to hurt you, did you?" she asked as she continued to review her notes. "I'm looking into a few things, seeing if there are additional charges we can pin on Kraft."

She looked up. "I understand there's been a suspicious fire with serious injuries at the Bontrager property and a poisoned horse at a neighboring property. A check of the tourist accommodations in the area revealed that Kraft's been in the area since two days before the barn caught fire. I'd say that's interesting timing. Fire marshal's pulling his report and faxing it over."

"Put him away for a long, long time," Chris said bitterly. "I don't know how he got out so soon, but he can't get out and hurt someone again."

"The attempted murder charge against him would have been enough to lock him away for a while, but the other charges'll mean additional time, especially since someone sustained an injury connected to the barn fire. I don't think you'll have to worry about him for quite some time."

"I didn't think I'd have to before and look what happened."

The officer nodded. "I hear you. We make arrests in the morning and they're on the streets before we get off our shift sometimes."

She flipped her notebook shut and tucked it into a pocket on her shirt. "You know," she said, giving him a direct look, "I figure all you can do is what you think is the right thing every day and hope for the best. That's all."

She nodded when his eyes searched hers. "I did a tour in the Middle East myself. I know about what happens when someone dares to speak up."

Draining the last of her coffee, she stood. "Well, that's it. Let's go upstairs and see if the family knows anything yet."

❧

Pain.

There was so much pain. It was overwhelming—as if her arm had exploded and the side of her stomach was on fire.

But pain meant she was still alive, praise God.

Hannah felt sheets with her hands and something lumpy on one side of her body. And she couldn't move the arm that hurt. It felt like it was strapped to something hard and when she tried to move it, even a little, the effort nearly made her pass out again.

The air smelled antiseptic, too, and something beeped. Hospital! She slowly remembered she'd been shot. She must be in the hospital now.

But dear God, how could one survive this kind of pain?

Hannah moaned and tried to open her eyes. Voices came to her, familiar voices.

"I can't, Jenny!"

Chris? Was that his voice? Was that really Chris? That awful man hadn't hurt him?

"Come on," Jenny said. "People can hear even when they're unconscious. Hannah needs to hear that you're all right. You don't know what I had to do to talk the head nurse into letting you see Hannah."

Hannah wanted to tell them that she could hear them. She could hear them too well. Her head hurt almost as much as her arm and her side. That didn't make sense. She remembered being shot, remembered falling. Maybe she hit it on the road when she fell. She couldn't remember—couldn't think.

"It's not important that I'm all right," Chris said. "It's only important that she is."

"You can help her by talking to her. Now sit and talk to her. I got you five minutes and that's it."

"I shouldn't take away from the time you and Matthew get—"

"I want to see if I can get him to eat something in the cafeteria."

Someone took her hand and it was a big, warm, rough hand.

"Hannah? Can you hear me?"

Chris!

She tried to tell him she could hear him, but she was so tired only a whisper came out.

"What? Sweetheart, please, wake up. I want to tell you that I'm sorry. I want you to yell at me. Anything. Just wake up."

Sweetheart? He'd called her sweetheart? And why was he sorry? He hadn't done anything.

"Tell me you forgive me."

She managed to get her eyes open and stared up into his face, his dear, dear face. "You—you didn't do anything wrong."

The effort to speak took everything out of her, and she fell asleep again.

When she awoke later, Jenny and Phoebe were standing beside her bed, smiling.

They exchanged glances and then both of them gave her a hug, careful not to jar her.

"We heard you woke up," Jenny told her as she pulled up chairs for Phoebe and herself. "We're not allowed to stay long."

Hannah glanced around, then toward the door.

Jenny laughed. "I think she's hoping Chris is here," she told Phoebe.

"He hasn't left?" Hannah tried to sound casual.

"No, he's helping Matthew."

"He was leaving that day."

"I know. He thought if he did that he could keep Kraft from hurting anyone else."

Hannah shifted, trying to get comfortable— the movement took her breath away. She bit her lip, trying to keep from crying out and she tasted blood.

"I'll get the nurse," Phoebe said and quickly left the room.

"C'mon, use the pump," Jenny advised, curling Hannah's fingers around it. "Breathe through it. You can do it."

When the pain subsided, Hannah opened her eyes and realized tears had streaked down her cheeks.

"How—how did you get through it?" she asked, her voice shaky.

Jenny stroked her hair back. "It'll get better. I promise." She stared at Hannah intensely. "You're a lucky girl."

"I don't feel so lucky."

The nurse came in, checked the pump, and nodded. "You need anything else?"

Hannah shook her head. "*Danki.* I mean, thank you."

The woman smiled. "I knew what you meant."

She turned to Jenny. "Got some experience in using one of these, eh?"

"I sure do."

"Used to watch you on the news," she told Jenny. "Glad you're doing well now." With that, she left the room.

Phoebe came in and took her seat again.

"You're lucky because you survived despite losing a lot of blood. The fact that Chris knew what to do about the nicked artery in your arm and that he kept his head probably saved your life. The bullet just grazed your side and didn't hit any vital organs."

"But—" Hannah hesitated and then took a deep breath. "What about having babies? What if the bullet hit—Jenny, what if I can't have babies?"

Jenny squeezed her hand. "I know, you're worried because you have a lot of pain in your side. But the surgeon said he doesn't feel there's any reason why you won't have children. The bullet didn't hit your reproductive organs."

She stopped for a moment, then went on. "He wouldn't lie, Hannah. They tell you if it's doubtful."

Now it was Hannah's turn to squeeze Jenny's hand. Each month that Jenny didn't conceive she felt sad for days. The doctors hadn't been encouraging with her because the injuries from the bombing had been so severe.

But somehow, despite the monthly disappointments, Hannah knew that her brother remained steadfast and believed that if it was God's will then he and Jenny would have more *kinner.*

"Let's just get you well and back home."

Phoebe nodded. "It's too quiet there without you. You bring life to the *haus*."

"You're so sweet. Speaking of quiet, you're not saying much today," Hannah told her.

"I'm just a little tired."

"You need to go home and get some rest."

"I agree," Jenny said, getting to her feet. "And we need to let you get some rest too." She leaned down to kiss Hannah's cheek. "Matthew will be by after supper to see you. Maybe he'll bring—" she stopped, looked at Phoebe.

"Jenny, if you don't mind I'd like to talk to Hannah for just a minute."

"Sure. I'll be downstairs in the lobby."

Phoebe pulled over a chair and sat down beside the bed. "No one's saying it, so I guess I'll have to."

Hannah looked away from the sympathy in Phoebe's eyes. "He's gone, isn't he?"

"No, he hasn't left. Not yet."

"Then—" she stopped. "I'm not going to ask why he's not coming to see me. I told myself that I wouldn't ask."

"But you don't understand, do you?"

Hannah's eyes filled with tears. "I thought he cared for me."

Phoebe patted her hand. "Oh, dear one, he does. He does. I'm sure of it. But he blames himself for what happened."

"But he didn't do it!"

"He came looking for you that day. He was leaving because he wanted the man to follow him, to take him away from here. He was afraid you'd be hurt. Then exactly what he feared happened."

"But he didn't do it!" Hannah repeated. "It isn't his fault I got hurt."

Sighing, Phoebe nodded. "But he blames himself. I think you have to be prepared for him to stay away." She smiled. "So I guess you know what you need to do, don't you?"

"Get better and get out of here," Hannah said slowly. "And then I want to go see Christopher Matlock. I have a few things to say to him."

"*Gut*," said Phoebe and she smiled.

Hannah lay against her pillows, closed her eyes, and let exhaustion overtake her. It seemed no matter how much she slept, she needed more. She was beginning to despair that she'd ever go home.

⌘

The air in the jail felt cold and dank and, if she were fanciful, smelled of despair.

Hannah was glad she'd never done anything to land herself here. A jail officer sent her through the security checkpoint and then made her take off her sling to check that she wasn't carrying weapons.

"Hey, Bill, she's okay," another officer called over. "She's a victim. It was in the news last week, remember?"

"She could be here to hurt him," Bill said, not impressed.

The other officer rolled his eyes. "Yeah, right. When's the last time you heard of an Amish person who did something criminal?"

"Never make assumptions. There's always a first time." The officer showed no expression as he glanced up at Hannah. "No offense, ma'am."

"None taken," she said, awkwardly sliding the sling over her arm again.

"The D.A.'s gonna have a cow," she heard one of the officers say as she walked away.

"Why's that?"

"You remember . . . it's that forgiveness thing they do."

Malcolm Kraft waited behind a glass window, one of a long line of them. People who had been arrested sat on one side and visitors sat on the other.

He looked different than the last time she'd seen him. He'd been so consumed with anger at Chris—and mad at her for interfering. The ball cap and sunglasses had obscured much of his face and his eyes, but there had been no hiding the deadly intent of the man—especially when she saw the gun in his hands.

She'd been afraid of him then. Maybe not enough, she thought now, as her arm ached and she cradled it against her in an effort to get comfortable.

Now, he sat with his shoulders slumped and his face took on a pained look when he saw her. With some reluctance, he picked up the telephone as she sat and lifted the one on her side to her ear.

"What are you doing here?" he asked, his tone unfriendly.

"Thank you for seeing me."

He sighed and wouldn't meet her eyes. "I almost didn't. They told me it was you again and not—" he stopped.

"Your wife?"

His eyes finally met hers and she saw defeat. "I don't blame her for not wanting to have anything to do with me. I don't deserve her or my son after what I did."

A shaft of pain lanced through Hannah's heart as she thought about his little boy.

"Look, I'm really sorry for what happened. I didn't mean to hurt you."

"But you brought a gun to hurt Chris."

He nodded.

"Why were you not in prison? The article I read said you were in prison."

"My lawyer got the verdict overturned." When he saw her frown, he explained, "They decided I wasn't guilty."

"But you are."

He glanced around, then leaned forward. "You trying to get me to say I did it? Well, I won't. I'm not giving anyone a chance to prosecute me for that again."

"That's not my intention," she assured him. "But it seems like you got a second chance," she said slowly.

He shrugged. "Yeah. I guess. So why are you here?"

Reaching into her purse, she withdrew the article she'd printed that day at the library. She folded it so that the photo of his little boy, Jamie, was the only thing that showed, and she held it up so he could see it.

His face crumpled and he began crying. "Why are you doing this? "

"I don't want to hurt you, Mr. Kraft. I want to know why you were so angry with Chris that you forgot this little boy who needs you."

He raised his eyes and wiped away tears with his knuckles. "Like my wife is ever gonna to let me near him again." He stood. "I'm sorry for hurting you, but if you don't mind, I'm going back to my cell now."

"Mr. Kraft! Don't hang up!"

When she saw him stop, she took a deep breath.

"If you got another chance—"

"A third chance? Yeah. Right!" He started to hang up the phone again.

"What would you do with it?"

"People don't get those."

She nodded. "Maybe some people don't. Would you be able to remember what's important this time and do the right thing?"

He must have sensed that she was serious because he sank into his chair. "What are you talking about?"

Hannah shifted in her chair. Her arm throbbed. Maybe Jenny was right. She'd said it was too soon to be out doing this, but when Hannah insisted, she'd driven her there in the buggy.

"I forgive you for hurting me," she said quietly. When he went still, she nodded.

"People don't do that. You got hurt because of me. Why would you do that?"

"Because if I don't forgive you, how can I ever expect God to forgive me?"

"Like you ever do something you need to be forgiven for!" he said, his laughter disbelieving.

If he only knew . . . Hannah had been guilty of discontent, of feeling unhappy with her life. Maybe that wasn't on the same level as what he'd done, but that was beside the point.

"It doesn't matter," she told him. "We don't believe in judging."

"You're saying you can sit there hurting because of something I did and you can forgive me?"

"Yes," she said simply. "I already have."

⁂

"Mr. Benton?"

The assistant district attorney looked up at Hannah, ran his hands through his thinning hair, and gave her a baleful look.

"Yeah?"

"Hi, I'm—"

"I know who you are," he said, standing. He waved at the chair before his desk. "And I know why you're here."

"Really?"

He sighed heavily. "Yeah. I hear things. And going by my past experience with the Amish, you're here to tell me you don't want me to prosecute Kraft."

Hannah nodded.

The assistant district attorney sighed again, shuffled the papers on his desk to find a file, and pulled it out.

"Ma'am, this man set fire to your brother's barn, which injured one of his workers; poisoned the horse belonging to the elderly woman you live with; and shot you, seriously injuring you."

"Yes, I know that," Hannah said calmly. "But I don't want to press charges. I understand I have that right."

"You do, but I can also prosecute a crime that others witnessed, even without your permission."

Chris. He'd witnessed her getting shot. Hannah sighed inwardly. She didn't think she had a chance of convincing him not to prosecute Kraft after all he'd been through with him.

"I'm sorry, ma'am," the man continued. "But I'm not willing to let someone like that waltz out of jail and do more harm to our community. It's been my experience that the Amish have been reluctant to prosecute for religious reasons. Attempted murder's a much bigger deal than vandalism or petty theft."

"But I don't want to press charges," she said again.

"It's one thing for your brother to refuse to prosecute Kraft for setting fire to the barn, but I don't understand why you and Eli Yoder won't go after him for injuring both of you—especially you."

He got up and walked to the coffeemaker on a side table. "Can I get you some?"

"No, thank you."

He seated himself again, took a sip of the coffee, and made a face that indicated it tasted bitter.

"Is this man intimidating you? Has he contacted you to talk you out of pressing charges?"

"No."

She watched the man rub his temples as if he had a headache. It wasn't her intention to stress him, but this was important. She didn't intend on changing her mind. She wasn't about to see Kraft get locked away again when there might be a chance for him to salvage his life.

He tapped his pen against the file that sat on the desk before him and tried to look stern. It didn't work, in Hannah's opinion.

"I have a report in here from the doctor who operated on you. He said your injuries were life-threatening, that your blood loss led to shock and heart arrhythmia."

"I know all that. The doctor told me."

"Then how can you think Kraft shouldn't pay for doing what he did to you?"

She sat up straighter. "I'm not against prosecuting Mr. Kraft because I'm not aware of what he's done here, but there has to be an alternative to incarceration, some middle ground we can reach."

"You're asking me to—"

"I looked into it, and there are some programs where he can get probation and counseling. And if he violates any of the conditions of the probation, he suffers the consequences."

They stared at each other for a long time.

Finally, the man sighed and shook his head. He reached for a folder and pulled out some forms. "Okay, this is what I'm willing to do."

If he stayed here a hundred years, Chris didn't think he'd ever understand the Amish.

"You have to talk to Hannah!"

Matthew looked up from forking hay into a barn stall. "Why?"

"I just heard that she's not pressing charges against Kraft."

"It's not our way."

"But he shot her!"

"I'm well aware of that."

Chris paced. "She could have died."

Matthew winced. "I'm well aware of that too."

"I thought she'd bleed to death before I could get help for her." He felt sick at the thought and sank down onto a hay bale.

His glance went to the loft. Everything had changed from the time he'd climbed up there, fallen asleep, and awakened to find Hannah's wide eyes staring at him. She'd been shocked to find him there, and the surprise had caused her to lose her footing.

He remembered how it had felt to see her fall, to grab at her and feel her hand slip in his before he could grasp both of hers and lift her up. It had taken quite a while for his heartbeat to steady after he hauled her over the edge of the loft and made sure she was okay.

He hadn't been the same since.

This Plain woman, so different from any woman he'd ever met, had intrigued, puzzled, and annoyed him beyond measure. He'd been in a state of anxiety the whole week she recuperated in the hospital and only when he saw her being brought home—pale, her arm in a sling—had he begun to relax.

And now she wanted to let out the man who had hurt her, almost caused her to lose her life?

Matthew laid his hand on his shoulder. "I know it's hard for outsiders to understand. But in my opinion, it's probably the central, most important tenet to our beliefs. It doesn't mean we forget what's been done to us. But we remember that we don't have to understand God, just to trust Him and have faith in Him."

"I always wonder why God lets bad things happen to good people. Why would God let somebody hurt someone as good as Hannah?"

"Maybe because God Himself doesn't judge someone as bad—so why should we? I don't really know why. But I know that she truly can't be hurt by anything that happens to her."

"If that's true, how come she's got her arm in a sling?"

He heard the bitterness in his voice and got to his feet. "I'm sorry. I'm just angry that this happened."

"Angry at yourself or angry at God?"

Startled, Chris stared at him. "A little of both, I guess."

"I don't see how you could have prevented what happened. God allows for free will—for people to do things even when He probably wishes they didn't. And can you blame God when we don't understand why He allows things? He has His reasons and our job isn't to question Him."

Chris paced the barn again. "I tried to get her to leave, but she came back. She came back and put her buggy right in front of Kraft."

Matthew folded his arms across his chest and studied Chris. "I didn't hear all this before. I thought she just got in the way."

"Oh no," Chris said, spinning to glare at Matthew. "That crazy sister of yours decided she'd stop him from hurting me."

"She must love you even more than I thought," Matthew murmured, looking thoughtful. "Jenny said so, but I didn't believe her. Don't know why," he said, rubbing the back of his neck and giving Chris a sheepish grin. "She's always right."

Then his grin faded. "So now you have a lot of forgiving to do, eh? Kraft. Hannah. God. And yourself."

Chris slid his hands in the pockets of his jeans. "Yeah."

"You could talk to the bishop, you know. He helped me a lot when I felt angry at God."

"You were?"

"Isn't everyone at some point in his life? I experienced such anger when Amelia suffered such a terrible illness, enraged that He took her home to be with Him when we loved and needed her. I shouldn't have been left by myself to raise our *kinner*. They shouldn't have lost their precious *Mamm*. *Ya*, I was angry. It took a long, long time and a lot of talking to the bishop to get over that."

Chris thought about how he'd been so angry with God when he watched buddies get hurt and sometimes die during his tour. He'd been angry and hurt when his superiors and the men he served with didn't back him up to see that Kraft got prosecuted. All of that was bad enough.

Then, with a week to go before he got out, he'd been hit with a roadside bomb. Now he figured any woman would run screaming if she saw the scars on his body in the daylight.

Joshua ran into the barn. "*Daedi! Aenti* Hannah needs help—"

Chris felt his heart jump into his throat. "What's wrong? Has he come back?"

"What . . . who?"

"The man who shot her." His voice rose. "Has he come back?"

"*Nee*." Joshua looked from Chris to his father and then back at Chris. "There's no man. She just wants *Daedi* to come over and help move something."

He turned to his father. "Hannah says Phoebe's going to do it if you don't get there quick!"

Matthew thrust the hay hook at Chris and hurried out of the barn, muttering about some women taking on more than they should.

Chris's heart settled back down where it should be. He finished Matthew's task, then fed the horses. Joshua followed behind him, giving the horses fresh water to drink.

~✥~

"You need to go see her."

"She doesn't want to see me."

Chris avoided Jenny's eyes and wondered how he'd allowed himself to be trapped into talking to Jenny. When she'd asked him to help her carry the refreshment tray back to the house, he'd been suspicious but didn't know how to refuse.

Then, when they reached the porch, she indicated that he should sit in a chair, then drew another chair over and sat beside him.

"She does."

Chris drained the glass of iced tea and set it down on the table beside him on. "She can't possibly want me to visit her after I was responsible for her getting hurt."

"That was Kraft's fault, not yours. I know you care for her— I saw that. And she cares for you too."

His heart leaped at the thought, but just as quickly he tamped down his feelings and shook his head. "It doesn't matter. How could that work with our differences?"

"Which differences would those be?"

He stared at her as if she'd grown three eyes. "Religious, cultural."

Her gaze went to the fields, and he looked in the direction she did and saw Matthew.

"It's worked well for us," she said slowly, and she looked at him again. "I'm not saying it hasn't been hard adjusting sometimes even though my grandmother was Amish and I visited during some summers."

She smiled and set her glass on the tray. "Matthew was the boy next door I had a crush on and never forgot."

He watched her absently rub at a faded scar on her hand. It no longer felt strange to see this woman he'd seen at the veteran's hospital wearing Plain clothing, doing chores around the farm, and stealing time to write while the children—her children now—were at school.

"Not everyone was accepting of our getting married," she told him with a smile.

They looked at each other and at the same time said, "Josiah."

She laughed. "Yes. Apparently you and I are in a unique society for his . . . mistrust. But he's grown to accept me even if he doesn't approve of me. It'll take time for him to accept you."

"You act like I'm staying."

Getting to her feet, she reached down and patted his cheek. "Yes, because even though you're a man, I think you're smarter than that."

"Hey!"

She stopped at the door and turned around. "Look, I shouldn't have teased you. It's scary loving someone. But do you really want to walk away from Hannah without even trying to see if it'll work?"

She didn't wait for him to answer.

Good thing, he thought, because he didn't know what to say.

Hannah sat with her quilting circle, trying to stitch a section of the Sunshine and Shadow quilt she'd started for Chris before she was shot.

It was fortunate that she was right-handed and it was her left arm that had been injured. But the awkwardness and occasional pain shooting down her arm as she worked didn't make things easy.

She didn't know why she was still working on this. Why should she give him a quilt when he wouldn't visit her—even now when only a field separated them?

The other women had offered to help her complete it, but she always finished what she started. First, she'd finish the quilt.

Then she'd have a talk with him and he'd hear how she felt about him not coming to see her.

Then she thought, why not now? The time was right—right now!

She marched to the door.

"Hannah? Where are you going?" Phoebe called to her.

The other ladies looked up from their quilting.

"I need to go next door for something. I'll be right back."

She found Jenny in the kitchen, sitting at the table, writing on a big yellow pad.

"Well, hello! Are you through with the quilting already? I can fix us some tea—"

"So what does 'sweetheart' mean?" she asked without preamble.

"You know what it means."

"Tell me."

"Okay. It's a term someone uses when they love you."

"The meaning hasn't changed?"

Jenny stared at her. "No. Why?"

"I'll be right back."

Hannah turned on her heel and stomped outside. But she didn't see Chris in the fields with the other men.

Joshua was working in the yard.

"Where's Chris?"

"He left just a few minutes ago," Joshua told her.

"Left? Where was he going?"

"I don't know."

Hannah scanned the fields. It seemed to her that the harvesting had been completed for all practical purposes. Had Chris gone into town—or had he left for good?

"Do you need something, *Aenti* Hannah?"

"I'll say. I need to tell that man—" She stopped when she saw the curiosity on Joshua's face. "How long ago?"

"Just a little while ago. I could go try to catch him for you."

"Never mind," she said, gritting her teeth. "Can you hitch up Daisy for me?"

"*Schur.*"

They walked over to Phoebe's barn.

"Do you want me to go with you?" Joshua asked as he led a fully recovered Daisy out with the buggy. "You need help, don't you?" He waved his hand at her sling.

Such a sweet boy. She hoped he didn't grow up to be a man who drove women crazy like Chris.

"I'll be fine. *Danki*, Joshua." She climbed into the buggy and Daisy started off.

Hannah muttered to herself as they traveled, rehearsing what she wanted to say to Chris. Okay, so apparently they weren't going to have the relationship she'd hoped they would, but weren't they at least friends? Didn't friends visit each other when they were ill or when they came home from the hospital? Didn't they wish each other well?

And if he was leaving for good, couldn't he at least say good-bye to her? She deserved that, didn't she?

Halfway to town, she saw his lone figure ahead. His long legs were putting more distance between them. *You just can't get away fast enough, can you?* she wanted to ask him. She urged Daisy faster so that she could pull up beside him.

He glanced up as the buggy came level with him, and his eyes widened in surprise. "Hannah!"

"I want to talk to you!"

"Okay."

He joined her at the side of the road after she'd pulled the buggy over. She remembered the last time she'd seen him on this road, remembered what had happened, but she pushed that memory aside.

"What's up?"

"What's up?" she burst out. "What's up?"

"Yeah. You okay?"

"You'd know if you visited me!"

His expression became shuttered. "I didn't think you'd want to see me."

"Well, you thought wrong!"

He blinked. "Evidently you have something to say. Maybe you should just say it."

"So you figured you'd just waltz out of town without saying good-bye?"

"I wasn't—"

"I thought we were at least friends," she snapped, using the line she'd rehearsed on the ride to find him. "Friends don't treat each other this way!"

"No, they don't," he agreed, stepping closer.

"I asked Jenny what 'sweetheart' means."

"You did?" he asked, looking wary.

"Yes. I checked to see if it had the same meaning I thought it did—that it hadn't become something like 'babe' or 'chick.' Like the town of Intercourse nearby."

"So Jenny was right."

"Yes, she said the meaning—"

"No," he interrupted. "I'm talking about what she said the day you were put in the hospital. She said that people can hear sometimes when you think they're unconscious. You heard me."

She nodded. "You call me sweetheart and then you leave? If this is the way people treat each other in the *Englisch* world then I'm glad I'm here!"

A police cruiser approached from the opposite side of the road. It slowed and the officer leaned out the open window.

"Any problem, folks?"

"Hello, Officer Lang," Chris said.

They knew each other? Hannah wondered where the attractive officer had met Chris and felt a stab of jealousy as she saw how friendly the woman behaved toward him. She bit her lip.

Then inspiration struck.

"He's not supposed to be leaving town, is he, Officer?"

"Pardon me?"

"Well, I mean, you haven't wrapped up your investigation with the shooting, have you? Isn't he supposed to stick around until after it's done?"

"I—" The officer looked at Chris and then back at Hannah.

"Well, no, everything's not all tied up," the woman said slowly. "He needs to stick around for a while."

"I do?"

She nodded. "I'll be checking back."

A voice squawked out something on the communication system in her car. She tilted her head and listened. Then she turned to look at them. "Gotta go."

"But—"

She glanced back at Hannah. "It'll be interesting to see how this works out."

The car accelerated down the road, and the lights flashed and the siren came on.

"I think you need to see something," Chris said. Taking his backpack off, he opened it. "Look inside."

Wary, she peeked in as he requested. She saw a wallet and the library book he'd borrowed along with a plastic bottle of water. There was nothing else.

Confused, she looked at him.

"I was taking the library book back. They found it in Kraft's room. Thought I'd return it. Didn't want you to be in trouble with that librarian. She scared me."

Hannah smiled slightly. "She's pretty careful who she loans books to."

He nodded. "I'm thinking of getting my own card."

"I—don't understand."

"I'm sticking around. You didn't think I could go anywhere you're not, do you?" he asked quietly

She saw something in his eyes she hadn't seen before.

"I—don't know. You haven't said anything."

"What could I say?" he asked. "I kept telling myself I couldn't feel the way I do for you, that it wouldn't work. I did it even up until maybe a few minutes ago."

"Then—what changed?"

She held her breath, waiting for his answer.

"Then you came speeding up, demanding to know where I was going. Refusing to let me go."

He grinned and leaned closer, careful of her arm, and then he kissed her.

"I love you, you impossible woman. And I'm hoping you love me. I think you do."

"Impossible?"

He kissed her again. "Yeah. Impossible. I don't think you'll be the easiest wife, but I'm willing to give this a try."

"Wife?"

"Yeah, wife. I talked to Phoebe. She told me to go speak to the bishop."

He tilted his head and studied her when she just stared at him. "I do believe I've rendered you speechless. Never thought I'd see the day."

"It's likely you won't again," she said, reaching out to touch his cheek.

"I gather that I have months of instruction in the Amish faith, so we can't get married until next year. But I figure that'll just give us a chance to get to know each other better."

She nodded, wondering at the strange turn of events. Who would have thought such a thing would happen, that a man like him would come into her life, that she'd come to care for him so much that she'd walk in front of him to protect him? That he'd stand beside her on a dusty road and talk about marrying her.

"Why don't you let me drive us back home?"

He helped her climb into the buggy, and she handed him the reins when he sat beside her.

He leaned over, and she leaned away from him.

"I just want another kiss."

She glanced around. "Not here!"

"Yeah, here." He grinned at her and started to reach for her then stopped. "I'm afraid of hurting you."

"You'll only hurt me if you don't hold me," she whispered, leaning closer. "I'm so glad you came here."

"I'm not entirely sure I know why I came here," he said slowly, caressing her cheek. "I thought it was because I wanted to talk to Jenny about Malcolm and how I felt like my life would never be the same. We didn't know each other long, but I felt like we really connected at the hospital—" he hesitated— "as friends," he said firmly.

"Go on."

"I knew she'd had to make a lot of adjustments to life after she came home from overseas. We wrote each other a few times, and she seemed so happy here. Then one day, I was sitting in the hospital, watching TV, and this show came on about the area and I just felt compelled to come here."

He looked out at the farmland surrounding them. "I felt something settle inside me the moment I got to Paradise. And even though things were anything but peaceful when I met you, well, I couldn't help being attracted to you."

"We have this expression," she said, smiling at him. "People kept saying it to me: 'There's a man God set aside for you.' But I got to doubting that when time passed."

A car approached from behind them and slowed beside the buggy. It was the police officer again. She glanced inside the buggy, grinned when she saw how closely they were sitting— Chris's arms around Hannah—and then she sped off.

Hannah watched the car until it went around the bend in the road.

"I want to talk to you about not pressing charges against Kraft," Chris said.

She stiffened. "I'm not changing my mind."

"I'm not asking you to. I want you to help me understand. I talked to Matthew and I'm trying to understand."

"I'll try," she told him. "Just not today. All right?"

"No. Not today."

"Let's go home and tell everyone our news."

Chris spoke to Daisy and she made a U-turn in the road.

"Very impressive," Hannah told him.

He shot her a grin. "*Ya*," he said. "You'd think I had grown up Amish, wouldn't you? Say, do you need a driver's license for these things?"

Her laughter floated in the air as they made their way home.

The End

Glossary

aenti—aunt
allrecht—all right
bauch—stomach
boppli—baby or babies
bruder—brother
daedi—Daddy
danki—thanks
dawdi haus—addition to the house for grandparents
eldre—parents
en alt maedel—old maid
Englisch or Englischer—a non-Amish person
Es dutt mir leed—I am sorry
fraa—wife
gem gschehne—You are welcome
geyan schona—so willingly done
gwilde—quilt
grossdochder—granddaughter
guder mariye—good morning
gut—good
gut nacht—good night
gut-n-owed—good evening

haus—house
hungerich—hungry
kaffi—coffee
kapp—prayer covering or cap worn by girls and women
kich—kitchen
kichli—cookies
kind, kinner—child, children
lieb—love
liebschen—dearest or dear one
mamm—mother
mann—husband
nee—no
Ordnung—The rules of the Amish, both written and unwritten. Certain behavior has been expected within the Amish community for many, many years. These rules vary from community to community, but the most common are to not have electricity in the home, to not own or drive an automobile, and to dress a certain way.
Pennsylvania Deitsch—Pennsylvania German
redd-up—clean up
rumschpringe—time period when teenagers are allowed to experience the *Englisch* world while deciding if they should join the church.
schul—school
schur—sure
schwei—sister-in-law
schweschder—sister
sohn—son
verdraue—trust
wilkumm—welcome
wunderbaar—wonderful
ya—yes

Discussion Questions

Caution: Please don't read before completing the book, as the questions contain spoilers!

1. Autumn is the season when the Amish get married (after the harvest). Hannah experiences mixed emotions as she contemplates another fall without being engaged and planning to wed. She doesn't envy others for their marriages and children, but she wishes God would show her "the man He set aside for her" so she can share her love, be married, and have children of her own. Did you have to wait longer than you wanted (like Hannah) to meet "the man God set aside for you"—or are you still waiting?

2. Hannah and Chris are opposites in many ways, but they share some similarities. What are they?

3. Chris feels let down by his friends and fellow soldiers when he feels he must "do the right thing." Have you ever gone "against the tide" and done the right thing only to have others disagree with you—even shun you?

4. Just when Chris's tour of duty was nearly done, he sustained severe injuries. Now, in spite of not being a vain man, he wonders if anyone will ever want him. Have you ever experienced self-esteem issues? How did you deal with them?

5. Many people travel to Amish communities to absorb the sense of peace and order they feel there. Chris does this and hopes to talk to Jenny about how she has overcome many obstacles. What place gives you a sense of peace and order?

6. Many people admire the simplicity, the connectedness, and the spirituality of the Amish lifestyle. How can you achieve this in your life?

7. Hannah moves in with Phoebe, an older woman who is a longtime friend and has become family to her not just by marriage but also by friendship. Do you have friends who are like family to you? How did they become like family?

8. After her brother's first wife died, Hannah moved in with him to take care of her nieces and nephew. Once he remarries she's not needed in that capacity anymore. Have you been the family caretaker or a parent who has experienced the "empty nest syndrome"? How did you feel when you were no longer needed in this capacity?

9. The title for the book comes from Ecclesiastes 3:1: "To every thing there is a season, and a time to every purpose under the heaven: A time to be born, and a time to die. . . ."). Hannah chafes at time passing and she feels she may become an old maid. What or who have you wanted but still don't have?

10. A man hates Chris and pursues him to Paradise. Have you ever had an enemy? Why did this person dislike or hate you? How did you react to this?

11. The Amish practice forgiveness, believing that only by forgiving others can God forgive them for anything they do. Hannah decides to forgive a man who has seriously hurt her. Do you think you could do the same thing? Why or why not?

12. Healing isn't just a physical state. It's also an emotional one. Describe a time when you were feeling challenged or you were searching for something. How did you deal with it?

A Time for Peace

∽✑✑

1

*I*t was official.

She wasn't a saint.

But Jenny had never claimed to be a saint. None of her Amish brethren did, either.

She knew she should be grateful for her family, and she was. Her husband's *kinner* were as much hers as they were his, especially young Annie who had been so young when her mother died that she didn't remember her and thought of Jenny as her *mamm*.

But for the past three months, since Hannah had announced that she and Chris were having a baby, Jenny felt the unaccustomed, and very unwelcome, emotion of envy. They'd only been married a year. She and Matthew had been married for three.

It wasn't fair.

Almost immediately, she felt ashamed. But she couldn't seem to help it. She wanted a baby of her own. A *boppli*. She loved that word. It sounded so sweet. So happy and bouncy. So cherished.

Instead, so many months had passed and still she didn't become pregnant. She wouldn't be carrying a baby close to her heart. She wouldn't share the miracle of creating life with Matthew and watching it come into the world.

Sometimes she wondered if she was showing God she didn't appreciate all He had brought into her life. After all, He'd brought her back here to have a second chance with the man she'd never forgotten. She'd gone through such a valley of despair when she'd been seriously injured during her work as a news reporter covering children in war-torn countries.

Yet Matthew had seen past that, cherished her, and shared the most precious children in the world with her.

God had even found a way for her to continue to write about the children affected by war, who she'd grown to care so much for, right here on a farm in the heart of peace, love, and simplicity.

She and Matthew had talked about how she felt when she didn't become pregnant. He'd been kind and understanding, and he had tried to comfort her—the perfect husband.

He wasn't unhappy that they hadn't had children together yet. He reminded her that before they were married, he'd told her he didn't care if her injuries prevented her from having their child. He had three to share with her, he'd said, and if they were meant to have a child together, God would send one. It was a matter of God's will, he told her. And he seemed content.

But she wasn't. Even if she tried not to think about it, every month she found that she hadn't become pregnant.

And this was the way she rewarded Him. With a lack of gratitude, with mental whining. With tears when she found that another month had come and gone and a tiny glimmer of life hadn't begun to form in her.

Sighing, Jenny threw down her pen and got up from the big table that dominated the kitchen. She was tired of working, and she couldn't seem to stay focused on her writing. Best to just get busy doing something else. Idleness wasn't encouraged here.

Not that she'd ever been an idle person. But everyone contributed here, from small children with chores appropriate to their age and ability to older family members doing what they could after they moved into a *dawdi haus*.

She glanced at the clock. Half an hour before the *kinner* got home. Time to do something constructive. If she couldn't write, then she should at least get supper started or *redd-up* the place a little.

Funny how she'd gotten to where she thought in Pennsylvania *Dietsch*, she thought. If anyone had ever told her that one day she would return to her grandmother's house here in Paradise, marry her girlhood crush, and become Amish, she would never have believed them.

But she had, and here her dreams were coming true— dreams of having a husband, having children who loved her, and having a writing career as well.

Her life was nearly perfect.

Nearly.

Sighing, she got up from the table. *Nearly* was a lot better than what much of the world has. She knew that better than anyone after her job as a TV news reporter.

Every time her own family gathered around this big wooden kitchen table and she saw how healthy and happy they were, how they had so much abundance of food and love and security, she made sure she thanked God.

Spring was coming. The cold of the winter had passed and she'd seen little green buds on the trees around the house that morning when she said good-bye to her family as they rushed off to work and *schul*. That was probably why her thoughts had turned to new life.

She was only in her early thirties and had years to have a baby, her doctor told her. Women could have them safely into their late forties, he'd told her.

But though she tried not to worry about internal injuries she'd suffered from the car bomb, there was still that little niggle of doubt in the back of her mind each month she didn't get pregnant.

Determined to push those thoughts aside, to remember to be grateful for what she had, she put away her writing things and changed to "*mamm* mode" as she called it.

Supper went into the oven—Matthew's favorite ham and scalloped potatoes. She'd endured a lot of teasing the first time she'd made it. Microwaved food had been her specialty before she became an Amish *fraa*. Now she cooked from scratch with recipes her grandmother handed down to her.

She turned from the oven when she heard a commotion at the door. The Bontrager children were sweet as can be, but when they came in the door after *schul*, they sounded like a herd of buffalo.

They swarmed into the kitchen and engulfed her in hugs. They charmed her into giving them the cookies she'd baked earlier that day along with big glasses of milk.

"Three? They're small," said Annie, giving Jenny her most charming smile.

"Two," she said. "They're big."

Seven-year-old Annie normally talked so much no one else had a chance to talk for a few minutes at the end of the *schul* day, but with her mouth stuffed with cookies, Joshua and Mary were able to talk.

"I helped Leah with John and Jacob today. They're still having trouble with math. It was fun."

"Maybe you'll be a teacher one day."

Mary smiled. "Maybe."

Jenny looked at Joshua. "And what did you do today?"

"I got a 100 on my science test."

"Very good. All your studying paid off." She knew to be careful with praise. *Hochmut*—pride—wasn't encouraged here.

Joshua didn't do as well at school as the girls. Annie had decided she wanted to be a writer like Jenny and Mary enjoyed teaching the younger children, so they both worked hard at lessons. Joshua liked working with animals and with his *daedi* in the fields and didn't think schoolwork was all that important.

The snack finished, the children got up, put their plates and glasses in the sink, and set about doing their chores. Mary began mixing up a bowl of cornbread, and Joshua went to help his *daedi* in the barn.

Jenny glanced out the window as she washed up and set the plates and glasses in the drying rack. She hadn't seen Phoebe all day. Usually she came over in the afternoon to have a cup of tea and a visit.

Wiping her hands on a kitchen towel, she turned to Annie who stood on tiptoe to get dishes out to set the table.

"Would you go over and see if Phoebe would like to have supper with us?"

"*Ya!*"

"And don't charm her into giving you more cookies."

Annie's face fell. "Not even one?"

Jenny's lips twitched as she tried to keep a straight face. "Not even one. We'll be eating soon."

"Okay." She dragged her feet out of the room and left the house. But when Jenny turned and looked out the kitchen window, she saw her race across the field that separated the two houses.

A few minutes later, Annie slammed the front door and rushed into the kitchen.

"Whoa, a little quiet—" Jenny started to say and then she saw Annie's face.

"*Mamm*, I can't wake Phoebe up."

A chill ran down Jenny's spine. "She's taking a nap?"

"On the kitchen floor! I think she's sick! I think she's sick!"

Jenny reached over and turned the oven off, then called to Mary.

"Come help me see what's wrong with Phoebe. Annie, you go get your *daedi*. He's out in the barn."

Jenny lifted her skirts and ran across the field with Mary in tow, praying that nothing was seriously wrong with her grandmother. She had looked a little tired when she visited the day before but insisted she was fine when Jenny asked her.

But then again, Phoebe always acted like she wouldn't let the passing years slow her down.

"Phoebe! Phoebe!" she called as she ran into the house.

Just as Annie had said, Phoebe lay on the floor in the kitchen.

Amish Peanut Butter Spread

This spread is a favorite for after worship services in the Amish community. Enjoy it on bread, especially homemade bread.

2 cups brown sugar
1 cup water
2 cups peanut butter
1 pint marshmallow creme
¼ cup dark corn syrup

Bring the sugar and water to a boil. Cool. Mix in the rest of the ingredients with a mixer.

Recipe by Mary M. Miller, Sarasota, Florida

~ From *Taste of Pinecraft . . . Glimpses of Sarasota, Florida's Amish Culture and Kitchens* by Sherry Gore. Pinecraft Press. Used with permission from the author.

Cheeseburger Soup

½ pound ground beef
4 tablespoons butter, divided
¾ cup chopped onion
¾ cup chopped carrots
¾ cup diced celery
1 teaspoon dried basil
1 teaspoon dried parsley
3 cups chicken broth (note: canned is fine)
4 cups diced potatoes
¼ cup flour
8 ounces Velveeta cheese
1½ cups milk
¾ teaspoon salt
¼ teaspoon pepper
¼ cup sour cream

Brown ground beef; drain and set aside. In a 3-quart or larger saucepan sauté onions, carrots, celery, and spices in 1 tablespoon butter until vegetables are tender. Add broth, potatoes, and beef. Bring to a boil, reduce heat, cover and simmer for 10 minutes or until potatoes are tender. In a small skillet, melt 3 tablespoons butter. Add flour. Cook and stir for 3-5 minutes. Add to soup and cook 2 more minutes. Reduce heat to low; add cheese, milk, salt, and pepper. Heat until cheese melts. Remove from heat and add sour cream.

Recipe by Mrs. Henry N. (Edna) Miller, Fredericksburg, Ohio
    and Miriam Good, Elida, Ohio

~ From *Taste of Pinecraft . . . Glimpses of Sarasota, Florida's Amish Culture and Kitchens* by Sherry Gore. Pinecraft Press. Used with permission from the author.

Amish Starter

1   package active dry yeast
½ cup warm water
2   cups warm water
2   cups all-purpose flour
1   tablespoon granulated sugar

Mix yeast with the ½ cup warm water and sugar. Set aside for 15 minutes. Mix in 2 cups warm water and flour, cover and set in warm (not hot) place. Stir several times for several days. Starter should smell sour and have bubbles on the surface. It will take 5 to 10 days (fewer if it's warm weather, more if it's cool). When it's ready, put in a jar. Refrigerate.

As you use the starter, add ¾ cup each warm water and flour and 1 teaspoon sugar. Must be kept refrigerated.

This is a simple starter that is quick to make and which will keep on providing starter (as you replenish) for delicious rolls.

Recipe can also be used to make Cinnamon Bread by placing the rolls in three greased loaf pans.

Amish Cinnamon Rolls

It might surprise you to find that using the Amish starter (often used to make Friendship bread) does not produce a sour baked product. These cinnamon rolls are sweet and tender and will become a favorite.

Rolls

1	cup starter
½	cup sugar
1	tablespoon salt
½	cup vegetable oil
1½	cups hot water
½	tablespoon dry yeast
6	cups flour

Cinnamon filling

½ cup cinnamon

1 cup sugar (light brown sugar will produce a warm, dark filling)

2 sticks butter, melted

Glaze

4   cups powdered sugar
½ cup cream or milk

Mix ingredients for the rolls, cover the bowl with a cloth, and allow to rise in a warm but not hot place for at least an hour (two hours is even better). Turn out on flour-covered surface, sprinkle with a little flour and then pat or roll to a thickness of about ½ inch. Spread with melted butter, then mix the cinnamon and sugar and spread that on top. Roll the dough up and then slice into 2-inch pieces. Place into greased baking pan and bake at 350 degrees for approximately 25 minutes. After baking, spread glaze on top and eat!

Breakfast Casserole

1 pound bacon (1 pound of sausage may be substituted)
1 onion
8 eggs, beaten
4 cups frozen shredded hashbrown potatoes
1 cup Swiss cheese
1 cup cottage cheese
2 cups cheddar cheese

Preheat oven at 350 degrees. Dice bacon and onion and sauté in a skillet until bacon is browned. Drain. Combine the remaining ingredients in a bowl. Pour into a greased 13-inch x 9-inch x 2-inch baking dish; add bacon. Bake for approximately 35-40 minutes. Let rest for 10 minutes, then cut into portions. Serves 12.

An Interview with Author Barbara Cameron

Q: What inspired you to create the Quilts of Lancaster County series?

Barbara: I have loved learning about the Amish since I took a trip to Lancaster County years ago. They inspire me with their desire for a deeply spiritual, simple way of life. For the Quilts series, I wanted to explore how a young woman who was in love with the life and with a young man could adapt to that life after a devastating injury that affects her belief in God.

Q: Is there anything specific about the titles you chose?

Barbara: I wish I could take credit for the titles. My wonderful editor, Barbara Scott, read the first manuscript and saw that I mentioned Ecclesiastes ("a time to love, a time to . . .") and wanted to change my titles. She was very sweet in her e-mail, saying sometimes authors get attached to their titles. Well, we do sometimes but not when someone else comes up with something so much better! Then she said the editorial committee discussed how quilts were used in the book (Jenny wakes in the hospital covered by a quilt made by her grandmother). Barbara said each of them had memories of quilts—even the sole male committee member—and it felt like everything fell into place.

Q: How much research did this series take?

Barbara: Tons! I wanted to make certain that I caught the way of life, the search for a deeper meaning to life, not just the focus on ourselves and the endless search it seems the *Englisch*, as the Amish call us, seem to have for things. In my research, I met an Old Order Amish woman who would graciously agree to read my work. I wanted to make sure I didn't offend the Amish, or make a mistake—readers who like Amish fiction know a lot about them. When she called to tell me that it was obvious I loved the Amish, that she had enjoyed the first story I sent her, I sat down and cried. I felt like I'd done the job I hoped to do.

Q: What elements do you think readers will find they can relate to even if they're not familiar with the Amish culture?

Barbara: Reading is a very individual experience so there may be different things that resonate for different readers. One thing I know for certain is that I have found it easier to trust God's will, something the Amish feel is an important part of their spiritual life.

Q: How do you as the author connect with the characters in the series?

Barbara: I didn't base Jenny on me, but I was able to use my experiences with wondering what God wanted me to do with my life when I experienced a big change in it. And oh, did I ever relate to her struggles with physical therapy because I'd had an injury the year before and dealt with it. I also loved to write about the children in the story as they grow and become even more dear to Jenny and the family.

Q: Do your characters begin to take on a life of their own as you write?

Barbara: They sure do! My daughter came home from school one day to find me sitting and crying at my computer. I told her that so-and-so had died. She said she didn't know I had a friend with that name. It was a character. (I can't tell you the name of the character—spoiler alert!)

Q: Can you give us a teaser as to what we can expect in the future?

Barbara: There are three books in the Quilts series but who knows . . . maybe there will be more. And my editor has also bought Stitches in Time, a three-book Amish series (one of the books is set in an unusual location . . .).

Q: What message would you like your readers to take away from *A Time to Heal*?

Barbara: Maybe the first and most important is that there is always hope—hope that we will grow even closer to God through any time we experience when we feel alone with a challenge. And we never know when and where we may find love.

**If you missed the first book of
the heartwarming Quilts of Lancaster County series,
enjoy this excerpt from** *A Time to Love*

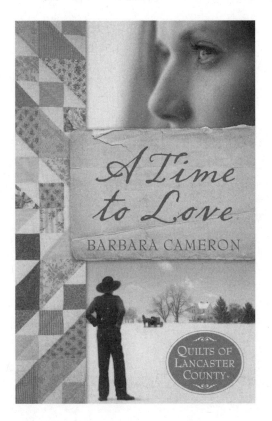

War correspondent Jenny King thinks she's just a temporary guest in her grandmother's Amish community while she recuperates from the devastating injuries sustained in a car bomb attack that changed her world. But when she meets Matthew Bontrager, the man she had a crush on as a teenager, she wonders if God has a new plan for her. Jenny has emotional and physical scars. Though she feels she has come home to this man and this place, she's not sure she can bridge the difference between their worlds.

A Time to Love, Barbara Cameron
Available now from Abingdon Press
www.AbingdonPress.com/fiction and bookstores everywhere

Bonus chapter from Book 1 in the "Quilts of Lancaster County" series

A Time to Love

ೕಬ

1

Jenny woke from a half-doze as the SUV slowed to approach a four-way stop.

"No!" she cried. "Don't stop!"

"I have to stop."

"No!" she yelled as she lunged to grab at the steering wheel.

David smacked her hands away with one hand and steered with the other. The vehicle swerved and horns blared as he fought to stop. "We're in the States!" he shouted. "Stop it!"

Jenny covered her head and waited for the explosion. When it didn't come, she cautiously brought her arms down to look over at David.

"We're in the U.S.," he repeated quietly. "Calm down. You're safe."

"I'm sorry, I'm so sorry," she whispered. Covering her face, she turned away from him and wished she could crawl into a hole somewhere and hide.

He touched her shoulder. "It's okay. I understand."

Before he could move the SUV forward, they heard a siren. The sound brought Jenny's head up, and she glanced back fearfully to see a police car.

"Pull over!" a voice commanded through the vehicle's loudspeaker.

Cursing beneath his breath, David guided the SUV to the side of the road. He reached for his wallet, pulling out his driver's license.

A police officer appeared at David's window and looked in. Jenny tried not to flinch as he looked at David, then her. "Driver's license and registration, please."

David handed them over. "Officer, I'd like to explain—"

"Stay in your vehicle. I'll be right back," he was told brusquely.

When the officer returned, he handed back the identification. "Okay, so you want to explain what that was all about—how you started to run the stop sign and nearly caused an accident?"

"It's my fault," Jenny spoke up.

"Jenny! I—"

"Let her talk."

"You can't stop at a four-way," she told him in a dull voice. "You could get killed." She drew a quilt more tightly around her shoulders.

"You look familiar," the officer said, studying her face for a long moment. "Now I got it. You're that TV reporter, the one who was reporting from overseas, in the war zone—" he stopped. "Oh."

He glanced at David. "And you're that network news anchor. What are you doing in these parts?"

"Taking her to recuperate at her family's house."

The officer glanced back at Jenny. "Didn't know you were Amish. Thought they didn't believe in television."

Jenny fingered the quilt. "It's my grandmother," she said, staring ahead. "She's the one who's Amish."

She met the officer's gaze. "Please don't give David a ticket. It was my fault. I freaked and grabbed the steering wheel. I didn't want him to stop. But it won't happen again."

The officer hesitated then nodded as he touched the brim of his hat. "I have friends who've been through the same thing. Be careful. You've been through enough without getting into a car accident."

She nodded. "Thank you."

After returning to his patrol car, the officer pulled out on the road and waved as he passed them.

Jenny looked at David. "I'm sorry. I just had a flashback as I woke up, I guess."

"It's okay," he told her patiently. "I understand."

She sighed and felt herself retreating into her cocoon.

He glanced in his rearview mirror and got back onto the road. They drove for a few minutes.

"Hungry yet?"

She shook her head and then winced at the pain. "No."

"You need to eat."

"Not hungry." Then she glanced at him. "I'm sorry. You must be."

He grinned. "Are you remembering that you used to tease me about being hungry all the time?"

"Not really," she said. "Lucky guess, since we've been on the road for hours."

He frowned but said nothing as he drove. A little while later, he pulled into a restaurant parking lot, shut off the engine, and undid his seat belt. "It'll be good to stretch my legs. C'mon, let's go in and get us a hot meal and some coffee."

"I don't—"

"Please?" he asked quietly.

"I look awful."

"You look fine." He put his hand on hers. "Really. Let's go in."

Pulling down the visor, she stared into the mirror, and her eyes immediately went to the long scar near her left ear. It still looked red and raw against her too-pale skin. The doctor had said it would fade with time until she'd barely notice it. Later she could wear extra-concealing makeup, but not now, he'd cautioned. The skin needed to heal without makeup being rubbed into it.

"Jenny?"

She looked at him, really looked at him. Though he was smiling at her, there were lines of strain around his mouth, worry in his eyes. He looked so tired too.

"Okay." With a sigh, she loosened her hold on the quilt and rewrapped her muffler higher and tighter around her neck. Buttoning her coat, she drew her hat down and turned to reach for the door handle.

David was already there, offering Jenny her cane and a helping hand. When she tried to let go of his hand, he tightened his.

"The pavement's icy. Let me help," he said. "Remember, 'Pride goeth before a fall.'"

Her eyes widened with amusement as she grinned. "*You're* quoting Scripture? What is the world coming to?"

"Must be the environment," he said, glancing around. Then his gaze focused on her. "It's good to see you smile."

"I haven't had a lot to smile about lately."

His eyes were kind. "No. But you're here. And if I said 'thank God,' you wouldn't make a smart remark, would you?"

She thought about waking up in the hospital wrapped in her grandmother's quilt and the long days of physical therapy since then. Leaning on the cane, her other hand in David's, she started walking slowly, and her hip screamed in pain with every step. Days like today she felt like she was a hundred instead of in her early thirties.

"No," she said, sighing again. "I think the days of smart remarks are over."

The diner was warm, and Jenny was grateful to see that there were few customers. A sign invited them to seat themselves, and she sank into the padded booth just far enough from the front door that the cold wind wouldn't blow on them.

"Coffee for you folks?" asked the waitress who appeared almost immediately with menus. She turned over their cups and filled them when they nodded. "Looks like we're gonna get some snow tonight."

"What are you going to have?" David asked.

Jenny lifted her coffee cup but her hand trembled, spilling hot coffee on it. Wincing, she set the cup down quickly and grabbed a napkin to wipe her hand dry.

David got up and returned with a glass of ice water. He dipped his napkin in it and wrapped the cold, wet cloth around her reddened hand. "Better?"

Near tears, she nodded.

"She filled it too full," he reassured her.

Reaching for an extra cup on the table, he poured half of her coffee into it. "Try it now."

Jenny didn't want the coffee now, but he was trying so hard to help, she felt ungrateful not to drink it.

"Better?"

She nodded, wincing again.

"Time for some more meds, don't you think?"

"The pain killers make me fuzzy. I don't like to take them."

"You still need them."

Sighing, she took out the bottle, shook out the dosage, and swallowed the capsules with a sip of water.

"So, what would you like to eat?" asked the waitress.

Jenny looked at David.

"She'll have two eggs over easy, bacon, waffles, and a large glass of orange juice," he said. "I'll have the three-egg omelet, country ham, hash browns, and biscuits. Oh, and don't forget the honey, honey."

The waitress grinned. Then she cocked her head to one side. "Say, you look like that guy on TV."

David just returned her grin. "Yeah, so I'm told. That and a dollar'll get me a cup of coffee."

She laughed and went to place their order.

Growing warm, Jenny shed her coat and the muffler. She sipped at the coffee and felt warmer. When the food came, she bent her head and said a silent prayer of thanks. Then she watched David begin shoveling in food as if he hadn't eaten in days, rather than hours.

She lifted her fork and tried to eat. "I like my eggs over easy?"

He frowned and stopped eating. "Yeah. Do you want me to send them back, get them scrambled or something?"

"No. This is okay."

"How did you eat them at the hospital?"

She shrugged. "However they brought them."

Deciding she might have liked eggs over easy in the past but now they looked kind of disgusting, half raw and runny on the plate, she looked at the waffle.

"I like waffles?"

"Love them."

Butter oozed over the top and the syrup was warm. She took a bite. It was heaven, crispy on the outside, warm and fluffy on the inside. The maple syrup was sweet and thick. Bliss. She ate the whole thing and a piece of bacon too.

"Good girl," David said approvingly.

"Don't talk to me like I'm a kid," she told him, frowning. "Even if I feel like it."

He reached over and took her free hand. "I'm so proud of you. You've learned to walk again, talk again."

"I'm not all the way back yet," she said. "I still have memory holes and problems getting the right word out and headaches and double vision now and then. I have a long road ahead of me."

David looked out the window. "Speaking of roads . . . as much as I hate to say it, I guess we should get back on it as soon as we can."

Jenny turned to where David was looking and watched as an Amish horse-drawn buggy passed by slowly. The man who held the reins glanced over just then and their eyes met. Then he was looking ahead as a car passed in the other lane, and the contact was broken.

He looks familiar, she thought . . . *so familiar.* She struggled to remember.

David turned and got the waitress's attention. As she handed him the check, she noticed Jenny, who immediately looked down at her hands in her lap.

"Why, you're that reporter, the one who—"

"Has to get going," David interjected. "She needs to get some rest."

"Oh, sure. Sorry."

She tore a sheet from her order pad and handed it to Jenny with a pen. "Could you give me an autograph while I go ring this up?"

She hurried off, sure that her request would be honored.

"Could you sign it for me?" Jenny asked David.

Nodding, he took the paper and quickly scrawled her signature, then added his in a bold flourish.

"Here you go, two for one," he told the waitress when she returned. He tucked a bill under his plate and got up to help Jenny with her coat.

The SUV seemed a million miles away, but she made it with his help. Once inside, she sank into the seat, pulled the quilt around her again, and fastened her seat belt.

"It'll take just a minute to get warm in here," David told her.

Jenny stroked her hand over the quilt. "I'm not cold. . . . I hate those pills," she muttered and felt her eyelids drooping. "Making me sleepy. The waffles . . . lots of carbons."

She opened her eyes when he chuckled. Blinking, she tried to think what could be so funny.

"Carbs," she corrected herself carefully after a moment, frustrated at the way the brain injury had affected her speech. "Lots of carbs. Don't think I used to eat lots of carbs."

"So take a nap," he told her. "You talk too much anyway." He grinned to prove he was teasing.

Smiling, she tried to think of a snappy comeback. They were always so easy for her, especially with David. But then she was falling into a dreamless sleep.

Sometime later, she woke when she felt the vehicle stop. "Are we there?"

"Stay here," she heard David say, then she heard his door open and felt the brief influx of cold air before it closed. She couldn't seem to wake up, as if her eyes were stuck shut. The door on her side opened, and she heard the click of her seat belt, felt arms lift her.

"I can walk," she muttered.

He said something she couldn't quite grasp, but his voice was warm and deep and so soothing that she relaxed and let him carry her. And then she was being laid on a soft bed, covers tucked around her.

Home, she thought, *I'm home*. She smiled and sank deeper in dreamless sleep.

What they're saying about...

Gone to Green, by Judy Christie

"...Refreshingly realistic religious fiction, this novel is unafraid to address the injustices of sexism, racism, and corruption as well as the spiritual devastation that often accompanies the loss of loved ones. Yet these darker narrative tones beautifully highlight the novel's message of friendship, community, and God's reassuring and transformative love." —*Publishers Weekly* starred review

The Call of Zulina, by Kay Marshall Strom

"This compelling drama will challenge readers to remember slavery's brutal history, and its heroic characters will inspire them. Highly recommended." —*Library Journal* starred review

Surrender the Wind, by Rita Gerlach

"I am purely a romance reader, and yet you hooked me in with a war scene, of all things! I would have never believed it. You set the mood beautifully and have a clean, strong, lyrical way with words. You have done your research well enough to transport me back to the war-torn period of colonial times." —Julie Lessman, author of *The Daughters of Boston* series

One Imperfect Christmas, by Myra Johnson

"Debut novelist Myra Johnson ushers us into the Christmas season with a fresh and exciting story that will give you a chuckle and a special warmth." —DiAnn Mills, author of *Awaken My Heart* and *Breach of Trust*

The Prayers of Agnes Sparrow, by Joyce Magnin

"Beware of *The Prayers of Agnes Sparrow*. Just when you have become fully enchanted by its marvelous quirky zaniness, you will suddenly be taken to your knees by its poignant truth-telling about what it means to be divinely human. I'm convinced that 'on our knees' is exactly where Joyce Magnin planned for us to land all along." —Nancy Rue, co-author of *Healing Waters* (*Sullivan Crisp* Series)
                    2009 Novel of the Year

The Fence My Father Built, by Linda S. Clare

"...Linda Clare reminds us with her writing that is wise, funny, and heartbreaking, that what matters most in life are the people we love and the One who gave them to us."—Gina Ochsner, Dark Horse Literary, winner of the Oregon Book Award and the Flannery O'Connor Award for Short Fiction

eye of the god, by Ariel Allison

"Filled with action on three continents, *eye of the god* is a riveting fast-paced thriller, but it is Abby—who, in spite of another letdown by a man, remains filled with hope—who makes Ariel Allison's tale a super read."—Harriet Klausner

www.AbingdonPress.com/fiction